T0354521

THE
HUNTRESS

Pixie Birkitt

Order this book online at www.trafford.com
or email orders@trafford.com

Most Trafford titles are also available at major online book retailers.

Printed in the United States of America.

ISBN: 978-1-4669-6053-4 (sc)
ISBN: 978-1-4669-6052-7 (e)

Trafford rev. 10/04/2012

 www.trafford.com

North America & international
toll-free: 1 888 232 4444 (USA & Canada)
phone: 250 383 6864 ✦ fax: 812 355 4082

CHAPTER 1

The Call Out

A nother book finished and just as it always has done, the play written in book form has caused a spark of questions within me. Shakespeare's Romeo and Juliet but what is this love he speaks of within the play? What emotion could be so powerful to cause such an unfortunate ending?

No matter how many books I seem to read that speak of this emotion, I never truly understand it. From what I have seen in my short life, only hatred, death, war and despair remain in this world.

Something like that can't be found in a world such as this one, a world engulfed in the hatred. I glance out of the window to see that sunrise is near, the Call Outs will be soon and I may be dead by this afternoon. I climb out of bed and return the book to the shelf. I stare down at it proudly for a moment, it's one of the few connexions I have with my mother. Silently, I hope that if I survive the Call Outs, one day I'll be able to find her, speak to her, perhaps maybe develop a mother and daughter bond with her just like the ones I've read so much about.

From what I've been told, she was highly intelligent and agile, that's why she was chosen in the Call Outs. They've never aloud me to see the video of her year, never even aloud me to see a picture of her. All I have is the hologram but even then, I can barely make out her face. I know she has the same black hair as me, but sometimes I wonder whether my emerald eyes come from her, or my elven blood. There are so many things I wish to know about her but unfortunately, the only way to gain answers is by surviving this day and we're all in the same situation.

Each of us separated from our parents at birth just as our parents were, trained from being a small child, having to survive experiments that change your genetic structure for this. This day.

The alarm bell rings as sunrise arrives and the wall, in front of my bed, opens up to reveal a silver suit and several silver weapons. We have until just after sunrise to arrive at the training hall otherwise we are exterminated in our rooms. I move quickly, knowing I don't have much time, I take down the silver suit and begin to put it on.

It's armour.

It's feathered into a skirt at the bottom to make it easy for me to move and the metal never seems to make a noise. Upon the chest plate, which reminds me of a corset, are strange, elven symbols carved into the flexible, unique metal.

Swiftly, I grab the black belt and have it resting on my hips before I begin placing the throwing knives into place. I slip my feet into the silver, knee high boots that also have the markings. I throw the silver quiver over my shoulder and grab my bow. I'm ready.

As I approach the door, the hologram begins playing and automatically I panic. *Have I taken too long? Are they going to exterminate me?*

"Dear Miss Devotion, you have proven yourself to be quite devoted and well organised, are you ready to leave for the Call Outs?" The hologram of my mother says in a strange robotic female voice, the voice I've heard all of my life and now seems unusually comforting to my ears.

"I would appreciate it" I mutter and the doors open. I rush out of the doors and straight to the training hall to find myself being the first one there. Nothing new then.

"Miss Devotion, do you wish to train?" The hologram asks, and I nod. I remember how they had told me that they had based my hologram on my mother but even still I don't know what her eye colour would be or whether she would be of elven blood or not. All I know is that her is long and black and from what I can make out, her skin seems unusually pale. Her face in the hologram is distorted and so I can't quite make out what she would look like.

A dummy seems to grow out of the floor and appear in front of me. I take out the first arrow and begin shooting, soon I find myself shooting arrow after arrow. Never missing where I aim. The second candidate arrives and stares at me.

"Devotion, aren't you scared?" Asks the shy, young voice of the second candidate. She's no taller than five foot and her long fiery red ringlet hair is tied back into a ponytail, leaving only her block fringe in her face. Her skin is pale and her cheeks are rosy, giving her the illusion of innocence. She stands there, shaking nervously. Both of us know what could become of our fate.

"If I must be honest with you Innocence, I'm terrified" I reply as I draw back the string of the bow. I exhale slowly and release the arrow.

"You've always been one for training, if I'm betting on anyone being chosen, it'll be you" Innocence replies

"I hope that I will be and the same for you," I reply as I retrieve the arrows from the dummy, "you are by far the best among us when it comes to traps"

"Thank you" she says with a nervous smile. The dummy returns beneath the floor as the room floods with nervous teenagers. All of us are seventeen to eighteen years old and each of us are clearly terrified of what could possibly become our fate. The hall seems to fill with a feeling of dread that hangs heavily in the air. I take a large gulp of air as we begin to file into perfect lines and stare up at the wall. It opens to reveal a group of males and females behind a glass shield all of them were once in the games, each of them once survived the Call Outs.

A male stands proudly in the centre and begins to speak, "Hello my training champions, you each know of the two possible fates that may become yours. You have each proven your strengths and proven that you are each strong however many of you have shown weaknesses and this is something that can't be accepted within the fate you all wish upon yourselves," my mouth becomes bone dry and I clutch the bow with all of my strength. "Elves and humans, no matter what race you are, you have proven your worth and you should each be proud of what you have achieved" the man steps back and a female steps forward.

"I am Delusion, a huntress from the fourth games," the woman begins, "I proved myself worthy to become a huntress through my illusions and deceptive ways. I am of elven blood just as many of you will be. The first of you whom has proven yourself, in physical strength and cunningness is Conquer"

I look behind me to see Conquers large, muscular build. His jaw clenched at first but soon relaxes and his dark sinister look, deteriorates. He is safe. I step out of the way and allow the largely built human male to step past me. His long, shaggy black hair covers most of his face, hiding it from the world, his dark skin makes him seem almost like a shadow as he moves towards the wall. He places his sword and guns on the floor and the wall opens. He steps through and the wall closes again so that no one can follow him.

The woman steps back and a male steps forward, "I am Fusion, a hunter from the twelfth games. I proved myself worthy through my strength, speed and ability to kill with my bare hands. I am of human blood just as many of you will be. The second of you whom has proven yourself, in intelligence and speed is Innocence" I look to my right and smile proudly at Innocence as she takes a sigh of relief.

She looks to me and smiles comfortingly, "good luck" she whispers and I nod. I watch as she walks towards the wall and places her rope and knives on the floor. The wall swallows her up and silently I pray that I too will be chosen.

The male steps back and another male steps forward, "I am Embers, a hunter from the third games. I proved myself worthy through strength and fire magic as well as intelligence. I am of elven blood. The third and fourth whom have proven yourselves, in strength and magic are Inferno and Frost"

I stare blankly at the screen, four have already been chosen, my luck is slowly running out, there are eight more places, I could fill one of them though. I cling onto hope.

The male steps back and female steps forward "I am Ice, a huntress from the sixth games. I proved myself worthy through intelligence, speed and my ranged attacks. I am of elven blood. The fifth and sixth whom have proven yourselves, in speed and range are Bullet and Ivy"

Six more spaces. I must cling to hope.

I slowly become oblivious to the world around me. Only listening to the names called.

"Nymph"

"Darkness"

"Burned"

The names continue until its time for the twelfth name to be called and a woman steps forward, "this year there shall be a difference, this difference shall be explained in a moment but first. I am Devote, a huntress from the twelfth games. I proved myself through all of these things, from magic to strength to range to intelligence but I proved myself through the same way you shall. This year, a twelfth candidate has not been chosen, instead this is your chance to prove yourselves through a blood bath, the last alive shall be the last candidate"

No! My mind screams as everyone already begins in their fight to survive. Immediately, I find myself dodging the first attack. A male charges towards me, wielding a sword in his hand, I gasp quickly as the breath rushes from my body and in a swift movement I dive out of the way and roll back on to my feet. I take an arrow out of my quiver with an inhuman grace and speed before I aim at the male and take my first kill.

With a quick movement I grab one of the throwing knives out of my belt and turn as I hear the footsteps approach me. I spin with incredible speed and with little time to aim, I throw the knife and with perfect precision, I take my second kill.

I hear a gun shot, and with a swift movement that I never thought possible, I dodge the bullet. *What can I do? I have to survive! I have to!* My mind screams as instinct begins to take hold. I take another arrow, and with perfect concentration, I fire the arrow at a large group that are fighting for survival. The arrow head catches fire in mid air and when it embeds itself in a males head, the fire engulfs the entire group.

Magic! How I love you at times! My minds voice says as a quick burst of joy floods through my body. *That's a few less people to kill.* I hear another gun shot and again I move but this time I'm not quick enough, the bullet skims my thigh, sending immense pain through my leg but I force myself to continue.

Blood soaks the floor, bodies begin to pile up. The dread has been replaced by the need to survive.

I move swiftly on my feet, gliding through the air as I approach the preoccupied human, using a gun. It is him whom has been attempting to shoot me. He shoots down another victim just as I appear behind him. I cup his jaw with my hand, take out a knife from my belt and slit his throat. His body drops to the floor lifelessly and blood pours out from his throat, and splatters on my legs and feet. He gurgles slightly as he struggles to breath and that is the only indication that he is still alive.

I turn and look to the final male standing. His eyes look dark and sinister, hatred burning in his eyes as he glares at me. He takes his sword and begins to approach me at a remarkable speed. With little thought, instinct taking hold of me completely

I take out my arrow, aim and fire. I can see the realisation in his eyes and watch as the hatred floods from his eyes and is replaced by fear and dread before the arrow embeds itself in his head. Killing him almost instantly.

Suddenly, that I am the last standing.

I have survived the blood bath and I shall become the twelfth huntress in the games.

With no control over my body I approach the males body in the centre of the room, unsure of whether I should be proud that I am the last standing after those whom I have grown up with have been slaughtered. Some of their blood shall forever soak my hands. How could they have wanted to view such a thing?

I look up just as the camera zooms in on my face, "congratulations Devotion" Devotes voice says, "you should be proud of your achievement, you have proved yourself worthy"

I stare up at the glass in the wall, my mind completely blank of thought as I find myself shocked and horrified after what I have had to do to survive but this is what I was born for, what I was created for. Soon the last few moments begin repeating in my mind. My body shakes slightly and I feel physically sick.

Finally, a thought comes to my mind, *this is what I was born for, I was created to kill, nothing more.*

"Come through child," a male commands and before I have chance to think, I find myself placing the weapons on the floor and approaching the wall. It opens up and swallows my body. Within the wall is a beautiful hallway, the walls are a blood red colour with gold chains hanging from the walls. Upon the cold stone floor is a scarlet carpet and the room itself is lit by candles.

I walk through the hallway and to a large room where my fellow hunters and huntresses await. The room is similar to the hallway only it had black chairs and a black sofa along with a TV that has come through the wall.

I notice Frost glaring in my direction, her eyes fuelled with anger but there's nothing new about that, for years she has hated me for no apparent reason.

"Devotion!" Innocence shouts as she runs towards me and wraps her arms around my waist "you made it! You were chosen too!"

"I wasn't chosen" I say in a tone as cold as ice and as sharp as a knife, the images still playing in my mind "I had to prove myself," anger burns deep within my stomach and I struggle to control it, to extinguish the burning flame within me.

Perhaps this anger shall help me in the games, help me become a champion I wonder silently.

"What do you mean?" Innocence asks.

"They forced us to slaughter each other until there was one remaining, I was the last remaining" I reply.

"So they repeated the twelfth year this year?" Inferno says and I nod, "looks like Devotion must be as strong as Devote" he laughs and I giggle.

"No one could ever be stronger than Devote, she's said to have been the strongest known huntress" Frost snaps, "powerful in magic, her strength is said to be incredible considering her size and build and her speed is said to be amazing, Devotion could never compare to Devote.

"She's right, remember the footage from twelve years ago?" Innocence says as she backs away from me and looks around, "Devote killed half the island without assistance, she didn't even join a group even though they offered her a place, she remained solo throughout the entire thing, its

"The strongest ever known" I mutter.

"You have each achieved extraordinary things, you should each be proud," a familiar voice speaks, I turn to my left to see Fusion enter through the wall. His shoulders are broad and his build is large as he towers all of us accept for Conquer. The large, strong muscles of his arm flex angrily as he stares at me, his mossy green eyes burn with annoyance and something else, something I don't quite understand.

Have I done something wrong? I wonder.

He nods his head to me respectively, his shaggy long brown hair falling in front of his face as he does so. His skin is coated in a dark tan.

I reply with a simple respective nod and a soft smile. Silently hoping to break an uncomfortable ice between us both.

"Congratulations Devotion, you have proved yourself worthy and strong just as Devote did, nineteen years ago" Fusion says, his voice has a strange hint of a tone, one that I don't recognise ever being spoken in. It sounds restrained yet caring. "Come, former champions are excited to meet each of you"

We follow him as the wall opens again, and we enter a large dining hall, the walls are decorated in red silk and upon the large wooden tables are gold and silver cutlery. At the table are several past champions along with the makers, our teachers and our trainers. The first to rise is Embers, his long dark red hair is tied into a ponytail with slight curls and waves, some of his fringe falls out of the ponytail and in front of his face, his eyes resemble the embers of a fire and his skin is coated in a very dark tan. Somehow he seems to remind me of the embers of fire, his presentation, his eyes and his hair. It all seems strange to me.

No wonder he's called Embers I think to myself as I examine him with my eyes.

His pointed ears twitch slightly before he speaks, "Greetings candidates" he says with a soft smile, his voice filled with wisdom and his worn, wise eyes seem to light up like a flame as he looks at each of us and his eyes settle on me.

"Greetings," we each reply, nodding our heads in respect. He shakes everyone else's hands whilst I stare absently into the flame of a candle.

His hand touches mine and pauses. "You should be highly honoured and proud, you have done well in proving yourself" he mutters quietly so that none of the others can hear him.

I nod respectfully, "I am" I reply, "thank you"

Delusion is the next to approach us, she smiles to Innocence, "you must be a cunning and intelligent one" she says and Innocence giggles nervously, her rosy cheeks burning brighter than usual.

"I've studied your traps and watched the spells you cast, I find them incredible. They're amazing, I especially appreciate the Scuttle Fish spell you created" Innocence replies.

"I am honoured to know that a worthy candidate has studied myself and my year, I hope you use what you have learnt in this years games" Delusion replies. Innocence releases another nervous giggle. Delusion looks at both I and Innocence as we stand closely together, I can feel her shaking. "Innocence, I shall be training you further in traps and combat. Devotion, I shall be teaching you spells of delusion and trickery but only for the first few days whilst Innocence, I am your permanent trainer, I shall be advising you before the games begin"

"I am honoured" I mutter with a slight nod of my head.

"As am I" Delusion replies.

"And I shall be teaching you in the art of fire magic but again it is only for the first days" says Embers as he touches my shoulder gently.

Ice is the next to approach us, her short white hair glimmers like snow in the dim light, "You showed great skill in ranged attacks, Devotion. I shall assist your training within these but for a short time" she says with a large smile placed on her blue icy lips, her voice sounds cold and hateful, its almost as if she could strike me with ice just by speaking to me and even though she seems to be attempting to be pleasant, her voice still remains like ice. Her greys eyes remind me of the lake outside the training centre in winter, when it is coated in frost, ice and snow. "I shall be doing the same for you Bullet and Ivy, we shall arrange training sessions for every day until the games arrive"

"Thank you" I mutter.

"Ice, I am so privileged to meet you!" Ivy begins, her voice filled with an unusual enthusiasm.

Devote steps passed the others and stands before me, "it's a pleasure to meet you, after seeing how you manage to wield such powerful magic, and your aim with knives and arrows is superb, I am honoured to meet such a skilled Huntress" she says, her voice sounding as restrained as Fusions had. She smiles softly, "child, would you sit with myself and Fusion at the table"

I glance to Innocence and her smile gleams, "go for it! It's a massive honour!" She encourages.

I force a smile and nod before I walk between Devote and Fusion. I sit between them both at the wooden table, the seats cushion feels sturdy as I sit down, and my legs suddenly relax. I realise how much strain they have been under because of how much I've been shaking.

"You're not a person of many words are you?" Devote says

"It's been an eventful and surprising day" I reply.

"I understand how you must feel, I was in the same place as you once" Devote replies.

Innocence sits opposite me, beside Delusion and smiles, "Delusions going to be my prime trainer" she says excitedly, her red ringlets bobbing as she moves.

"Congratulations, your hero will be training you," I mutter.

I look down the table to find each of my fellow candidates are sat beside their prime trainer and I find myself wondering whom mine shall be. I look to Devote and then to Fusion.

"I shall be your prime trainer, Devotion" Devote says in a clear, strong voice, causing all the candidates to go quiet and stare at me.

"Your so lucky!" Innocence encourages yet for some reason, I don't feel lucky. I feel as if I should have fallen with the others in the training hall.

A large feast is placed on the table, filled with a banquet none of us have ever really known. I stare at the large turkey in the centre of the table, its perfectly cooked brown flesh looks delicious in the dim light and the smell that radiates from it, calling to me causing my mouth to water and my stomach to grumble loudly. The smell of freshly baked bread and gravy soon invades my nose. A plate is placed in front of me and I force myself to wait until everyone else has begun filling their plates before I begin filling mine.

I fill it with as much food as I can, piling it up on my plate and eat in silence, allowing the flavour of each food to burst in my mouth and my stomach to fill with rich food that I have never truly experienced. Whilst I drink wine for the first time in my entire life.

CHAPTER 2

The Beginning

I awake the next morning. My head feels unusually cloudy as I lay there, my temples throb angrily and my eyes have become abnormally sensitive to the light. I search my new room for a pair of sunglasses to block out the light. Gently I place the very same armour I wore last night and leave my room. I know I don't have long until we begin travelling and training. What awaits me is unknown for now, every year it changes. I walk towards the dining table to find Devote and Fusion waiting, patiently. They're murmuring something to quiet for me to make out the words.

Devote jumps as I step towards them. She looks to me, caution and warning burning brightly in her eyes. She seems startled by my arrival. "Good, you're up" she says, her body relaxes and her hard facial expression softens with a smile yet it doesn't seem to melt the icy feeling in my heart and the horrid feeling of warning in my gut. I find myself prepared to fight as I cautiously continue to approach them.

"I am," I mutter.

"You must be like Devote, she finds herself up at sunrise every morning" Fusion says, his voice completely relaxed.

"Its an old habit from when I was training just as you have trained all of your life. I often found myself waking earlier than most for training," Devote explains, her voice seems comforting and soft yet it doesn't calm me. I still find myself wary around them.

"I found I got in the habit many years ago," I mutter.

"Then your name explains a lot. You are as devoted as Devote to being the best" Fusion replies.

"I wouldn't say I'm the best, I'm far from it" I reply, my voice remaining quiet.

"We'll find out just how strong you are in the games" Delusions voice appears from behind me as she enters the dining hall. She yawns and I notice deep bags under her eyes from where she manages little sleep.

Devote stands up and approaches me, "we have a long journey ahead of us" she begins before she hands a book to me, "they informed me that you appreciate reading, lets see if the knowledge you have gained from all those books you've read, pays off"—Delusion laughs—"I want you to study this book, it has several things that may be useful for you when it comes to the arena. We shall commence training when transport arrives"

Silently, I find myself wondering what the transport shall be like. It can't be a small vehicle, how are we supposed to train?

I sit beside Fusion and open the book before I commence reading. I notice that there are several things on rope tying and trap making as well as spells.

"Hold up tiger, you will want to eat breakfast before you begin studying, you're going to be doing a lot today," Fusion says with a laugh at the end of his sentence. "You don't want to be burning yourself out"

"Yes, we wouldn't want that now would we?" Delusion says in a sarcastic tone. I notice the sudden competition rising between the ex candidates.

"We don't want her put off her game" Devote replies, her voice suddenly snappy.

"We both know Innocence will prove herself and come out on top, she will be the Huntress to win, she's smart with traps and other things" Delusion replies with a laugh "this girl has nothing on her, she didn't even manage to prove herself worthy over years of training.

"No but she proved herself worthy by being the last standing whilst Innocence has never killed in her life, you don't know how she'll react to her first kill" Devote replies, suddenly her voice sounds strangely cocky which doesn't seem to suit her.

"Humph, I know she'll react just as I did, with a lust for more"

"Are you sure you're not just saying that because she reminds you of yourself?" Fusion asks but all Delusion does is glare.

"What's for breakfast?" I ask, in a strange attempt to draw away attention from the argument but my attempt seems futile, instead another adds to the argument and competition between the previous Champions. I sigh before I stand up and slam my hands on the table "hey! Do you guys have to argue? Your going to put all of us off our game and we don't need that!"

"She's right" Innocence says as she appears out of the shadows "but she is often right, you're going to affect our concentration by arguing, we need to be focussed on the games not how competitive you seem to becoming over whose candidates will be champions and whose shall not"

Everyone seems to go quiet and I find myself suddenly letting out a laugh, "I realise this is a competition to prove our strength and rid this world of crime along with other things but you don't have to take it out on each other and out on us" I say. I sigh and sit back down as the touch screen appears on the table.

"Looks like breakfast!" Says Conquer in a joyful voice before he rushes to the table and begins placing in an order. "Hey Frost! They have bacon! They have frigging bacon! And eggs!" Suddenly his mouth is drooling as he begins pressing frantically on the screen. I look at the menu and find myself choosing nothing more than a cereal bar and some fruit. I need to keep my fitness up.

"Such a child," Frost mutters as she watches Conquer before she looks to me, "and so pathetic and childish for one to only think of themselves and not allow the big girls and boys to play competition"

"Shut up!" I growl, feeling annoyed by her words and annoyed by those whom claim to be our trainers.

*   *   *

I sit outside the training centre. It's the first time I've seen the abnormal train station, perhaps its because I've never been passed the training centre or maybe its because they never let us leave the training centre. I find myself studying the book carefully, learning as much as I possibly can and excitement building inside of me. The excitement of trying out some of these knots and traps.

I wonder what a person would look like if trapped in one of these. How would they escape? This must be something Innocence knows well from plenty of practice. I imagine a man hanging helplessly from a tree by his ankle, screaming for help as I move in to give my final blow. That unlucky man wouldn't be the survivor at the end, that I know for sure.

Looking up from the book, I see Delusion teaching her main candidate, Innocence, of different poisonous foods that may be in the arena. Foods that she must stay clear of.

Suddenly, the sound of squeaky breaks snap me out of my small fantasies and I look up to see the train park in front of us. "Devotion!" Devotes voice calls sharply and I jump from the sound of the sudden commanding voice. I swiftly move towards her and follow her on the train, with only the book and armour as my possessions. "Training room, now!" She continues and I find myself following her straight down the narrow corridor and to a large room that I wouldn't have imagined possible on a train.

"What will I be training in?" I ask.

"First, this is your time table for when we arrive at the destination in three days time," Devote hands me an A5 slip of paper, "this is your time table for whilst we are travelling," she hands me a second time table and I nod before I look at the time and then to the time table.

"Hand to hand combat is first" Fusion says.

"Who will I be fighting?" I ask with a slight nervous gulp of air.

"Me" Fusion replies and my eyes widen. "We will be training for an hour before you begin practicing advanced magic, is this understood?" I nod, "once you have your first two training lessons, it is a break and you will be checking your mail and having something quick to eat. Your break won't last long"

"How longs my break for?" I ask

"Thirty minutes, no longer than that," Devote replies and I nod. I understand that the training will be stricter than anything I have ever known before. "You did well this morning, choosing a healthy breakfast, of course you are thinking a head. Whilst the others will be come sluggish and their training hours will relax, yours will remain as close to the same as they were before"

"Understood" I reply.

Devote steps out of the way, allowing Fusion to step closer to me and as soon as he's in arms reach, he throws a punch at me. Immediately, I find myself diving and rolling out the way of Fusion's blow. Within seconds he reacts, moving like a tiger, pouncing on its prey. He wraps his arms around my throat and has me completely trapped. I struggle against his grip but it is little use. I feel vulnerable and defenceless.

After a moment he releases me, "you need to move quickly, throw your blows before someone has chance to trap you. You never know what they could do, from what I did I could have knocked you unconscious with little effort," Fusion says.

I nod and recover myself before I rise to my feet. I prepare myself once more, this time I'm stood so that I have much more balance. I clench my fists. This time when Fusion begins his attack, I find myself working of the deadly impulse drummed into my body from a young age, I block his attack and twist his arm so that its forced behind his back. I wrap my free arm around his throat and prepare to squeeze.

"Good, you must always be on guard in the games, you never know when you may be attacked," Fusion says before he uses an incredible strength and manages to free himself from my grip. I fall to the floor, "now you must never let down your guard, even if you have them trapped," he moves towards me, his movements filled with aggression and violence.

My instincts take hold and I roll out of the way and back onto my feet. In a swift movement, I run towards the wall and use it as a way to jump over Fusion I wrap my arms around his neck and my legs around his waist. My hands automatically position themselves so that they're prepared to snap his neck.

I hear Devote clap in background, "good, your using your speed and agility against him," she applauds but I don't allow it to take my concentration. He struggles against my grip until my back is against the wall of the train, I push against it and use my weight to bring him to the floor. Suddenly, the train jolts us forward as it begins moving. I remain in the perfect position to snap Fusions neck. Devote gently places her hand on my shoulder, pulling me out of an unusual hypnotic state, something I've never known before. "You're doing well, you're allowing your instincts and impulses to kick in, this is good" she pulls me off Fusion and I keep my eyes on him. Never allowing my guard down as I await his next attack.

*   *   *

My bodies left aching with bruises after training in hand to hand combat with Fusion and I find myself smelling of smoke and scorched hair after training in magic with Devote. "You did well, you're picking this up quite quickly child" Devote encourages but I feel to battered and bruised to believe her.

"Your life training has prepared you well," Fusion continues to encourage but I find my mind else where.

How am I supposed to master all these advanced skills in such little time. We've never used or learnt half of the magic Devote is trying to teach me and Fusion is much stronger than most of those I have trained with all of my life.

I look at my time table to see that I am supposed to be training with Delusion next in illusion magic. Devote throws a cereal bar at me, "You need to keep up your strength" she says as I catch it.

"My body already feels battered and bruised, how am I meant to do this until the games?" I ask.

Devote touches my shoulder gently, "I asked my trainer the very same thing but she kept pushing me. She gave me a tip though," she replies.

"And what was that tip?" I ask.

"Plenty of water, healthy food and ice cold baths at night" Devote replies and I shudder slightly at the thought. Remembering how I would have such a bath when my muscle ached after training most the day away.

"These next few weeks until the games are going to be very long aren't they?" I mutter.

"You have no idea, none of us know what the company have in store for you this year," Fusion replies.

Devote returns to being professional once more, all signs of comfort leave her voice, "After you have trained with Delusion, we are going to look at footage from previous years, you need to study how the prey may react. You must understand how unpredictable they can be and how to tackle just about everything"

"You expect me to watch thirty years of footage over a few weeks when these games can last up to three weeks?" I reply, completely stunned.

"We've selected certain prisoners and hunters/huntresses for you to study, it is incredibly important you understand what you could face in the arena," Fusion replies.

"Is this what your trainer did?" I ask Devote but Fusion is the one who answers me.

"No, my trainer did this for me and it helped me come second in the games," Fusion stares at Devote, his eyes suddenly filling with what I can only compare to passion and lust yet it seems much more beautiful than lust could ever be.

"We think it could assist you to make it into the top three. It doesn't matter if you win, you have to be in the top three," Devote continues, her eyes never leaving Fusions. Her emerald green eyes, that seem too much like my own for comfort, sparkle brightly as she stares deeply into his, almost as if she can see into his soul and she likes what she sees. Within her eyes are something I don't quite recognise from seeing in the world I have grown up with but it resembles something I've seen in books.

Can this be the love I have read so much about? Can love be possible in this world?

They look at me with something knew in their eyes, something I certainly don't recognise. Their eyes seem to be filled with some sort of kindness and care. Devote smiles to me, her beautiful peachy lips seem incredibly smooth and loving whilst her eyes are completely lit up with what I can only describe as pure joy.

"What?" I find myself asking.

"Nothing," she mutters with a slight laugh.

Fusion looks to his watch and sighs before he takes Devotes hand in his, "its time Devotion went to train with Delusion, her break time is up," he says with a sad look in his eyes. Devote sighs as well and her smile falters slightly.

She looks at a piece of paper and looks back to Fusion, "I'm to train Frost next, something I doubt I will find at all amusing, she strikes me as very unfriendly even towards her fellow candidates," she says.

"She's never been nice," I mutter under my breath. Devote laughs and I know that she has heard what I said.

"I can tell," she replies before she walks towards me and ruffles my hair, somehow acting as if I'm a small child.

"I'm with Conquer next, I look forward to this, he strikes me as a brilliant hand to hand combat fighter," Fusion mutters before he approaches Devote a kisses her lightly on the cheek. Secretly, I know he's right about Conquer and his natural talent in hand to hand combat, he is the best of our year when it came to it. He has the physical strength and enough speed to match his opponent and come out on top.

"Have fun," Devote commands in a light hearted voice.

"I will, try to have fun with the ice queen" Fusion replies.

"I'll try" Devote replies and Fusion leaves the room.

"Ice queen?" I ask.

"No time for questions, you have to meet Delusion in less than five minutes," Devote replies.

"Where will she be?" I ask just as Frost enters the room.

"Just follow the hallway, you'll see her name planted on one of the doors" Devote replies.

"Shouldn't you be leaving Devotion! It's my turn with Devote," Frost snaps, "and you're cutting into my training time"

"I am leaving, I was just asking for directions," I reply honestly, my voice surprisingly calm.

"I don't give a flying monkeys, your cutting into my training time!" Frost snaps, "and I need my training time! More than you do!"

"Urgh!" I reply before I leave the room and begin to walk down the narrow hallway of the train. Soon I come to Delusion's room and knock on it gently.

"You're late!" She snaps through the door, "I don't like lateness, get in here!" I sigh and press my finger on the touch screen so that it can scan my finger print. The door opens automatically and I step through. Silently dreading my time with Delusion.

*   *   *

Soon the dinner bell rings and every hunter and huntress rushes out of training as quickly as they can, moving faster than I'd ever seen them move. I walk slowly, approaching the room where dinner has been set out, to see every candidate is sat at the table and is already beginning to gulp down food like there's no tomorrow.

Remember, fitness! Healthy eating is the key! I think to myself as I sit between Innocence and Conquer. I look at the buffet and choose the healthiest foods I can think of. Jacket potato with nothing more than butter on it to add extra flavour. Broccoli and a small scoop of chicken tikka so that I'm getting some meat in my diet.

"Is that all your eating Devotion?" Innocence asks.

I nod, "Yes, I'm keeping up the healthy diet we've been on since we were children, as much as I can" I reply.

"Smart idea," Innocence replies, suddenly she looks distracted as she stares at Conquer, "by God he must be hungry, I've never seen anyone eat that much in my entire life"

I giggle, "Slow down cowboy! You'll give yourself the hiccups!" I joke. Conquer looks at me and smiles before he begins laughing as my words seem to settle into his mind. His mouth is still full of food.

"What would you know Devotion?" Frost says, in her usual cold, snappy voice. Clearly wanting to try digging at every single thing I do in order to affect my confidence.

"It was just a joke Frost," I reply, innocently before I take a mouthful of chicken tikka. "Maybe you should grow a sense of humour, it would benefit you by far"

"Funny, coming from the huntress that wasn't even chosen because she didn't manage to prove herself," Frost continues with a smug look on her face.

I remain still, concentrating on each mouthful of food I take, trying my hardest to ignore her and trying to push aside the flash backs of what occurred in the Call Outs.

"If anything Frost, she proved herself worthy more than the rest of us, she fought to death against the others that were to be terminated and she won!" Innocence snaps, her voice sharp as she stands up and slams her hands on the table, "and she certainly out did you, I don't even know why they chose you for this because your certainly not worthy of the title *huntress*!"

"And what would you know of proving yourself, Innocence? All you can do is create pretty little traps," Frost replies, her voice becoming smug and cocky. "You can't even use a weapon!"

"Actually, traps can be quite useful and efficient. They can be more deadlier than any weapons at times," I mutter, causing everyone's eyes to leave Frost and Innocence and focus on me, yet again. I fidget uncomfortably under the silent stares, "it's true," I mutter, hating the fact that I spoke and managed to pull everyone's attention on to me. For a moment, I truly hate myself. "Some traps can be deadly and bring the worst of deaths upon a person. I mean which would you prefer? Having your throat slit or a bullet through your head or would you prefer hanging upside down by your ankles from a tree to slowly dehydrate or starve to death?"

"I'd prefer the bullet," Conquer replies after he's swallowed his mouthful of food.

"Exactly my point, so in effect, Innocence proved herself to be cunning and smart and strong whilst what did you do to prove yourself to be worthy of the title *'Huntress'*?" I ask as my gaze falls back on Frost and I can feel everyone's stares have left me and moved to back to Frost.

"Through strength and magic" Frost mutters.

"Well then, you have not proved yourself in intelligence and so you can't speak up and say that I have not proved myself and question my intelligence especially at a joke," I reply before I return to eating my food. Everyone remains quiet for a moment before they return to the conversations they were having before the feud between Frost and myself. "Thanks for standing up for me," I mutter to Innocence.

"You shouldn't be thanking me, I should be thanking you, you stood up to the biggest cow of this decade and not only for yourself but for me as well," Innocence replies, "how you didn't get chosen I don't know. You showed so much intelligence just then"

PIXIE BIRKITT

"Who knows how the makers think" I mutter.

Innocence sighs, "Your right there, no one knows how the makers think and I'd prefer not to find out" she whispers.

"I wouldn't either, I imagine their minds to be quite dark and sinister," the words leave my mouth and as they do, I see an unusual image flash past my eyes. Suddenly, I'm stood in a jungle and instinctively I know that this is in the arena. I step carefully, with a pistol in my hand.

Hang on! I don't use guns! I think to myself, as I step with grace and caution. I hear a sudden movement and almost instantly, I'm prepared to kill. He is in my sight. I'm ready.

Suddenly, I feel a surge of pain throughout my body, I feel unusually hot and my skin feels as if its burning. I look down to see that my entire body is engulfed in flames. I panic. The image fades.

I stare at my half eaten jacket potato and take another mouthful, trying to act normal. I can feel the butter melt on my tongue, bringing a beautiful flavour along with it. I sigh. Could that have just been my imagination caused by thinking about the makers and the possibility of their minds being dark and sinister.

Silently, I hope that it is the a case and that what I saw isn't the fate of one of my fellow candidates.

*   *   *

I sigh, as I watch through the past games, my mind is else where though. All I can think about is the image that had appeared in my head. *It had to have been my imagination, I've had it before but never about the games, only about training. It can't be real* I think as I watch Delusion in her youth as she uses her strengths to counter her weaknesses, causing her to be the strongest in the games. I haven't seen her use hand to hand combat throughout the entire games and silently I wonder whether that's one of her weaknesses but it doesn't matter. All I need is strategies.

I note each strategy used by each Champion. Delusion stayed within the trees, using her traps, bird calls and illusion magic to trap each enemy. Devote remained on her own, never joining a group and slowly picked at prisoners in groups until there were none left. She'd remained hidden in the shadows, using the night to her advantage.

Two common strategies, remaining hidden, using the darkness of the night and the shadows of trees to your advantage.

I sigh, my mind wandering once more. Three days our journey will take and so far it seems like an eternity has past on the first day.

I stare out the window to see the night drawing in, the stars sparkling beautifully in the sky. I had always wanted to witness them properly, not through a window and I hoped that in the arena I would get that chance. The chance to witness the stars in the sky properly as they twinkle. I approach the window and open it slightly, allowing a strong gust of cold night air to surround me and fill my lungs. The winters night looks beautiful as the distant moon glistens on the snow far in the distance.

The icy wind whips through my hair with a powerful force. Instinctively, I lift my hand and manipulate the energies so that it begins whipping around my hand causing my skin to go numb, but I don't care.

"Hey! What do you think your doing?" Frost snaps as she approaches me, "Practising when not in training! You know that's against the rules!"

I release the energies and turn to see her standing at the doorway, anger blazing in her eyes, "I'm not practising anything, I was just admiring the view" I reply, the wind causing my hair to whip around my face.

"Then why is there a strong gust of air?" Frost snaps in a sarcastic tone.

I sigh, *you've got to be kidding me! The window is open!* I think.

"The frigging window is open," I reply pointing at it. Frost glares at me as I close it an smile sarcastically, "they didn't by any chance extract pieces of your brain when they were conducting the experiments did they?"

She huffs and begins to twitch away when I let out a quiet giggle, *such a spoiled brat at times but so funny! Oh how I remember how some of the trainers used to spoil you, Frost* I think before I turn off the TV and approach my room. The door slides open with a simple touch of my finger on the touch screen, it scans my fingerprint and I step into the dark room. The lights flicker on and I look around. A beautiful wooden bow with black arrows hangs on the wall, along with a dozen throwing knives. I take a gulp of air and stare at the powerful weapons. The blades glisten with a deadly sheen that draws me closer to them, gently I touch the razor sharp blade and allow it to slice open my fingertip, the blood trickles down my finger and I find the blades still calling to me. This is what I was created for, this is what I am. A killer.

The warmth of my blood runs down into the palm of my hand and silently I wonder whether it will be like this in the arena only another persons blood on my hands. The thought sends shivers running down my spine. I step away from the weapons, wipe away the blood and settle into bed for the night.

*   *   *

The next day is almost no different, training most the day, a cold bath to sooth my aching muscles and the bruises that are forming on my body. When tea arrives, I find myself feeling as if I'm starving. Everyone sits, muttering quietly to one another as we eat and I find myself eating in complete silence. Throughout the entire day, the image from yesterday have been playing on my mind. Its as if it has some meaning to it that I don't quite understand. I sit in pure silence.

"Penny for your thoughts?" Innocence says with a smile as she holds up a very old looking coin. Rust has almost deteriorated what was once on it but when I look closely, I can see the image of the old queen with her head held proudly.

"It's nothing," I mutter

"It seems more than nothing, your not talking at all," Innocence replies.

"I've never really been the talkative type, you know that"

"I know but it still seems off, even for you"

"It's just something I saw in my head yesterday, like I said, it's nothing"

"Hmmm," Innocence suddenly seems lost in thought, after a moment of silence she changes the subject, "so, have you thought of a strategy your going to use in the arena?"

"Not really, we don't know what it'll look like or what the makers are wanting to happen in the arena," I reply

"Good point, we don't," Innocence admits, "I'm kind of nervous to find out what they have in mind for us"

"So am I," I admit, "but there's nothing we can really do about it, it's what they've chosen for this year"

"I'm hoping we'll be in some sort of jungle or somewhere with plenty of places to hide traps and hide yourself, best places to be really. I wouldn't like to be in a desert land like the seventeenth games"

"From what I've seen, it comes in handy when there are places to hide yourself," I pause for a moment, "and your traps"

"Yea, Delusion has me practicing ways to stay hidden and confuse the enemy"

"Fusion has me watching previous games to see how the enemy can react and the best course of action to take when they react in a particular way, but then, people are," I pause as I search my mind for a particular word, "unpredictable"

"That they are," Innocence agrees, "so what have you learnt from your times watching the previous games"

"Stay hidden, stay safe, don't get injured, and don't join forces with a large group and don't attack large groups, take them down one by one because in several years, hunters and huntresses have become injured through making such attacks," I reply.

"Yea, a large group can take a lot of the kills from you if your in the group," Conquer suddenly speaks, his voice low and quiet so that the others can't hear him. "There are twelve of us, a lot of the time in the games, six will join forces and very rarely do one of them become one of the champions"

"Who do you think will end up teaming together?" Innocence mutters.

Conquer looks around the table, "Frost, Ivy, Bullet, and Inferno are going to team up, they work together and if you notice they seem a little too close," he looks back to us, "Darkness and Nymph have been best friends for years, they'll no doubt be working together. Burned is a bit of a loner like yourself, Devotion, he'll probably start in a group and then go his separate ways if that"

"What do you reckon Devotion will do in the arena?" Innocence asks curiously.

"Devotions an unpredictable person, she'll do what it takes to win for she is Devotion after all and she will have several strategies ready for when the games come," Conquer replies.

"You know people far too well" Innocence mutters.

"Its body language, not exactly difficult to read," Conquer replies. "Just look at how they act together or a part, if they're stronger in a group or on their own, how they study and how they work"

"I guess you're right," Innocence replies.

"Devotion and Burned are loners, they stick to themselves most the time and don't talk much but they tend to rush to the rescue of other people, for example, when Frost began attacking you with insults, Devotion was immediately to the rescue. That's how they work. Whilst several others tend to attack in groups or show off," Conquer continues to explain.

"But no one came to Frost's rescue," Innocence replies.

"Of course not, no one really likes her if I must be honest with you," Conquer replies. With that, the conversation ends.

I finish my tea and return straight to analysing previous games, my mind still fixated on the image, it seems as if the makers are trying to make this years games almost completely different. Trying to make it a surprise, even for us, the ones trained for it the moment we could walk. Innocence soon enters the room and sits beside me.

"So you're doing this straight after tea?" She asks and I nod "Interesting, I bet you've learnt a lot"

"The best lesson I've learnt is not to get injured or trapped in other hunters/huntresses traps, it could be fatal" I reply.

"How many fatalities have you seen so far?"

"Of hunters and huntresses? At least a dozen, maybe two dozen," I reply, "most that get injured during the games, get infection and die. Some have forgotten to use the chemicals to clean the water before drinking it and have died. Some have gone through dehydration, others infection. The odd case is that the enemy has killed them, not caring that they will be killed immediately"

"This is our fate, hey?" Innocence mutters

"It was made our fate the day we were born," I reply.

"Your right, we just need to prove ourselves even further"

"Just one thing"

"What?"

"There have been three cases I've seen where hunters and huntresses have turned into cannibals and tried eating other hunters and huntresses, so we best be on our guard throughout the games, we can't trust our own kin," I reply.

"Thanks for the heads up," Innocence replies. "I'm hoping the makers don't change it that much this year, I know they like a twist but we've already had an *entertaining* change in events"

"It's a repeat of the twelfth games but I have a feeling this isn't the only drastic change that's been made this year, I get the feeling they're trying to spice it up again, make it different and keep the games the talk of every last inch of the world," I reply.

"If that is the case, what are we going to do? What other changes could they have made?" Innocence wonders, clearly more to herself than to me.

"We survive and we fight" I reply, unable to stop myself. I remember having to fight to the death to earn my place and survive. "We survive at all costs, we can't forget that"

"Agreed," Innocence replies with a soft smile, clearly painted on her face and not a natural smile. Her eyes look strained and tired as she looks from the screen to me.

"Don't worry yourself, we'll get through this, we've survived this far. We survived the experiments when we were children that killed at least a quarter if not half of our year, we survived sickness and the Call Outs, we can survive this last obstacle" I encourage.

"You're right, if we survived all that we can survive this as well"

"Exactly," I mutter with a false smile planted on my face, in a comforting fashion. I try to comfort her as much as I possibly can before the games, even though my gut screams things at me, tells me things about this years games. They're going to change a lot of things, I can feel it.

Her eyes light up once more and her smile seems to become genuine.

"So what do we do before the games?" She asks.

"We train and we train pretty damn hard, I'm determined to become a champion," I reply.

"I guess that's why they called you *Devotion,* you're pretty damn devoted to this"

"You can bet your bottom dollar I'm devoted to winning," I reply and she laughs, "what?"

"You sound almost like Conquer, you are both obsessed with being the champions, I guess that's why you were both given the names you got," Innocence replies.

"I guess," I mutter with a small laugh.

"Devotion, if you spent as much time studying as you did showing up other candidates and laughing, maybe you would stand a better chance at becoming a champion," Fusion's voice echoes throughout the small room, its coming from behind us. The strict tone in his voice sends shivers down my spine and the hairs on the back of my neck to stand on end.

"Sorry, I was just keeping her company, we were discussing the games," Innocence replies before she gives him her cutest puppy eyed look that not many people could stay angry at but it seems as if it doesn't affect Fusions determination, for me to study, in the slightest.

"Innocence, I would appreciate it if Devotion studied the previous games, it will help her when it comes to the arena, is this understood?" Fusion asks.

Innocence shudders slightly, clearly she feels uncomfortable under his glare, she glances at me and nods, her auburn curls bouncing slightly before she dashes out the room.

"Devotion, stay focused!" Fusion commands. Instinctively, I nod and return to watching the games, analysing every last strategy used that had assisted a hunter or huntress to become a champion.

*   *   *

The final day on the train finally arrives and it feels as if we've been travelling for a dozen eternities. It begins with a slack morning, almost no one is training, mostly they're studying or eating. I sit between Innocence and Conquer, with a soft smile planted on my face to reassure Innocence that everything will work out. That the makers won't have changed that much of the games.

The train goes underground to travel passed the water and to the island where our enemy will be kept.

"Devotion!" A familiar voice calls as I begin to dig into the toast I ordered for breakfast. I look up to see Devote looking down at me. Her pitch black hair hiding her face, "There is much preparation that must be done today, you need to make an impression on the crowd and on the enemy," she begins and I nod. I catch a glimpse of her beautiful emerald eyes to find deep bags underneath them, which tell me she hasn't slept well. She motions for me to follow her, I grab my plate and begin following her through to my cabin which is filled with unusual people, "we are expected to arrive at six this evening, the makers will announce the few changes you will know about at six thirty. You will be interviewed by the press at seven thirty and will be dining at eight"

I nod as she speaks, I try to eat my toast whilst being hurried towards a strange chair in the centre of my room. Once I've sat down, an unusual male stands in front of me. His long black hair is braided and at the bottom are small skull and bone beads. His eyes are such a dark brown colour that they're almost black and his muscular build makes him look almost completely terrifying.

"What is it you want me to do with Devotion?" He asks, his voice is deep and rough as he speaks with a very strong accent.

"I want you to give her the illusion that she's dangerous but also beautiful," Devote replies to the male.

He nods his head slightly, "Understood," he replies before he steps closer to me, "she already has a beautiful complexion so this shouldn't be too difficult," he nods to me, "my name is Levi and I shall be ensuring you give the impression that your trainer wishes you to give," he says as he holds out his dark coloured hand to shake mine. I take it and gulp, feeling unusually scared of what he's going to do to me in order to make me look dangerous but also beautiful.

"I have written up what it is I want you to do, pleasure ensure that she looks threatening in order to scare the enemy slightly but not too much," Devote says her voice sounding unusually cold as she speaks the words. I watch cautiously as she leaves the room.

"Don't worry, I have an idea of what to do with you child," Levi says with a smile.

"What are you going to do?" I ask, my voice sounding cautious and unusually frightened as I speak.

"Get me the dresses designed for Devotion!" He commands and swiftly, two young females rush out of the room to return with several dresses in their arms. "When I'm finished, you will look absolutely stunning yet as threatening and dangerous as Devote wishes you to look," he continues. The first of the girls steps towards Levi with caution, her long strawberry blond hair held up in a perfect ponytail, her full fringe falling just above her pale blue eyes. Her eyes stand out even more so because of the hot pink eye shadow and black eyeliner.

"These ones sir?" She asks, her voice shaking slightly. Levi nods and the pale girl sighs in relief. I glance at her clothing to see that she is wearing a full, black jump suit with flames on the legs that climb up her body making her look as if she is a campfire in the middle of the night. I glance to her companion to see that she is wearing the very same thing. My name is embroidered in scarlet red above both of their left breasts along with another word that is so small that I can't quite read it due to the distance between us.

"Put them on the bed," he commands and she does so. Suddenly, his voice becomes calm once more when he turns to speak to me, "now, Devote wishes for you to look dangerous yet beautiful and so, what I suggest is a dress such as this"—he picks up a long, purple and black lace dress that reminds me wenches wore in olden times, with the corset style at the front—"a beautiful dress, is it not?" He asks and I nod in agreement.

Suddenly, I'm pushed to my feet and the same two girls that got the dresses, begin to undress me. Instinctively, I begin to fight them a way.

"Hold up tiger, we need to dress you in this beautiful thing," Levi says, I pause and stare at him, "trust me, no one is going to hurt you, I doubt they would be able to anyway, everyone saw how you fought in the Call Outs, you certainly were exceptional," he continues. I gulp and allow them to undress me. My training clothes fall to the floor and Levi seems to examine my body uncomfortably close, "I believe a corset would do your body a lot of justice in order to give you a sexy appeal"

The second girl moves at lightening speed as she approaches Levi with a black corset. Her short, dark red hair is cut into a pixie cut and her side fringe falls in front of one eye, hiding it away. I stare at her for a moment and take in the details of her appearance. She has deep blue eyes and pale skin and seems to have some resemblance to the blond haired girl. Their eyes are the same shape and they look as if they could have been twins if it weren't for the difference in hair and eye colour.

"Would this do sir?" She asks, her voice equally as shaky just like the other girls had been. Their voices sound unusually similar, both soft and light in tone even when it is clear that both of them are petrified.

"That's perfect Selene," Levi replies, she smiles, hands the corset over to Levi and steps away. "Now, I want a bra that will boost up her breasts to make them look perkier and slightly, only slightly, larger," the first girl moves quickly and hands a bra to him, "perfect, you're both better at this than you were last year" he compliments with a comforting, soft smile. "Dress her," he commands after the girls have giggled for a moment, his voice is once again strict and to the point, causing the girls to quiver in fear once again.

With an unusual speed, they begin to move. My training bra is replaced by a padded one and soon enough the dress is slipped over my head. The corset hurts as they begin tightening it around my waist, causing me to appear curvier than I am. I find it difficult to breath once they're done and it feels quite uncomfortable but I know I have to deal with it.

I stare in the mirror to see that my head has been placed onto the figure of an absolutely gorgeous and sexy woman.

"Magnificent but we can't waist time, hair and makeup must be done! Accessories must be added!" Levi says.

"W-what would you l-like us t-to d-do first?" Selene stutters.

"Accessories, you fools! I thought you had learnt from last year! Hurry!" Levi snaps. Selene and the other girl move quickly. The other girl grabs a belt with throwing knives held firmly on it, she rests it on my hips so that it gives off the effect that I am indeed, dangerous.

CHAPTER 3

The Prison Hull

Hours have passed and finally they have finished my hair and makeup as well as applying accessories to the outfit. I stand in front of the mirror to see a complete stranger staring back at me. My long, straight black hair has been made wavy and two braids have been created either side of my face and tied round like some sort of unusual circlet that only goes around the back of my head. Feathers have been braided into the braids so that they hang down freely at the back of my head.

My makeup has been done in order to make my eyes look larger and draw attention to them. They look dark and sinister yet the emerald green colour brings an honesty and innocence to the unusual look. I have been kitted with weapons for accessories and an unusual silver, tribal bracelet that have been pushed all the way up to my upper arm. Upon the silver, strange symbols have been engraved that mean nothing to me yet remind me of certain animals such as the wolf and the dolphin.

Upon my wrists have been placed small, silver wrist bands that seem almost plain compared to the tribal bracelet. Beautiful silver rings have been placed on my fingers and a beautiful forest heart necklace has been placed around my neck.

I feel uncomfortable with my pointed ears on show and so I slouch slightly.

"Stand straight," Levi commands in a soft voice and immediately I do so. My snow white skin seems to radiate an unusual glow as soon as my posture becomes straight, "stand proudly, show no fear, show nothing. You are a proud huntress, you are dangerous and you fear nothing, stand and prove this is who you are"

You're basically saying for me to stand straight and show pride in what I've been created for, what I am to become, a killer I can't help but think the words. Somehow I manage to push them to one side and give a soft smile. My lips have been painted a blood red colour which seems to have made me appear even paler than usual.

"That's better," Levi comments before he checks his watch and smiles, "its almost time, you better go grab yourself something small to eat to keep you going," my stomach growls at the thought of food and I realise just how hungry I am.

"Thank you," I mutter before I rush out of the room and towards the dining hall. It seems completely empty and I take the time to grab some bread rolls and some chocolate. I stare down at the chocolate, wondering what it would taste like. Swiftly, I butter the bread and begin eating as quickly as I can, knowing that I don't have much longer until the train arrives at its destination.

The butter melts in my mouth and the texture of the bread becomes soft. The train comes to a sudden stop as I begin to fill my mouth with the rich taste of chocolate. I can feel it melting softly in my mouth and swiftly I swallow. The train jolts forward slight before it begins lowering down. I look out the window to see people watching the train with awe. Camera lights flash as pictures of the train are taken.

Is this what it's like every year? I wonder as I place my hand on the cold window, feeling curious and confused yet I don't allow this to show in my face in case they can see me. I put on a strong facial expression to give the illusion that I am powerful and dangerous beyond their possible capabilities.

"Candidates! Boys and girls! Gather at the doors ASAP!" Delusion commands in a powerful voice that seems impossible to come from her considering her small build. It seems so surreal. I approach the doors and stand at the back of the line that is beginning to form. "Out in the order you were called out in," she commands and every last candidate moves so that we are in the same order we were called out in.

The train doors open and the first to exit is Conquer. For a moment, he seems blinded by the lights and deafened by the sudden commotion of questions. I watch as he holds his head up high and ignores every last one of them as he walks towards the large guarded building. The next to follow is Innocence whom talks to very few of the journalists whom are bombarding her with questions, every so often she curtsies and flashes her cute and innocent smile in their direction. I watched how each of them reacted, each of their responses were different.

Frost steps out of the train, and as she moves, she flicks her silky golden hair and took on the sexiest pose I have ever laid my eyes upon. Her lips have been painted blue with lipstick and streaks of her hair have also been painted blue with a substance I am unfamiliar with, this has probably been done in order for her to take on the appearance of frost. She smiles a beautiful perfect smile towards the audience, her glossy pink lips seem to look almost flawless as she moves in her short light blue dress. Her dress barely reaches her knees and flares out like a freshly blossomed flowers petals. Her dress has one long sleeve and one short and upon the short sleeve rests a deep blue rose, still in bloom.

She curtsies before she enters the building and the next candidate follows her. I can't help but feel a twinge of jealousy at how well she seems to have performed with her twitch for a walk and her gorgeous smile.

Just stay calm and cool, you are both dangerous and beautiful, you can do this, you can make a standing impression on the audience I encourage myself silently. *Remember, in that arena you need weapons, the more powerful and suited to you the better, to get weapons you need votes and to get votes, you need the audience to love you and you need to make a good impression so make one!* Soon, my turn arrives. With care and precision, I step out of the train and glance at the crowd with a fierce look painted on my face.

"How do you feel after having to fight to the death for your place in the arena?" A male journalist shouts.

"How does it make you feel knowing you have made it this far?" A female shouts.

"Do you feel proud of yourself for making it into the games?"

"Have you thought of any strategies you may use in the games?"

The questions fly from left and right. Gracefully, I walk towards the building when a question catches my attention, "Devotion! Have you ever been in love?" A male asks.

I stop and turn to look at him, unsure of what to say but then the words seem to flood out from my heart in a stern voice, "I have never experienced such an emotion and at times I find myself questioning its existence. I have read the Romeo and Juliet play script, and books such as *The Reckoning,* and the *House of Night novels* and in each of these books from the distant past, I have noted that they all speak of how love conquers all, even death"

"Do you find yourself afraid of feeling any such emotion? My readers will want to know," the journalist replies, flicking his shaggy, long wet hair out of his eyes.

"I fear nothing, especially not an emotion. I am a huntress after all, and a huntress fears nothing," I reply.

"Would you mind if I took a quick picture?" He asks.

"Not at all," I reply. I rest my left hand on my hip so that I can feel the knives under the palm of my hands, I pose so that it looks as if I am prepared to throw the knives. I stand in a deadly pose, ensuring that I look ready to kill.

"Perfect, beautiful! Threatening and dangerous!" He says with a smile before he is swarmed by the rest of the crowd. I stand straight and proud once more before I continue walking towards the heavily secured building. I gently caress the knives and step into the building. The door bangs as it shuts and locks immediately. I can hear the sounds of several locks settling into place. Leaving us securely shut in with little escape. The thought of us being trapped inside sends shivers down my spine.

I force myself to remain calm, keeping the same illusion created by Levi, threatening and dangerous yet beautiful and sexy.

I glanced around the long, daunting, dark corridor, the large grey walls seem to grow narrower as I walk down it, until they seem claustrophobically close together. I rub my left upper arm in a comforting fashion for a moment before I continue forth through the corridor.

With an unusual sense of caution, I enter the unusually well lit room that seems to clash with the darkness of the corridor. White paint has almost been completely chipped away from the walls, baring grey concrete walls that has been covered in graffiti. Names written and crossed out whilst other names written on the walls have been left untouched. It's almost as if it is some sort of hit list.

Suddenly, for some unknown reason, the room has become incredibly cold and unwelcoming. I hesitate for a moment as an ice cold shiver runs down my spine, the hairs on the back of my neck stand on ends and goose bumps rise on my bare arms.

The deceiving sweet smell of cigarette smoke invades me nose, the tempting scent calls to me but I know this is just an illusion.

My eyes settle on the long granite table that has been nailed to the floor, clearly for safety reasons both for the hunters/huntresses and the prisoners. The long table isn't far from the entrance of the room but as I step towards the table, time seems to have slowed down dramatically. An unusual darkness seems to linger in the dark shadows cast by various objects in the room.

I glance at each prisoners face as they take their seats on the opposite side of the table. With an inhuman grace, I sit down as I find my eyes drawn to one prisoner in particular. There's something about him which makes it seem almost impossible for me to look away.

His skin is a beautiful, flawless dark colour and his long black hair has been styled into long dreadlocks whilst the sides have been shaved so that they have elven tribal symbols shown clearly in the shaved sides. His hazel brown eyes seem to light up and glisten in the light as they meet mine. Immediately, I force myself to pull my gaze from his and look to the repeatedly scratched table, unable to stop myself from feeling a slight tinge of embarrassment.

I look up at the wall, forcing myself to keep a stern and dangerous look. I sit up straight and glare angrily for a moment before I allow myself to relax slightly.

My back still straight and my head held high with strength and pride, I wait.

The clock strikes six thirty and the head of the makers appears on a screen at the head of the table, his dark hair has been neatly combed back and gelled so that it can't come out of place.

"Welcome hunters, huntresses and prisoners," the head maker begins, "now as you may be aware this years games have already been changed slightly and there are several more changes in store for you. To update the prisoners with the recent happenings and changes that have occurred, I shall explain the first of the changes. As you may have seen on television in previous games, the hunters and huntresses have always been chosen however this year, a twelfth hunter/huntress wasn't chosen, instead it was a battle to the death where a particular huntress conquered all. Devotion, will you stand for them to see?" I nodded my head slightly and stand before all of them so that they can see me, "Devotion was the huntress to win the battle to the death, she showed great strength and intelligence in so many areas through the battle," he pauses for a moment, "you may sit down now, Devotion," once again, I nod, this time in respect before I sit down once more. "There are several more changes we have made this year, to begin, the hunters/ huntresses will train with the prisoners at certain hours in the day, you are expected to dine and socialise with one another. Prisoners will be given certain freedoms in areas of the training centre and within the games themselves there are several rule changes that shall be explained throughout the games. The rules will be changing multiple times in the games. Do each of you understand this?"

Each huntress and hunter nods whilst the prisoners seem to shout that they understand. They seem much freer than we are, it seems as if they don't hold a care. Like they don't care about the fact that there deaths are not far away, that they will be hunted one by one until the last is remaining. I notice through the noise that the prisoners are making, the dark skinned male with dreadlocks hasn't said a word, and yet again he seems to catch my gaze. This time he holds my gaze and this time I notice an unusual bright flicker in his eyes as if life as suddenly been added to them. As if life has suddenly entered his body.

I become unaware of the noise taking place around us and the head makers voice, I find myself unaware of everything around me but his eyes. His eyes seem to take on a new form, green appears in his hazel eyes and slowly they change from brown to a beautiful lily pad green. They seem to suck me in further until I feel as if I'm standing in a blanket of snow whilst the warmth of the sun rests on my skin, a sense of peace travels through my body, and my muscles relax because of the warmth that radiates from his eyes.

Suddenly, I feel the touch of a deathly cold hand on my shoulder, drawing the warmth from my body once more. I gulp a large breath of air as the ice floods into my veins and I feel the shock rattle through my body.

I pull my gaze away and look to the hand, following the arm I see Innocence stood, staring at me in concern, "The announcement is over Devotion, are you okay?" She says, her voice quivers slightly in concern.

I nod once, "I'm fine," I reply before getting out of my seat. We begin walking towards a large, old heavy metal prison door and I can't stop myself from glancing back at the table where I see the male still watching me, his eyes have lost the glistening life and the beautiful lily pad green colour and returned to hazel.

"Are you sure you're okay?" Innocence asks after the door has closes behind us with a loud thud, the sound of locks locking into place echoes through the large, dark corridor.

"I'm fine, don't worry," I reply.

"You seem distant, you can't afford to seem distant, not when your about to be interviewed. You need them to like you, to vote for you so you can get what you need," she says and I know she's right but all I can think about is him. His beautiful eyes, his glowing dark skin, his dreadlock hair, all of it seems to be stuck in my head. The warmth his gaze brought to me seems to call to me once more.

I want to feel it again and I don't quite understand why.

"Don't worry, I'll be okay," I mutter quietly as we approach the queuing hunters and huntresses. "You should go find your place, you were chosen long before I—" I struggle to find the words and I know the sadness I feel is creeping into my eyes, "I had to prove myself, I'm twelfth remember"

"The twelfth huntress and no doubt, the best of this years candidates," Innocence comments.

A quiet giggle escapes my lips before I manage to clamp them shut, "I'm sure that I'm not the best," I reply.

"Well I believe otherwise," she replies before she runs off in a hurry to find her place in the queue.

With patience I wait, slowly becoming nervous. I can feel my hands becoming clammy and my stomach seems to be performing gymnastics as I wait. The closer to the front I gain, the more nervous I become. I gulp down several breaths of air in an attempt to calm myself but it seems little use. I don't quite understand why I feel so nervous, I've never felt this nervous in my life.

I feel completely helpless and trapped if like a tiger locked in a small cage, circling it as it attempts to find a way to free its self and fight for freedom.

I think a tiger would have more chance of gaining freedom than I the thought circles my mind as my gaze falls on the heavily armed guards that surround us, watching us. I can't help but feel like someone's prized possession that they're terrified will be stolen by someone else. *Wasn't there once a show, they said it was originally a psychological study, a show just over a century ago that became a huge hit. Oh! What did they call it?* Suddenly the name hits me, *big brother, I feel as if I'm in such a place,* I think as I finally step to the front. My feet aching from standing for so long.

I must have been stood there for at least twenty minutes and now its my turn to attempt to make an impression.

"And now! The girl you have all been waiting for, the huntress that proved herself in all ways, the girl with the flaming arrow, please give her a warm welcome! It's Devotion!" I hear my name announced by a light male voice that sounds as if he could be homosexual. I step forth and male greets me, his hair is black with a blue streak, he's covered in so much fake tan that he's a bright orange colour. He welcomes me with a large grin painted on his face before he takes my hand and leads me further onto a large stage. The lights cause my eyes to feel as if they are burning as they leave me completely blind for a moment and I find questions surrounding me. The male leads me to a strange, blood red seat and motions for me to sit down. "Hello Devotion," he says and I realise the voice belongs to him. He sits down in a black seat close to mine and looks to me.

"Hey," I mutter in a voice that makes it seem as if I'm not bothered that he's speaking to me.

"Now there are a lot of questions everyone has for you," he begins and in the corner of my eye, I catch the glimpse of a large camera mixing among the flashing lights of photographic cameras.

"I bet they do," I reply.

"How do you feel, being the second huntress to prove yourself worthy in such a *gruesome* and *horrific* manner?" He begins, he seems to emphasise the words *gruesome* and *horrific* for more effect.

"I'm still trying to figure out if it were just a dream or not," I reply and several people laugh, including the strange male interviewing me. I had no intention of it being funny and because of this, pure rage begins to boil inside of me but I force it to one side.

"Now the first huntress was Devote, the second Devotion, it must be something in the name don't you think?" He replies.

"I'd say its something they put in the food, but that's just me," again people laugh and I can't quite understand why.

"I have a question!" A familiar male voice shouts from the press that seem to have formed some sort of audience.

"And that would be?" I ask, my voice suddenly sounding polite.

"Would you say you're really as threatening as you appear to be?" The male asks as my eyes adjust and I realise it's the same male I'd posed for outside.

"I guess you could say I'm more dangerous than threatening, but I'll leave it up to you to decide after seeing me in battle and in the games," I reply, my voice changing so that it sounds dark and deadly.

"You seem to strike me as more sexy yet deadly than dangerous and threatening," the male sat next to me comments. "You certainly have a beautiful complexion, I doubt your stylist needed to work on you as much as some of the rest in order to make you look beautiful"

"Why thank you," I mutter, my voice becoming dark and mysterious, "I guess you could say I am quite deadly"

And why does my voice keep changing? I wonder silently.

"I guess you could, after all, we've already seen how deadly you can be," the male beside me replies.

"I'm sorry, I didn't quite catch your name," I mutter quietly so that the audience can't hear me.

"James," he replies.

"Thank you James, can I ask what you thought to the fight that occurred at the Call Outs?" I reply.

"I thought it was enchanting how you moved so gracefully. Are you of elven blood?" James replies.

"That I am," I say.

"Well then it explains how enchantingly graceful, beautiful and sexy you are, I look forward to seeing you fight in the games"

"I look forward to killing in the games"

"I'm sure you do," he replies, "and sadly that's all we have time for today, I hope you enjoyed seeing Devotion! Unfortunately we are running out of time and this young lady is very busy tonight!"

I stand and leave the stage on the opposite side to where I entered as quickly and quietly as my legs can carry me without being obvious that I feel desperate to leave the blinding lights and screaming audience behind.

Innocence joins my side as soon as I step off the stage and we continue forth to where we're supposed to dine. Following the long, dark corridor, "You seem unusually distant even for you," she says once we've fallen behind the others. "Is it because of what happened the day of the call outs?"

"I guess, it's not fair how the expect us to be nothing but killing machines," I mutter.

Is it just me or does it seem like this world has no compassion and has no understanding of how precious life is? I wonder.

"It's not, but be grateful that you're still alive and after the games we'll have our freedom, finally we will be free to do as we choose, our lives will no longer be controlled by the company," Innocence replies.

"I guess"

"Think about it, we can drink all the wine we want, eat whatever we want, do whatever we want without anyone telling us we can't do it, no one will be trying to control us," Innocence continues as if I haven't spoken.

"But the others will never experience that, all they've known is strict training, painful experiments and death surrounding us, they will never experience freedom because they're dead, and some of those whom are dead, there deaths are on my hands," I reply.

"I know, but you must think of yourself, think of your own future and not what could have been the future of someone whom is dead"

"I guess you're right but their blood shall forever be on my hands, as shall the blood of murderers, paedophiles, rapists and others that are in the games, their blood shall be on our hands"

"They chose to do terrible things though, they deserve the fate that shall fall upon them for they must face the consequences of their actions," Innocence replies and yet again she's right, they have caused so much suffering, their fate is what they deserve.

"As usual you're right," I mutter and a gleaming smile grows on her face.

"I would have thought you would have realised that most the time, I am right," Innocence says, her voice sounding unusually cocky which doesn't seem to suit her.

"Come on, we have dinner awaiting us"

"I wonder what they'll have prepared, something tasty I hope"

"I hope so too, it would be nice to pig out again on a beautiful meal and maybe some wine"

"Do you think it'll be like the meal after the call outs?" Innocence asks.

"I hope so, the meal tasted absolutely amazing," I reply.

"I'm glad we agree on that, I can't believe that something could taste so good, it makes you want more doesn't it?"

"That is something else I must agree with you on," I reply and she laughs, "I wonder if the enemy have ever tasted anything so spectacular before"

"I doubt it, perhaps tonight they will as one of their final meals"

"Maybe," I reply suddenly hating the thought as we approach the door. As soon as we step through it, the heavy metal door closes with a large bang that echoes throughout the room and the sound of the mechanisms that lock the door seems squeaky and louder than the previous doors.

I take a quick glance around the room, the walls have been painted so that they show scenes of previous games. Each wall shows a different scene of a hunter or huntress killing the enemy in different ways and each painting seems almost perfect. Upon the ceiling is a painting of angels laying upon clouds, watching the scenes in awe, all of them seem pleased by what they see.

I look down to the floor to see another painting, one that seems to resemble hell itself with prisoners burning in the eternal flame, screaming in agony whilst hideous demons with red eyes and black bat wings and dark grey skin torture them. I notice each of the demons are bald with long, twisted pointy ears and some have sticking out noses. Most of them seem to have most of their ears pierced and some even have facial piercings.

Some of the prisoners in the painting of hell have hooks under their skin and the demons appear to be ripping them out one by one, whilst other prisoners are whipped whilst they labour for the demons and others burn and scream, their faces painted in agony.

I smell no food and see no areas to dine in the room. There is no furniture and the light seems to radiate from the pictures themselves especially the one of hell.

"Is this the room to dine in?" I ask Innocence quietly. Every last hunter and huntress seems equally as confused as I.

"I don't know," Innocence replies. Suddenly, a heavy metal door opens in front of us and the chaotic sound echoes throughout the room as the enemy enters. Immediately, I find myself searching for the male I saw earlier and when I catch his eyes, I feel the same warmth flood throughout my body as his eyes change to lily pad green once more.

The door closes automatically as soon as the enemy have filled the large room even further and locks. Finally, a third door opens and we each look to each other in confusion.

"I think we're supposed to go through there," Innocence mutters.

"Probably," I agree.

A female dressed in a military uniform steps into the room, her fair skin seems to glow in the light and her pointed ears are a clear sign she is elven. Her eyes glow an unusual grey and she appears to be miserable. "Prisoners, form a single line here," she commands, a hint of sadness in her eyes as she stands in a particular area. Immediately the prisoners scramble together to form a long line that reaches the very end of the large room and curves slightly in order to fit. There must be at least fifty if not sixty of them. "Hunters and Huntresses, form a single line here," she moves only slightly to the right, "in the order you were called out in," she continues. We each move with grace and form a perfect line. I look to the prisoner on my left to see it is the male I locked eyes with. Stood beside him, I can feel the same beautiful warmth radiating from him and entering my body, melting the ice in my veins once more. The warmth seems stronger than before, stronger than when I had gazed into his eyes and it seems to cause me to feel a tinge of happiness that no matter how much I try to push it to one side, I can't.

I wait patiently for the next commands, unable to stop myself from glancing at the male every once in a while and I notice that he doing the same to me. Is he trying to some up my strength and ability to fight? Does he find it hard to believe that I've killed people? Does he feel threatened by my appearance?

The woman turns, "Follow me!" She commands before she begins to walk down a long corridor that has been painted white and every few feet has an archway with different archangels carved into them, with different scenes of them fighting in battle. We follow her into another, much larger room.

This time the walls are painted in battle scenes, showing archangels fighting whilst others watch up above and the blood of the defeated soak into the earth. The floor of the room has been painted blood red and looks as if it is a sea of blood.

In the centre of the room is a large, oak table that has been nailed to the floor and food is laid upon the table. A large range of food awaits us, from chilly con carnie to chicken tikka and Sheppard's pie.

"You are to sit beside the person stood beside you and each hunter or huntress must have at least one prisoner on either side of him or her," the woman says. We each approach the table and sit at the oak benches that surround the table. A female sits to my right, her long greasy brown hair tied up in a ponytail and her crooked nose held high in the air, she looks down at me as if she sees herself as a higher being but soon her dark brown, almost black eyes seem to relax slightly yet something about her expression gives me the impression that she is disgusted by me. Suddenly, it changes so that it seems as if she is attracted to me in some unusual way. Deep bags under her eyes tell me that she hasn't slept much at all recently, if ever.

I notice the male beside me shuffles closer and glares at her, a low animal like growl echoes from deep within him before he looks at me. The room has already erupted into conversation as hunters and huntresses try to speak amongst themselves whilst prisoners either interrupt them or speak amongst themselves as well.

"Hey," the male beside me says, his voice is soft and compassionate as well as comforting, warm and welcoming.

"Hey," I mutter quietly, sounding unusually shy as I begin filling my plate with food.

"You're Devotion right?" He says and I nod in response, "I'm Callum"

"A pleasure to meet you Callum," I reply in a soft voice.

"How are you finding it here so far? I know its not the most welcoming of places," Callum replies, his full, dark lips seem to hold a strange temptation that seems to cause an unusual urge inside of me to hold a conversation with him.

"You can say it's a very unwelcoming, cold, dark place filled demons, death, hatred and is in great disrepair," I reply and he laughs, "do I keep saying funny things today?"

"It's the way you're so blunt about things, so forward," he replies.

"I wasn't as blunt in my interview and people were still laughing at what I was saying," I reply.

"Yea, I saw," his voice sounds cheerful and full of life as we begin talking properly. "How did you find James? You two seemed pretty cool with each other"

"He seemed like a nice guy, I liked him," I reply.

"I like him too," the female beside me interrupts yet Callum seems to ignore her, the only acknowledgement he gives her is the same animalistic growl from deep within his chest and immediately, she shuts up.

"I think you did pretty well in your interview, you're all definitely professionals when it comes to interviews," Callum says.

"Considering none of us have ever been interviewed before, I'll take that as a compliment to all of us," I reply, a small soft smile growing on my face as I begin to feel more comfortable. His eyes glisten with life once more as he looks at me and something deep inside of me begins to stir because of the life returning in his eyes.

"Well you wouldn't have believed it," Callum comments.

"Thank you," I mutter as I take the first mouthful of chicken tikka. The flavour explodes in my mouth and the spices dance on my tongue like a ballet dancer.

"Beautiful," Callum mutters quietly, drawing my attention from my food and back to him, he smiles and his cheeks burn so brightly they remind me of tomatoes, "t-the f-food" he stutters as he points to his plate with his fork, his mouth full of food.

"I'd have to agree," I reply. I look away and stare deeply into the fire of the candle in front of me and notice that the entire rooms lit by candles. Something about the flame seems to draw me in to it, helping me cope with the strange feelings that are beginning to stir, feelings I don't quite understand.

It's probably to make us seem more intimidating to the enemy, dim lights can cause such an effect in the right atmosphere and I'd say this is definitely the right atmosphere, my mind rationalises before I have chance to wonder why. I find myself completely drawn into the flame, losing every last piece of my trail of thought, as I watch it flicker whilst radiating warmth and bringing us light as well as giving me some sort of hope I've never really understood.

*   *   *

Time seems to have passed by so quickly and I find myself yawning before I get chance to settle into bed. All night I've been speaking to Callum, throughout most of the meal, which was at least an hour and a half long in the end, we were talking and he walked me to my room and throughout that we were talking. We were talking about random things, he answered many of my questions about the outside world, he told me all about how people go clubbing regularly at weekends where they get so drunk they can barely walk. He seemed so nice and genuine. Not like most of the prisoners at the table. The girl whom had been sat to my other side had kept interrupting our conversation and eventually I learnt that her name was Katy-Lea and she didn't strike me as a nice person. I noticed that every time she interrupted our conversation, Callum seemed to growl an human growl and that seemed to fascinate me.

My head hit's the pillow and as I lay there, all I can think about is Callum. *What could have possibly driven him to commit such a serious crime that he'd end up with such a fate?* I silently wonder. *He seems far to nice to have commit any serious offences but is it just an illusion?* Something stirs inside of me and my heart tells me that tonight he was being genuine and it wasn't just an illusion. I stare up at the ceiling for a moment before I turn on my side, curl up into a ball like a cat and close my eyes, and within minutes I fall asleep.

My dream begins so innocently. I'm laid in a field, surrounded by sunflowers, the sun shining brightly in the sky, its heat caressing my face gently. Everything seems so innocent, so beautiful, so perfect.

It's then, as the clouds block out the sun, and a chilly breeze runs down my spine causing me to shiver, I hear the scream. Instincts race through my body as I stand and begin to run towards a large set of woods, to investigate the scream. To help the owner of the voice. The scream carries such a fear that it blasts a breath of air from my lungs and the agonising pain it carries causes the hairs on the back of my neck to stand on ends.

I'm running with incredible speed, each step I take is equally as light as the step before. The scream comes to a sudden stop but I continue running in the direction it came from. The emergency that's flooding my body won't let me stop, adrenaline begins pumping inside of me, allowing me to run faster but it doesn't seem as fast as I can normally run. It's as if I'm someone else.

It feels as if I wouldn't be able to stop when I do eventually get to the source of the scream.

But when I do get there, I feel too sick by the sight that I have to stop running.

Organs have been thrown everywhere, the strong coppery smell of blood lingers in the air, invading my nose, blood soaks the autumn leaves on the floor and as my gaze follows the blood, it settles on the mutilated body of a young teenage girl. Her rib cage sticking out of her chest, every last organ has been taken out of her body and thrown randomly around the wood.

I clamp my hand over my mouth to stop myself screaming as tears burn my eyes and pore down my face. Something inside of me screams that I know her yet my heart tells me that I have never laid my eyes on her before.

Suddenly, the sound of a snapping twig grabs my attention, I look in its direction and I see her. Instantly, I know her.

Katy-Lea.

Her hair and clothes are soaked with blood so much so its dripping from her and to the floor, her hands are soaked in it and she's staring at me with wild, psychotic eyes. I know I could kill her if she tried to attack me, I've been training all of my life for such a task yet for some reason, I turn and run as quickly as I can.

For some reason, in this dream, I'm out of character. The sight of death, no matter how gruesome, has never fazed me so much before so why now?

Suddenly, the dream fades and I see flashing images of a male stood in my place, his face completely blurred out to the point where I can barely make out the colour of his skin, it changes to a court room where the same male is on the stand and then it shows Katy-Lea, locked up in a cell.

I wake up in a sweat, unable to make sense of it all. *What did I just see? Did that really happen? Did Katy-Lea actually murder a teenage girl and only get caught because of the girls screams and a nearby male? It can't be! It must have just been a dream,* my mind begins to rationalise it but something in my heart and in my gut tells me otherwise. It tells me it was real, and that it did happen. The sadness that seems to surround the male causes my heart to scream things at me, telling me that the girl was meant to meet him in that meadow, that they were young lovers.

I stare out into the darkness, as if it could bring me more answers. As if it could tell me something.

The sound of gunshots from the outside world, rattles through my body, grabbing my attention. I hesitate for a moment before I pull of the bed covers and my feet gently touch the ice cold tile flooring of the grey room. I step towards the barred window and glance out into the winter night sky, the large lights rest on a body, shot dead in the snow. Blood soaks it, turning it from white to a haunting scarlet colour.

Strangely enough the body doesn't look human nor does it look elven. Its skin looks more like scales than skin and its ears are larger and the points of the ears are more obvious, more so than any elf I have ever seen. I look to the crescent moon and watch as a scarlet dot seems to appear. There are more gunshots yet I can't see any other bodies, and as it happens, the moon slowly turns to a scarlet colour.

"A scarlet coloured moon, does it speak of the blood spilled upon this night?" I wonder, the dreadful sounds of agonising screams and the snarls as strange warriors fight echo throughout my room, tormenting my ears causing them to ring. They fight for something but for what is unknown to me.

The coppery smell of blood fills the room and I know from the mixtures of scents that I can smell that at least a hundred have been killed.

The gun shots come to a sudden stop and I listen for a moment but I hear nothing more. I back away from the window and enter the warm covers of my bed as I lay down and begin to wonder. I have never read of anything such as the creature I witnessed dead on the floor, never heard of such a creature. What are they?

In some sense, the creature resembled both humans and elves, the shape of the creature was like that of a human and an elves. If it weren't for the dark green scales, the long tail that resembles a devils tail and the unusually long ears, it would have looked completely human.

Could it have been the result of an experiment just like the elves were. We were a result of experimentation, couldn't they be a different result to experimentation? I wonder, they may have been wilder than any human, or something like that. They resemble animals in some ways. They could have been human if it weren't for the parts of them that seem to resemble animals.

My mind continues to wonder, constantly thinking of the creature when finally I fall into a deep sleep. Callum seems to creep into my thoughts before I manage to fall asleep. Somehow it seems like I can't erase him from my mind.

*   *   *

The gentle touch of the morning sun rests on my cheek, waking me. I open my eyes and for a moment I'm blinded by the sun light that fills my room. The warm touch of sun brings a more welcoming morning. The glistening snow outside looks beautiful and speaks of freedom. Inside, I realise that I long for freedom. To feel as if I'm not owned by someone.

I step out of the warm covers and into the cold, I grab the training clothes that have been hung up near the bathroom and quickly change. The training clothes consist of a black t-shirt with a silver stripe down both arms and *'Huntress'* printed over my right breast and *'Devotion'* over my left. Again upon my left and right arm guards, they say the same words.

The shorts are similar to the t-shirt. Black with a silver stripe on each side. I stepped out of the room to be welcomed by the sound of an alarm coming from every room in the hallway where the hunters and huntresses slept last night.

I watch as several of my fellow candidates step out of their rooms, ready to begin the day. Each of them look as confused as I feel.

The same woman from the last night arrives at the end of the hallway, dressed in the same military uniform, "Follow me," she commands immediately. Not something I'm not used to however it would be nice if she had welcomed us with a *'good morning!'*

Silently, I wonder what will be happening today. Will it be training or something more?

CHAPTER 4

Meeting the Prisoners

We move swiftly, following the woman until we arrive at a large training room. I watch as the prisoners herd into the room like sheep. Immediately, my eyes search for Callum, secretly hoping that last night wasn't a dream even though a part of me hopes that the creature I saw last night was nothing more than a dream, a figment of imagination.

I panic slightly for a moment until he comes into view, it seems as if he's searching for me as well and when his eyes finally lock onto mine, a small smile grows on his face and his eyes light up. The warmth immediately floods through my body and I have to force myself not to smile yet it seems so difficult not to.

The same woman steps into the centre of the room and speaks in a confident, firm voice yet it seems to hold a hint of fear, "Hunters and huntresses must train with prisoners today, you must socialise and you shall train until noon, breakfast shall be served in here shortly," she says before stepping towards a wall and standing straight, watching us.

I glance at my fellow candidates and wonder what they're thinking, no one seems to have made an attempt to step forward and begin training as well as socialising. I look back to Callum and in one, brave step, I find myself being the first to make an attempt to approach the equipment in the centre of the room, never mind the prisoners.

My gaze never leaves Callum's face as he too steps forward towards the equipment and into a stride that is at the same pace as mine. We stop at the table of equipment and pause for a moment.

I hesitate before I lift my hand and he takes mine in his and we shake hands. My hand tingles as I feel the warmth radiate from his skin and into mine in what feels as if it could only be magical. I notice an unusual black tribal tattoo around his wrist and forearm.

"Hey," he says in a soft gentle tone. His voice is welcoming and comforting with a slight hint of drowsiness. The slight bags under his eyes tell that he's tired yet they seem to be lightening up with life and energy once more.

I smile a soft, warming smile, "Hey," I reply, my voice sounding unusually welcoming and warm. We hold hands for a moment and for some reason I feel as if I can't let go. In my heart, I don't want to let go and I don't quite understand why but I can't stand the thought of letting go. My heart hammers against my rib cage because of his touch and I feel slightly dizzy and sick as my stomach performs back flips.

With an unusual force that I've never quite had to use before, I pull away and ignore the strange stinging pain in my heart. *Why is it so hard to pull away?* I wonder as I try to force myself to look away from his eyes but I can't. Suddenly, Innocence helps me look away when she touches my shoulder sending a shot of ice through my veins and destroying the warmth brought by Callum.

"Are you ready?" Innocence asks and I nod, unable to speak due to the lack of trust I have in my voice. I feel my body tremble slightly and my legs seem to be taking on the form of jelly. Shakily, I grab a bow from the pile of equipment and step towards the archery range before I begin shooting repeatedly.

Each time I hit gold as I listen to Innocence chat away to me as she begins throwing knives, she's not the best at throwing knives but at least she's putting in the effort to improve. Yet my mind is else where. My mind seems fixated on Callum. The warmth in his eyes and smile seem to stick in my mind.

I feel so confused.

How can someone cause me to feel such things? How can he be causing such a strange effect on my body? Why do I feel this way? How does he cause me to feel this? Jelly legs, butterflies in my stomach, my heart pounding in my chest with a simple touch, my eyes unable to look away from his, the warmth he brings to me. How can he be causing all of this? I'm a Huntress! I shall be hunting him soon! I can't afford to feel such emotions! My mind spins with thoughts and no matter what Innocence is saying, its not entering my mind. I find myself nodding every time she pauses. *What exactly am I feeling?*

Finally, her words break through the barrier of thoughts that have formed in my mind. As I approach the target to collect my arrows, she gently touches my hand and stops me pulling out the arrow, "Devotion, you're beginning to trouble me, you seem distracted if not distant. You have been unusually distant since we arrived here. I know normally you're quite distant and you keep yourself to yourself but at this moment, you're acting off even for you"

"I'm fine, I just have a lot on my mind," I reply quietly, keeping my voice as calm as possible.

"Is it what happened at the training centre? I've heard of Hunters and Huntresses being haunted after the games, it could be what's happening to you, oh what did they call it," she taps her chin with the finger nail of her index finger as she begins to think, "post traumatic stress disorder! That was it!"

"It's not what happened that's on my mind, I don't have post traumatic stress disorder, its something else, something I need to work out . . . on my own," I reply.

Innocence sighs, "Well if you need me, you know where I am," she replies.

"Thanks, I'll come to you sometime and talk to you about it but here isn't the place," I reply, shooting a glance at the camera filming us.

"Good point, the camera's are going to be glaring at us for a while until the games are long over," Innocence says.

I nod in agreement, "Exactly, I'm not going to speak about what's on my mind whilst camera's are about, watching our every move"

"We're going to be here for a few days as well according to the changes made by the makers"

"Sounds fun, we're going to be having a blast here"

"They're after drama in this years games, they want to spice it up a little so its changed dramatically to create the drama they want. It's to keep people interested, to keep the whole world watching and talking about us. Make us the highlight of every conversation in the world"

"Yea and so they want us to create some sort of bond with the prisoners or something don't they? So that we will fight for them until they're the last standing or perhaps cause a few tears when we kill them"

"Exactly, the makers are clever, they know what they have to do to create what they want," Innocence replies.

"And I have a feeling drama isn't the only thing they want in this years games," I mutter.

"Why? What else do you think they want?" Innocence whispers as I pull out an arrow and place it in the quiver on my back.

I glance over my shoulder and look to Callum, something in my gut tells me that the makers have something new in mind for this year and its something to do with him, "A lot of violence, gory deaths and anger, a lot of anger" I whisper. I notice that he isn't socialising with any of the prisoners, he seems to be keeping himself to himself as he lifts weights. I force myself to look away and return to pulling out the arrows once more.

"To create even further drama," she whispers in realisation and something in my gut tells me she's right. "They want strong emotions and the stronger the emotions the better for them"

"That's right, the more anger and sadness they can produce the more the world will be hooked to this years games"

"I wonder why they're creating so many changes this year, some of them don't make sense though, but I guess it will all fit into place in the games"

"Some of them don't and some of them we don't know about, we'll find out what else they're after when the games begin" I mutter. Gracefully, I take an arrow in my hand and prepare myself to pull it out the target when and image appears in my mind.

The image of an unusual radiant white blade slowly growing out the palm of someone's hand. It looks like a painful yet quick process as it moves and something about it tells me its deadlier than any weapon ever created by man. Blood trickles down the arm of the person, coming from an open wound caused by the blade. My mouth becomes dry and I can feel the rain as it hits my face.

I hold the glowing blade in my hand now that it is no longer in my palm and in a swift and graceful movement, I turn around and throw the blade into the throat of one of the male prisoners that I recognise from the meal. The prisoner falls to his knees, his eyes never leaving mine as his skin begins to crack around the blade.

The cracks begin to spread throughout his body and they begin to glow the same radiant white colour as the blade. The light begins to glow brighter and brighter and his skin turns a glowing orange colour.

Suddenly, his body explodes and blood splatters all over the trees and all over my body. The image fades and I return to the training room.

Innocence touches me gently and smiles a soft welcoming smile, "Are you okay?" She asks. My forehead feels drenched in sweat, my bodies shaking and my legs feel as if they will give way to my weight at any minute.

I shake my head, "I need to sit down," I reply. She nods and guides me to a chair, her arm around my waist as she supports some of my weight. I sit down, my head spinning and the palms of my hands burning as if they're on fire.

"Did you have some sort of vision?" Innocence asks after a moment of silence. I gulp down and nod before putting my head between my knees, suddenly feeling nauseated and dizzy, "what did you see?"

"A prisoner explode," I mutter.

"Which?" She asks.

"I don't know, I recognised him from last night at the meal, I swear he was sat next to Conquer"

"I have an idea who and I'm guessing it was in the games"

"Yes," I mutter, feeling even more nauseous the more I think about it. "I feel like I'm going to puke!" I whisper under my breath.

Out of nowhere, the sound of footsteps approach us, "Is she okay?" A familiar voice asks and immediately my heart begins pounding in my chest as I think of his name. Callum. The warmth he brings to me tends to the sickness I feel and seems to heal it almost instantly, as if he has some sort of healing abilities. As if he has some sort of magic.

No longer do I feel as if I'm about to throw up, if anything, I feel better than I had done before the vision.

"Yea, she's fine, this happens to some Hunters and Huntresses, its what we call second sight, Devotion is gifted with this—" Innocence says but before she can continue explaining I grab her arm and dig my nails into her wrist with an incredible strength. I feel her tense slightly as the warmth of blood touches my fingertips.

I look up and slowly release my grip.

"Sorry," she mouths and I smile.

"Second sight, sounds quite interesting," Callum says with a warm smile, his eyes stare at me in concern. "I've never heard of that in hunters and huntresses before"

"That's because its kept under wraps by the company, they don't like people knowing about the gift of second sight," I explain before looking to Innocence and growling the next words from between grit teeth, "I wonder why"

There is a long moment of uncomfortable silence before Innocence speaks, "Why don't you train with us? You seem to get on with Devotion and if she is fine with you then I trust her judgement"

"I would appreciate that, it's better than weightlifting whilst watching them"—he points behind him as he speaks—"they're constantly trying to show off their strength to one another, its quite boring really and they're little bastards at times"

"Bastards?" Innocence and I both reply in confusion, neither of us quite able to understand.

"Were none of their parents married when they were conceived and born?" I ask.

"Probably not but that's not what I meant," Callum replies, both I and Innocence look at him in confusion, "you don't quite understand do you?" We shake our heads, "it doesn't matter, anyway they like giving out the odd threat here and there, saying they're going to beat the crap out of you in the games or that they're going to kill you"

"Hmmm" Innocence mutters with a long, slow nod before she looks to me, "are you feeling better?"

"Much," I reply before standing up, at first I feel a little dizzy and lightheaded but soon I recover. Callum looks at me with concern clear in his eyes, "I got up too quickly," I explain and he nods before we continue forth and I finish collecting the arrows and return to shooting them.

"You're excellent, you never seem to miss," Callum says after a while.

"Thanks," I reply as I draw back another arrow, "it takes plenty of practise and training," I release the arrow and yet again it hit's the centre of the target, meeting the clump of arrows that have already grouped together.

"And it must take one hell of a good aim, not everyone could do that even with plenty of practise and training," Callum replies.

"From what I've been told about my mum, she had excellent aim," I mutter "its probably one of the reasons I was chosen when I was born, because she had a trait or two that they liked and they thought they would pass down to me."

"From what you've been told? Haven't you ever met your mum?" Callum asks.

"I've never met either of my parents, all of us were taken from our parents at birth," I reply.

"That must really suck, not ever knowing your parents, I guess its like not really knowing who you are," Callum says.

"At times it is," Innocence replies.

"But we know who we are, we have our own personalities," I say.

"And in a sense, we are our own family, we were raised together, taught together, trained together, so in a sense Devotion is my sister," Innocence says.

"Even though we are not sisters by blood, we are sisters by our hearts," I mutter as I draw back another arrow.

"Then it must have been even harder for you Devotion, to have killed your fellows," Callum says, solemnly.

A single tear falls down my cheek and my eyes burn, I gulp down the rest of the tears and with a quick, rough movement I wipe it away. I put my bow on its stand and take off the quiver, leaving it carefully balanced against the bows stand before I walk away, unable to face the build up of emotions in my heart. The emotions that seem to have attached themselves to the memory of the Call Outs.

"Don't worry, sometimes memories are too painful to face especially when they are filled with raw emotion," I hear Innocence say, her voice sounding wiser than her years could have possibly taught her.

As I walk away, I spot Frost glaring at me evilly. In her eyes I can see something that resembles jealousy but I ignore it. I ignore her.

I rush to the toilet and with a bang of the door and a quick movement of my hand on the lock, I lock myself in. Feeling the sudden rush of emotions flood my body, I collapse in a heap on the floor, consumed by my own sorrow and self hatred.

* * *

A knock on the door suddenly brings me back to reality, pulling me out of the memory that has replayed a dozen times in my mind. "Devotion, it's Callum, there's a queue out here and you've been in there for twenty minutes, are you okay?" A male voice emerges from behind the door.

I pick myself up off the floor and wipe away the tears that have been streaming down my face, I hold my head high before stepping towards the door. "I'm fine," I reply before unlocking the door and stepping out to see a large male stood beside Callum. He looms over me with anger burning in his eyes, and instantly I recognise him to be the male from my vision. His large build and the anger in his face is the same as from the vision. His broad jaw clenches and releases repeatedly, his golden tan brings a haunting appearance to his face. The darkness around his almost black eyes causes this appearance to greaten yet the threatening glare he gives me doesn't phase me.

I step past him and stand closer to Callum, silently wondering whether it will be me that shall kill him or shall it be another. *Will I be able to create such a deadly weapon with magic? I've never done such a thing in my life,* I think to myself. *Maybe its something Devote will teach me before the games.*

"Do you want to continue training with Innocence and myself?" Callum asks.

I nod, "So she told you her name" I reply.

We begin walking back towards the range equipment area of the training room, "Yes, we began talking about certain things, she has many questions about the outside world, she seems very curious about the freedom we have," he replies, "I always took the freedom for granted, believing that we were trapped and controlled by the leaders and by the company, the largest company in the world that seems to run everything but from what she's told me, none have you have ever experienced true freedom"

"We had never even tasted alcohol until the evening after the Call Outs, the taste of the wine was certainly unique and I hope to experience such a thing again," I pause for a moment, "and are you talking about the company that own, and organise the games?"

"Yea, I am, in the outside world, they control a lot of things and I bet you do hope to experience things like alcohol and drugs," Callum replies, "alcohol is certainly unique but it can cause you to do stupid things if you drink too much, and trust me, no matter what training you've had, it'll all go out the window if you get wasted"

"I'm guessing wasted is another term for drunk?"

"Yea, it is"

"What other things can you do in the outside world?" I ask.

"Get drunk, go to parties, get high, smoke, have sex. There are a lot of things you can do," Callum replies.

"All things none of us have ever experienced and our fallen brothers and sisters will never experience"

"Yea," Callum replies, his voice sounding slightly restrained with sadness.

"It will certainly be a shock and hard for all of us to get out of the routine of training, well at least it will be for me, after the games that is"

"In the games you'll be too focused on hunting us," his voice becomes restrained even further.

"There is always the prisoner that receives his or her freedom," I find myself attempting to comfort him due to an unusual urge that seems to be building inside of my heart.

"Yes but that's if you survive the hunting all the way to the end," he says solemnly.

"You doubt that you will don't you?" I ask in a soft comforting voice.

"I am unlikely to survive until the end, the odds are against me"

"The odds may be against you as are they to all of the prisoners but there's still the chance of you making it until the end"

"I hope so," he mutters quietly, he seems to know something I don't.

A part of me screams at me to tell him that I hope so to. A large part of me does hope that he makes it until the end and gains his freedom. Ignoring the pain that suddenly stabs through my heart at the thought of his death, I continue towards the archery range, pick up the bow and return to shooting.

"Aren't you going to have any breakfast?" Innocence asks.

"Not in the mood, I'll last pretty well until dinner," I reply.

"You should eat something," Callum mutters.

"Well I'm not going to because I'm not in the mood," I mutter.

"Please, you should eat especially after a vision, you can't train with nothing in your stomach," Innocence replies, her eyebrows raised at me and her eyes pleading.

I place down the bow for a second time, my shoulders hunch, "fine," I say in a voice filled with defeat.

*   *   *

Training passes quickly and soon lunch arrives and a long, well needed break. I watch as prisoners play drafts and chess. Keeping mostly to myself, I eat my food in silence that is until Callum approaches me.

"Want to play scrabble?" He asks, I glance to my left and right then over my shoulder to be sure he's talking to me.

"Scrabble? Never heard of it," I reply.

"It's a word game," Callum replies as he sits beside me.

"Doesn't sound interesting to me if I'm going to be perfectly honest, I've never been a person of many words," I mutter

"What? Scrabble? Scrabbles awesome!"

"It still doesn't interest me, I have no interest in word games nor do I have any interest in board games in general"

"So, all you do is train?" Callum mutters.

"No!" I say, my voice sounding defensive, "I do other things"

"Like what?"

"Sometimes I watch TV, like *True Blood* and *Supernatural*, they're pretty decent shows"

"They're almost a century old if not older"

"Well I like the old shows and some of the even older films like the *Carry On* films," I reply.

"I'd have to admit that the *Carry On* films are pretty epic," Callum agrees, "what's your favourite?"

"I'd have to say *Carry on Camping*, it's certainly a good laugh!" I reply with a shy giggle.

"It's my favourite too," Callum agrees, with a chuckle.

"I also appreciate fine art, and paintings of scenery like this one"—I take out an old photograph of a painting of a beautiful mountain scene with a clear blue sky and a gorgeous lake that moves through the valley's created by the mountains—"I've never been able to find out the artist but apparently it belonged to my mother, they say the artist is one of my ancestors on my mothers side"

"Do you have any idea who your mother is?"

I shake my head, "No, when I was growing up there was a hologram of her that followed me until the Call Outs but her face was never clear enough to make out and her voice was computerised," I pause for a moment, "one day, I want to find her and my father, I want to meet them"

"I bet you do, I've always wanted to meet my dad," Callum replies.

"You've never met him?"

"My mum says that he went to prison when I was only a baby, she said that when he got out he didn't want anything to do with her or me. Apparently, he had a new girlfriend and was starting a family with her or something like that," Callum says solemnly.

"That's horrible, hasn't he thought that a child may in fact need his father?" I reply, sadness clear in my tone.

"Clearly not" he mutters. With an uncontrollable urge, I move, wrapping my arms around his neck and holding him close in an embrace. I feel him hesitate for a moment before wrapping his arms around my waist.

"Then he is not worthy of the title *'father'*" I mutter, a single tear falling down my cheek.

"Thanks, I guess your right in a sense but it would still be nice to know who he is," Callum mutters.

I pull away and fidget slightly, unable to forgive myself for what I have just done. "I know that feeling"

*   *   *

The rest of the day consists of training and Callum and I talking about whatever we can think of and once night comes, I feel the flood of relief fill my body at the thought of going to sleep. I find myself falling into a deep sleep the moment my head hit's the pillow.

Morning arrives swiftly and I feel as if I have only just closed my eyes when the light hits my face. I open my eyes and glance out the window at the snow storm that seems to have taken its hold on the outside world.

I grab the fresh pair of training clothes that have been hung up once again, they look exactly the same as the pair from yesterday. Suddenly, I hear the alarm echo in my room and swiftly I change before standing outside of the room.

The same woman as yesterday greets us at the end of the corridor, "Today you have free range of what you're doing, consider it a day off," she says.

Yea, like Devote and Fusion would allow that! I think to myself before I remember that they have no rein here this year as decreed by the makers the night we arrived. *I think I'll start today with a healthy breakfast and then begin studying, I might find something that'll help me in the games.* I follow my fellow hunters and huntresses out of the corridor and into a large dining room.

"Devotion!" I hear Innocence call before she bounds up to me, "A day off! How are you going to spend the day?"

I pour myself a quick fruit smoothie and glance at what is on offer for breakfast, "I think I'm going to have breakfast and do some studying," I reply.

"I'm guessing you'll be in the library then," Innocence replies sounding slightly disappointed, "look at you, all your focussing on is the games," she pauses for a moment and her eyes lighten up before she mutters the words quietly, "or its an attempt to avoid a certain someone!"

"Shush!" I reply as I grab some toast, "I'm focussed on the games like you should be,"

"Oh come off it!" Innocence replies, "I saw the embrace yesterday, you," she pauses for a moment, "have a crush," she giggles.

"I do not have a crush!" I snap.

"You so do!" Innocence continues and I can feel my cheeks burning slightly. "Your cheeks are going pink, you're embarrassed because miss Devotion has a crush!" Her giggle becomes even more noticeable.

"I am incapable of such things," I snap.

"You may be an elf but you are still capable of a crush"

"I do not have a crush!"

"You do!"

"Shut up!" I growl angrily before slamming my plate on the table and sitting down.

"Devotion, stay calm! I was just having a joke," Innocence replies.

"I'm remaining focussed on the games just as you should be doing, I bet this idea of a day off is to distract us from our goals," I mutter quietly, my voice sounding much calmer now. "Our goal is to become the champion no matter what"

"Well they certainly didn't give you the wrong name, you're definitely devoted to the games and becoming the champion"

"Hence I'm studying for the first part of today, later I'll do further training and magic practising"

"I guess your right, I doubt none of the other hunters and huntresses at this table are as committed and devoted to this as you are," Innocence mutters.

"I'm not dropping my guard and I will work my hardest to at least make it to the top three if not the champion"

"And no doubt you'll not stop until you reach your goal, I guess I should leave you to it then"

"Thank you," I mutter.

*   *   *

Swiftly I hurry down the narrow corridor after finishing my breakfast and soon I realise that this prison is more of a maze than a prison. I follow the guards directions, left, then right, then take another left, then a swift left and then another right, follow the corridor after that, then at the end, take another left and it's the first large archway on my right. But as I walk, the corridors seem to get smaller and darker. But it isn't just the appearance that the corridor is getting darker, something about the atmosphere seems to be growing darker with every step I take. Gradually, I begin to feel nervous as I walk through the endless labyrinth called a prison.

Following the long corridor, I find myself running down a flight of stairs before arriving at the end. I take another left and glance around the much larger corridor. Suddenly, I see the large white archway with two cupids engraved into the wood, both cupids watch a large book engraved in the archway, awe written upon both of their faces. Clearly, they know that they will never truly be able to contain as much information as the large book holds.

I hesitate for a moment, unable to look away from the beautiful artwork. Silently, I wish I had a camera to take a picture and keep the memory of such work forever more, in a way that it shall not fade as quickly with time.

With one quick, brave step, I enter the large library. The comforting smell of old books welcomes me as I enter. I find myself surrounded by, what could only be, millions of books. More books than I have ever seen in my entire life.

The library at the training centre was nowhere near this large.

In complete astonishment, I continue forth, walking through the isles of books, completely unaware of anything but the books that surround me.

Suddenly, I bump into something that seems to be as hard as a brick wall and for a moment, my reflexes don't seem to want to work as I stand there staring blankly into the muscular chest of a male.

All I manage to do is step back in a daze and slowly glance up at his warm face, his smile growing as his eyes meet mine.

"I thought the Huntresses were always alert," he says with a little chuckle. The hazel slowly leaving his eyes and being replaced by a familiar lily pad green.

"I thought these books were wasted on prisoners because they didn't read, instead they worked on building their muscles so that they looks more intimidating towards other inmates, I believe we were both wrong," I reply, my voice sounding unusually defensive.

He chuckles a second time, "Well you need to be on your guard, where we're going is a dangerous place," his tone suddenly becomes serious and no matter how much I try to, I can't find a single hint of the humour that was in it just a moment ago.

"Which is why I can't start getting cocky, and I can't take a day off from training, not like the others are. I have to stay focussed," I reply.

"Your telling me, I know one of your Huntresses is getting a little too big for her shoes. Oh what's her name, winter, ice girl or something, whatever her name is—"

Unable to stop myself, I quickly interrupt him, "Frost, her names Frost."

"Okay, Frost. I can't decide whether she's cocky or just a bitch, one thing I know is she's getting a little too big for her boots. Earlier I saw her trying to make herself seem as if she's all powerful but that didn't work out too well," his smile becomes warm and welcoming again once more as he stares down at me, his gaze never leaving mine.

I can't help but return his smile as I begin speaking, "She's just a bitch, and don't worry, she's always been a little too big for her boots and that isn't exactly out of the ordinary," I reply and he laughs.

"I'm guessing she's always done that twitch for a walk as well," he chuckles as he speaks.

"Yup, she always twitches, she's never taken a normal step in her life," I reply.

"I'm guessing you two don't get on then?"

"She accused me of cheating on the train when all I was doing was what my trainer told me to do, and she's insulted me so many times, I've lost track of how many times she has insulted me," I pause for a moment, "so I guess you can say we've never got on and we never will get on"

"Well you never struck me as the type to be a bitch so no wonder you both don't get on," Callum replies.

"So what are you doing in a library? You don't strike me as the type that likes to read"

"Well clearly there's a lot of things you don't know about me little miss," Callum replies with a large smile on his face, "I've always been quite the book worm"

"Well you learn something new everyday"

"That you do," Callum pauses for a moment, "I was just seeing if I could find anything on that *second sight* thing Innocence said you have. I haven't really found much information on it though"

I raise my eyebrows at him, "Doing a background check on me are you?" I ask, my voice light with humour.

"I guess you could say that, I need to know who I'm up against if I'm going to be the prisoner rewarded his freedom so its best to know the enemy"

"Well then I should be doing a background check on you as well, I better know my enemy," he bursts into laughter at the end of my sentence and I giggle.

"No, I'm interested in what it is. No offence but none of you appear to be like humans and elves I've met, I've never heard of a human with second sight nor have I heard of an elf with it"

"I guess it must be unique to Hunters and Huntresses"

"Possibly, I found some information on it that came from a previous Champion of the games, her names Devote I believe," Callum begins walking as he talks and I follow him to a table filled with books. He glances at a page in a book and nods, "yea, her name is Devote"

"My trainer," I mutter

"Huh?"

"She's my trainer for the games, to turn me into this years Champion"

"That's weird, you both are named for being devoted and you both have second sight, kind of strange," Callum mutters.

"I know but it's a coincidence, she was as devoted as I am hence our names, the fact that we both have second sight is probably the reason she was made my trainer among other things, she also had to fight to the death to become the twelfth huntress," I reply, silently wondering whether there are far too many coincidences there.

"It's quite strange really if I'm going to be perfectly honest with you"

"It might seem strange, but that's how the games work for us, it's the strongest, the fastest, the most intellectual, the ones talented in magic, it is those whom make it into becoming the Hunters and Huntresses, so in effect its not really that strange," I reply.

"I guess that makes sense, and I bet when you were fighting you pulled back, you wouldn't have used a lot of your strength, speed, intellect and magic would you? That would be giving the game away in a sense," Callum mutters and immediately, I find myself looking back on the memory of the Call Outs and in a sudden realisation, I notice that I allowed the most of them to kill themselves off, using my intellect, knowing that it wouldn't be clever to take them all on at once. I used my speed to protect me, so that I wouldn't end up dead. I used little magic and little strength.

Instead, I held back. I knew if I used my all then I would be giving the game away, that they makers would know exactly what I was capable of and I couldn't risk ruining the surprise for them and the rest of the world. A move such as that could have been deadly.

The makers don't necessarily need a twelfth Hunter or Huntress and with the changes they made this year they could have easily made that a change if I'd ruined the entertainment.

"That doesn't matter, its in the past right?" I reply.

"Right," Callum agrees.

A long moment of silence passes before I manage to string a proper sentence together, in my mind, "Do you know if there are any books on magic here? Or books on previous games? Anything I can study for the up coming games?"

"Yea, I found some spell books earlier this morning if you want to take a look," Callum replies.

"Sure," I say with a smile. I follow him down several isles of books, the book cases seem to grow larger and larger as we walk until they're almost triple my height. I watch as Callum climbs a ladder and grabs several books before handing them down to me.

"The spells in a lot of these books should be useful in the games I would have thought," he says with a smile.

"I hope so, are there anymore?" I ask. He nods, his smile growing larger before grabbing even more books and climbing down. For a moment, it seems as if he was born to be some sort of librarian.

"These are all the magic books," he says, his smile gleaming as he begins carrying several books back towards the table. I follow him and place the books on a small clear area of the table, "do you want me to clear some books for you?" Callum asks after placing the books on the floor near the table, before he's finished asking the question, he nervously starts tidying away books.

With no control over my body, I grab his wrist and tug on his arm, using very little strength, "Its fine," I say with a soft, soothing smile on my face. "Sometimes its easier working with mess and chaos than clean and order"

Callum's eyes meet mine once more and seem to liven up, glistening brightly as if they are stars in the sky and not eyes. "I'll have to remember that one," he replies with a short chuckle, "I've never heard anyone say such an unusual thing"

"I guess you can say that I'm quite unusual then"

"I would say you're exquisite" Callum whispers quietly, his breath seems to be rushing out of his body as he speaks. "So beautiful yet so dangerous"

"That was the look Levi wanted to give me, well near enough anyway," I joke nervously. I can feel my cheeks burning bright red and my heart seems to be attempting summersaults against my rib cage.

"Levi?" Callum asks, disappointment growing in his eyes.

"My stylist," the words rush out of my mouth and his eyes lighten up once more.

"You get given a stylist?"

"Yea, we need to make an impression on viewers in order to get votes which means awesome weapons!" I reply with a shy giggle.

"Ah, for the hunt," Callum replies solemnly.

"Unfortunately so, but I do look forward to seeing what types of weapons we shall be provided with"

"Sounds interesting"

"I wish I'd be able to show you," our eyes seem to lock and my voice sounds strange as I talk but I don't care, something about him makes all of my worries vanish into thin air.

"I wish you could to, I think it would be interesting and impressive to see you use such a glorious and powerful weapon such as those that can be provided"

"It would be fun"

"That it would, it's a shame its unlikely to happen"

"It is indeed a shame," I sigh and pull my hand away before I begin studying the spells and noting certain ones down that I believe will be useful in the games.

*   *   *

The day flies by as both I and Callum chat and laugh. A small part of me dreads the day the games arrive and I will have to hunt him. That part of me screams for me to protect him in the games. To keep him alive at all costs but I know I can't.

And that part of me seems to be growing the closer I get to him.

I force myself pull away from him and finally return to bed after looking at the time. My plans for the day seem to have vanished as I became engulfed in spells and Callum.

As I lay my head down to rest, my mind is preoccupied with him. He's all I can think about. His beautiful eyes, how they change colour, his luscious lips and his dark skin.

Gradually, I fall into a deep sleep and even then I can't escape him.

My dream begins in a beautiful meadow, my head laying on a soft pillow of grass, the grass that surrounds my body, clings to my bare skin as the breeze caresses my face and blows my hair in wild directions. For the first time in my life I feel free.

I hesitate for a moment before sitting up, unsure of whether I dare move or not. The wind blows through my long black hair, lifting it from my shoulders. I glance down at the long black dress that clings to my figure, the small gems on it twinkle like the stars in the sky, glistening with confidence and beauty.

The sky explodes with colours as the sun begins to set.

Out of the shadows of the trees that surround the meadow steps Callum, his eyes glistening the same lily pad green as he looks to me. His smile seems to bring a new life and warmth to my body.

A warm, soft smile grows on my face as he approaches me. The warmth he brings seems to roll of his body and enter mine, growing stronger the closer he is. Eventually, he falls onto his knees in front of me and cups my face in his hands and stares into my eyes.

His face seems to lighten up with a new life and happiness as he stares at me. The part of me that seems to be growing warm to him, screams for him to kiss me. Something inside of me wants him to be mine.

His hands slip down my body and around my waist, pulling me into his arms and locking me into an embrace. Unable to stop myself, I wrap my arms around his neck, holding him close to me.

I stare into his eyes and seem to drift off into another world. A safer, freer world.

It's when he speaks that I return to earth, "It's a shame this can't last forever," he says solemnly and its then, my mind registers the sadness in his eyes.

"Maybe it can, one day," I whisper breathlessly, "a life for a life," its after I've said the final words that the dream begins to fade.

"A life for a life," he agrees. His words are the final piece of him that remain when darkness engulfs me and I'm pulled from the beautiful scene and back into the world of reality.

The bright light shines in my eyes awakening me just before the loud alarm rings throughout my room. I quickly change into some fresh clothing and stand outside my room and just as the same officer as yesterday, greets us.

"Today you shall resume travelling to the capitol cities," she says in the same commanding voice, "follow me!" Immediately we follow her towards the dining hall we'd eaten our first meal when we arrived. There, we meet with the prisoners and suddenly, I find myself walking beside Callum to the exit of the prison.

I notice that upon his wrists and ankles are what appear to be shackles which have a strange electronic buzz radiating from them.

"Looks like you've been all shackled up," I mutter quietly as we wait to leave the prison. Each of us exiting in the same order we were called out in. I catch a quick glimpse of flashing lights outside and instantly I know that it is further press.

"Does it give you ideas?" Callum jokes and I giggle shyly, my cheeks burning bright red once more.

Soon, our turn to exit the prison arrives and at first I find the flashing lights and bright sun almost blinding. The chaotic sound of questions fill my ears as they're shouted at us by the press.

"They seem a little too excited if you ask me," Callum mutters and I fight the urge to laugh, "they're about to watch people die and they're this excited and happy about it"

"What do you expect? Humanity is by far the most barbaric of kin" I reply, my voice remaining quiet so that none of the press may hear.

"You're certainly right about that one," Callum agrees, "sometimes I wonder if an animal or one of the creatures they perceive as monster such as werewolves, are less barbaric than humans"

"To be honest with you, I would say humanity is far more barbaric than a werewolf," I pause for a moment, "at least now it is, I don't think it's always been this barbaric"

Swiftly, we walk towards the train and in several quick strides, we escape the press and enter a silent, calm world once more. We walk through to a reasonable sized dining room and I take a seat beside the window, unable to stop myself from staring out the window and at the large crowd that have gathered outside the prison and surround the large train.

A member of the crowd steps towards the train and looks into the window directly where I'm sat. She's stood not far from me and when she looks up, allowing the light to pierce through the shadows of her black hood and reveal her face, I notice that she has strange green scaled skin, just like the creature that was shot the first night I came here.

She steps closer to me, her eyes never leaving my face. I glance over my shoulder to see that Callum seems preoccupied with having the shackles removed from his wrists and ankles.

I glance back at the woman to see that she is just outside the train, directly in front of me. Her unusually large, green eyes stare into mine, they seem to be the same emerald green colour as my own, they seem to hypnotise me somehow.

Suddenly, her hand rises to touch the window, I glance from her hand to mine before I gently touch the window, my hand above hers. Her hand would look completely human if it weren't for the scales.

With a swiftly movement, she bangs her hand against the window lightly, but its enough to make me jump and flinch away. *What is she?* I wonder silently.

She glances over her shoulder in a quick movement, as if something has suddenly startled her. She looks back to me, nods slightly before she rushes away, hiding amongst the crowd once more.

I stare into the crowd where she has disappeared, yet I can no longer see her.

"Devotion!" Devotes voice rings in my ears, causing me to jump. I look over my shoulder to see her looking at me with a gleaming smile on her face, "You did well, you're doing exactly what the makers want and you'll no doubt get the votes you need, you're doing everything you need to do"

"What do you mean?" I ask as Devote sits beside me.

"How close yourself and Callum have become has got most of the city talking, you have them believing that you're genuinely becoming friends and considering how well you have done in training when being filmed, people are impressed, people are beginning to talk and they want to see more," Devote explains.

"Which means what? What is it I have to do?" I ask.

"Befriend him further, make it seem as though you're truly building a friendship," Devote explains.

But what if I want to build a true friendship with Callum? What if I actually want to be friends with him? I don't want to be acting for their entertainment! My mind screams.

"Okay," I mutter in defeat.

"Good! Carry on with what you're doing, you're doing so well! I have never been so proud! It's as if they did something to you that prepared you for the games above the rest," Devotes smile grows larger as she stands, "you are the best candidate I have ever trained," she mutters before she leaves, "we'll start training tomorrow"

I sigh, wondering if I should pretend or whether I should allow what has begun to stir inside of me to continue. Can this be right?

Soon, Callum joins me with as many books as he can carry, "Still interested in spells?" He asks and I nod, "good because I found more books," he smiles and I can't help returning it.

"Well looks like plenty of studying for me then," I mutter.

He chuckles, "Yes and yet again, I'm here to assist," I giggle shyly after he speaks. I take out my notes and grab a book out the pile placed in front of me when Callum's hand brushes against mine, sending warmth throughout my entire body, spreading from his touch.

"Our arrival at the capitol of the United European Countries shall be in little over a day, enjoy your travels," a male voice echoes around the room, seeming to emanate from nowhere.

*   *   *

The day soon passes yet again and I settle into a dreamless sleep. The morning seems to arrive quickly, waking me with the first rays of sunshine as the sun rises from behind the hills. Today, I resume training with Fusion and Devote.

I shower and dress into clean training clothes, they're still the same as at the prison. I tie my long wet black hair into a ponytail and rise from my room. Quickly, I eat my breakfast and wait for Devote to arrive. It doesn't take her long.

"To begin, you shall be training with Fusion and Callum," Devote says with a smile, "don't forget we need to keep up this clever illusion," I nod as she speaks, "the cameras will be on you most of the day, remember this. Callum and Fusion shall be waiting for you in the training room, so hurry," her smile seems even brighter today than it did yesterday. I smile and nod once more before I begin heading for the door.

It's then she wraps her arms around me and hugs me tightly, for a moment I'm shocked before I hug her back, "I have never been so proud," she mutters and I smile.

"Thank you," I reply, she lets go off me and I hurry off to train beside Callum and Fusion.

I enter the training room, its smaller than the last train but still perfect for training and Fusion begins by putting me up against Callum in a fight. Immediately, I manage to tackle him to the floor and hold him into place. At first a low animalistic growl escapes Callum's lips but he soon realises and smiles.

"Well done Devotion, you have learnt quite quickly," Fusion comments with a smile, his eyes glistening with happiness, "Callum, you need to learn to stay on your feet!"

I giggle as I look into Callum's eyes and he begins to chuckle, "You're right, I better not get on the wrong side of you in the games," he replies with a large smile.

I can't help but return the smile as I stare into his beautiful, warm green eyes, "I doubt you will," I reply.

"I hope I don't," Callum whispers.

"I know you won't," I whisper quietly.

"Come on you two, we shouldn't be laying around, you both should be training," Fusion says in a playful voice.

I giggle before I force myself to pull off him and resume training. Throughout it all, we laugh and joke, clearly none of us care that the cameras are watching us. With Callum, I find myself feeling freer than I have ever felt in my entire life.

CHAPTER 5

The Capitol Votes

T he days pass me by in the blink of an eye. Time with Callum seems to pass so quickly and as the train stops outside the first Capitol city, I stand anxiously beside Callum, silently hoping to have gained a good standard of votes.

Patiently, I stand at the back of the line of candidates, shaking nervously. I watch as each name is called out and the line becomes shorter and shorter. The prisoners are to follow us out however Callum is beside me, clearly feeling as anxious as I feel.

Finally, my name is called by the voice of the head maker. I step into the doorway of the train, my ears are met by the sound of people cheering not only my name but Callum's as well. Cautiously, I step out of the train, careful not to tear the dress I'd worn the day we'd arrived at the prison.

I join the line of candidates and hear the prisoners as they follow to stand behind us. We all stare at the large screen in front of us as the first name is called. I gulp down a breath of air in an attempt to calm myself but its little use, nothing can possibly calm my nerves right now.

"Conquer!" The makers voice echoes around us as it blares from the large screen, Conquer steps forth from the line and bows to the screen in respect, "You received one hundred and fifty votes from the Capitol City of the United European Countries!" The crowd roars loudly, several shouting his name, others merely clapping and whistling. "Congratulations Conquer," there is a short pause before the maker speaks again, "Innocence, you received two hundred and eighty votes from the Capitol City of the United European Countries!"

The list continues for what seems like forever until eventually, my name is called, "Devotion"—I step forth, shaking nervously, the gathering crowd, staring at me in pure silence—"you received four hundred and eighty seven votes from the Capitol City of the United European Countries! Well done Devotion, you did exceptionally well," the head maker says. The crowd seems to go completely wild, screaming my name, banging the bars in front of them, whistling and cheering.

"What?" I gasp as I look to my fellow hunters and huntresses, "How is that possible?"

"You're clearly liked," Innocence replies with a cheerful smile. I glance over my shoulder to Callum and he nods in approval, smiling at me proudly. I return to standing in complete silence as the screen separates, creating a large doorway for us to enter. I hesitate whilst the others continue forth before I begin walking towards the large building for the evening meal before we continue travelling to the next Capitol City.

We step through the large doors and into a large white hallway. I continue beside my fellows whilst Callum is directly behind me. I feel nervous and no matter how much I try, I can't seem to stop shaking as the cold hallway seems to grow even colder. Goosebumps grow on my arms from the cold and I shiver slightly before we enter a large white room with a long wooden table in the centre. At the head of the table stands the leader of the United European Countries.

His slick blond hair tied back in a ponytail and his worn blue eyes stare at us for a moment. "Please, sit," he says in a rough, hoarse tone. His tanned skin is worn and old, wrinkles line his facial features. He yawns as another indication that he is very tired and as his hair hit's the light, I notice small streaks of grey.

Cautiously, I follow my fellows and sit between Innocence and Callum, Conquer sits on the other side of Innocence.

"Hunters, Huntresses," he begins with a quick bow in respect, we each bow our heads in response to his respectful gesture. "I am Nial, and I am the leader of the United European Countries, as you already know the past of how we became one country, I shall pass that part and welcome you with open arms. Today, depending on the amount of votes you received, depends on what you shall be given at the end of this meal, as you will know, these items will assist you in the games," he claps his hands only once and several servants come to serve us.

Chicken Tikka is placed in front of me, the scent of spices invade my nose causing my mouth to drool slightly. I look at the plate placed in front of Callum to see some sort of rice pudding, I glance at the other prisoners to see they all have the same type of food whilst my fellow hunters and huntresses have a range of foods placed in front of them.

They're trying to make them weaker for when they're placed in the games, I realise immediately, *its so that its harder for them to fight back*

"Please, enjoy and talk amongst yourselves," Nial says.

I glance from Callum to my food, "I don't think this is fair," I whisper quietly once everyone begins talking.

"What do you mean?" Callum asks.

"What I mean is, it's not fair that you're all being given food that will malnutrition you so that its harder for you to fight back in the games," I whisper.

"It doesn't matter though, only one of us will live, the rest will die," Callum replies, "so it won't matter if we weren't eating properly because we'll be dead"

You won't be, a part of me screams yet I push it to one side and ignore its shouts and screams.

*   *   *

Finally, the meal ends and I wait patiently as one by one we are handed small backpacks, each with our names embroidered on the back. Nial hands me the pack with my name embroidered in a scarlet red colour on the black material and nods his head in respect. I nod mine in response and he shakes my hand.

"It's a pleasure to meet such a talented and skilled Huntress," he says with a large wicked smile on his old warn face.

I smile softly, "It's a pleasure to meet the leader of the United European Countries"

"Good luck, I'm sure you will do well," he says, his voice seems to change to something that can only be compared to what I would imagine to be Lucifer's voice. His face morphs so that it looks disgustingly evil, his eyes filled with a lust for blood and pleasure from the thought of murder and death.

"Thank you," I reply, with a short gulp of air. The air around me suddenly turns cold and the hairs on the back of my neck stand on ends. Hatred emanates from his body and tries to enter mine, sending an uncontrollable shudder down my spine. I take in another short gulp of air as his eyes begin to burn with the lust for the spillage of blood.

Finally, he turns away from me and relief rushes through my veins. *How can someone seem to hold so much evil? How can he be a leader?* Questions rush through my mind and my stomach seems to clench.

I glance at Callum, attempting to throw questions telepathically at him, my eyes begging for answers. He nods as if he understands what I have just experienced, and something in his eyes tell me he can explain very little of how it could have occurred.

I glance down at the backpack in my hands, "Don't open them until you're alone," Nial commands, and we each nod to show that we understand before we begin walking in single file out of the building. Immediately, we are all bombarded by questions, most directed at me. The majority of them are about Callum and myself.

We ignore the press and enter the train once more, the prisoners soon follow and I find myself hurrying to my room. I enter the room just as the train jolts as it begins to move and pick up speed, forcing me to stagger slightly into the door.

I rush into my room, close the door and sit on the bed before I open the backpack, curious to discover what I have been given. I glance at the 500ml water bottle before I pull it out of the pack to discover the rest of the necessities within the pack.

"We shall be arriving at the capitol of Veniva in the next twenty four hours," a woman's voice announces.

I glance at the ceiling as the woman speaks before I continue searching through the pack. The next thing I pull out is a silver cylinder and open it to discover a strange white cream, I sniff it and instantly recognise the scent to be some sort of medicine.

In case of injury, I guess as I remember the amount of votes I received. I place my hand in the pack and grab a cold metal rod, I pull it out and slide the button to turn it on. Suddenly, a white blade appears, using some sort of unusual technology to glow radiantly. I use it in a swift motion and it slices through the material of my bed covers with ease.

I stare at the blade and the perfect tear it has just created in the cover. *That'll no doubt be of some use,* I think to myself as I turn off the strange knife and continue searching through the pack.

Within it, I find crackers and energy bars to eat whilst in the games, things I'll have to make last me along with other things to assist me in surviving whilst I hunt. I pack the bag once more and stare at the wall for a moment before I zip it back up and leave to go find Callum.

It doesn't take me long to find him, all I have to do is go to the library on the train and he's there.

"Anything interesting in the bag?" He asks, but his attention seems to be elsewhere.

"Nothing really, just necessities in order to survive such as food and medicine in case of injury," I reply as I sit beside him.

"I hope it doesn't come to you receiving an injury," Callum replies solemnly.

"As do I, there's enough in the pack to last one person months" I pause for a moment, "well that's what I reckon anyway,"

Keep him alive in the games! You can do it! You can keep him alive throughout the games! Easy! A piece of my heart screams but my mind knows that conducting such a move would be dangerous, it could endanger both my life and Callum's. I sigh and stare at him for a moment, he seems deep in thought, his face smooth causing it to look almost emotionless.

"What's wrong?" I ask, gently placing my hand on his shoulder but he flinches away, it seems as though I've just pulled him out of his thoughts.

"Nothing," he mutters quietly but even though I haven't known him long, I know that something is clearly wrong.

"Something's wrong," I whisper softly, my voice carrying warmth so much so that it sounds as if it has come from a strange and not from me. Suddenly, it dawns on me as I realise, he's thinking about his fate, its drawing closer with each day. Our fate is near. "You're thinking about the games aren't you?" I whisper.

"Yea," he mutters with a shrug.

"Callum, you'll be fine, I bet with the amount of intelligence you have, you'll be the prisoner to win his freedom"

"You don't understand, the other prisoners have a lot more strength than I—"

"Strength doesn't matter," I intercept.

"It does, a lot more than you think," Callum replies.

I rub his shoulder gently in a comforting matter, "Callum, I've been training since I was a very small child, I of all people would know if strength mattered or not and I know that it doesn't. Believe it or not but agility is of more use than strength when in combat, for you can dodge the blows. Intelligence is useful in the games, it has kept many prisoners alive in the past years," I reply.

"I guess"

I gulp a quick breath as I swallow the words that seem to be building up in my throat, the words my heart wishes for me to speak. I can't risk saying such things. No matter what.

I sigh.

"Everything will be okay, I hope," I mutter.

"As do I," Callum replies as he gently rests his hand on mine and smiles the same soft, comforting, warm smile. The smile that makes me want to melt into his arms.

No! My mind screams and I shudder slightly. I can't risk such emotions and this, this isn't right!

"So, Nial," I begin, the words tripping up over themselves as they leave my mouth, I cough and start again. "Nial, is it just me or is there something about him that seems rather sinister"

"No it's not just you and you wouldn't have been the first in his presents to react the way you did, I saw it happen in a previous year of the games, my mother made me watch it as a warning to try to stay away from him at all costs, unfortunately she used to work for him," Callum says.

"So you're originally from the capitol city of the United European Countries?" I ask.

"Unfortunately so," Callum asks before he continues speaking, "like I was saying, you're not the first to react in the way you did"

"Something about him, when you're looking at him and he's talking to you, its like hatred is literally rolling of his body, radiating from him and trying to enter your body. You can see the lust for blood in his eyes burning powerfully and the evil in his face," I shiver at the thought as I try to explain the unpleasant experience.

"That's what my mother used to say," Callum replies

"Well at least now I know I'm not just going insane from all the stress, killing and death," I reply.

"Nope, I'm happy to announce that you're not going insane," Callum replies, he pauses for a moment before his voice becomes much quieter, "but what you saw was right, he is an evil man, a corrupt leader if you will"

"Why don't the people just get rid of him?" I ask.

"Unfortunately, it doesn't work that way any more and hasn't worked that way for over thirty years, not since the games began anyway," Callum says. Suddenly, the door opens and the camera crew enter to film us.

I smile softly and look to Callum to see his eyes pleading with me for us to stop the conversation, I nod before I try thinking of something else to talk about. "So, have you ever tried learning how to play an instrument?" I ask.

"I play guitar," Callum replies with a smile, a rush of relief filling his eyes.

"What sort of music do you play?" I ask.

"A large range of music, before I ended up in prison with this as my fate, I owned four guitars, one for playing heavy metal and I tell you now, it sounded absolutely beautiful, another for playing country music and it goes on from there"

"So, I'm guessing you have a wide variety of music that you listen to?"

"Yea and I used to make a living from it, anyway what about you? Do you play any instruments?" Callum asks.

"Flute, guitar, keyboard and recorder," I reply.

"Where do you get the time for all this? You read, you study, you train and you play four instruments"

"Don't forget our schooling, we had to do instruments as part of our music lessons"

"Ah, now I get it, sort of anyway," Callum replies and I giggle, "what type of music do you listen to?"

"I like a bit of blues here and there, symphonic metal, heavy metal, country, a large variety to be honest," I reply.

"I'm guessing it depends on how you're feeling at the time?"

"A little," I mutter.

"How are you feeling now?" Callum asks, his voice holding a hint of seduction and lust that he's clearly trying to hold back.

My soft smile grows slightly, "Happy and content at this moment in time," I reply, with nothing more than pure honesty.

"So what sort of music would you be listening to?" Callum asks, suddenly seeming completely oblivious to anything else but me.

I giggle and glance to the floor, trying to hide my face with my long black hair as they slowly begin burning bright red. "Probably country and symphonic metal" I reply.

We continue chatting about useless things, things I would have considered boring whilst it appears many of those out there would find brilliant as both a Huntress and a prisoner grow closer.

*　　*　　*

Time seems to fly by quickly as soon we arrive at the second capitol city, the capitol city of Veniva. Once again it is the same, a meal, socialisation, the camera never seems to leave both Callum and I for very long. They seem completely focused on our conversations and our actions. How we approach each other, how we interact, it all seems to have them fixated on us.

Once again, I've received the highest amount of votes, and now I know that it is because of how close we have gained in such a short period of time. The crowd seems to adore us but is it because of the friendship or are they seeing what is happening in my heart? What I'm trying to keep at bay?

I wait patiently, completely lost in thought as I speak to Callum. The games are gaining closer, we only have two more Capitol Cities and the short journey to the arena before the games begin. The thought of the games sends an unusual feeling of dread and anxiety throughout my entire body. The thought of Callum being killed sends stabbing pains in my heart.

Finally the meal ends and yet again, I rush to my room with a large case in hand, curious to know of what is within the large case because of the large amount of votes I've received. I stare at the letters embroidered in the same scarlet red colour on the case, the letters spelling my name. Gently, I trace my fingers along the embroidered letters.

I hesitate for a moment before flicking the latches and opening it. Laid within the case is a black water proof jacket, with my name embroidered across the left breast. I pick it up to find its incredibly light and seems to make no noise. Again, I trace my fingertips along the embroidered letters. I look back at the case to see that beneath it is a beautiful piece of black armour, in the shape of a dress, the bottom frills out like petals of a flower and upon the black armour are thin, scarlet red lines that take the form of beautiful symbols.

Elven symbols.

I pick up the armour to find just how incredibly light it is and it appears to make no noise as it moves. The back of it appears bare but when I go to put my hand on it, I find a thin layer of metal that can't be seen too clearly.

I notice some black metal boots that match the armour, they appear to be knee high and very light. Easy to run in.

I place the armour and jacket back in the case and before I go to close it, I notice a black circlet on the lid of the case, staring at me. Within the centre is a blood red stone. Upon the black metal, are the same symbols as the ones on the armour, in the same thin, scarlet lines.

Secretly, I understand why they have made my colour be blood red, its because they believe that I am nothing more than a cold hearted killer. That's what the makers and the leaders believe yet I'm unsure whether I should believe the same as they do.

I close the case and leave it beside my bed before I leave the room to find Callum. Again, he is in the library.

"What was in the case?" He asks in a soft, quiet tone, clearly worried that he will be heard.

"Armour," I whisper.

"Cool," Callum says.

"Its black, so its harder for people to see me at night time," I reply.

"Cool, enough for two?" He jokes and I laugh.

"I wish there were, the armour itself looks quite feminine"

"Hey, I'd wear anything if it kept me alive in the games," I giggle at his joke and he smiles, the warmth radiating from his body once more and entering mine.

Again, the camera's enter and focus on both of us and once again, we result to mindless chatter and even then, we seem to gain closer.

*   *   *

We arrive at the third Capitol City, in the early hours of the morning and are rushed out of our rooms as soon as we are ready to be presented to the leader of the capitol. We leave the train, in a strict order and await for the amount of votes.

"Congratulations Devotion, you seem to be taking this world by storm with another 541 votes," the maker says on the screen. I glance to Callum as he smiles and nods in approval. It's only because of him I'm receiving so many votes.

I glance at my fellow hunters and huntresses to see Frost staring at me evilly, her glare is filled with pure hatred and what seems to be a message. '*If your going to play at this game, so am I*'

I shiver under her stare as one by one, we walk towards the large building to be greeted by an unusual woman as soon as the large doors close behind us. We stand in the large white room, all staring blankly at the woman.

Her hair is a long, silver colour that reminds me of the moon and her eyes have taken on an unusual grey colour. "Welcome," she says with a warm yet crooked smile. Something about her strikes me as untrustworthy, something tells me she is like the leader of the United European Countries and that in itself, sends shivers down my spine. A spark of pain appears in my thigh, reminding me of the injury I received in the call outs and telling me that it is still there even though it is healing quickly, but there is something about the pain in my thigh. It feels as if something is pulling out the blood so that it goes towards the female.

It's as if she's trying to draw something out of my injuries.

I stand there and wait, ignoring the unusual sensation in my leg.

"I am the leader of the capitol of Seneria, a place which was once called Singapore. My name is Leanne, I welcome you to this place and I hope that you enjoy your meal," she continues.

We sit and yet again, we begin socialising and eating. The camera's focusing on both myself and Callum. I wait patiently until it comes to receiving the items that shall assist me in the hunt.

Finally, the time comes to line up and one by one, we are given different sized cases. The woman that has presented herself as Leanne approaches me, her long, black lace dress dances around her ankles as she walks in her tall black high heels. She flicks her grey hair over her shoulder and shoots a crooked smile in my direction.

She stands in front of me, and her eyes seem to change so that they seem to resemble fire and hell more than a comforting grey. Her smile grows even more crooked and she looks down her small nose at me.

"It surely is a pleasure to meet such a beautiful and graceful huntress, the way you fought the day of the Call Outs can only be described as perfect. Your elven grace certainly compliments your beauty," she nods her head slightly in respect and I copy, "such manners, such beauty and such grace," I stare closely at her face to see just how warn and old her face is yet she still seems to present herself with a powerful beauty.

"Thank you, it is a pleasure to meet the leader of Seneria," I reply with a false smile.

She laughs, "Thank you" she replies before she hands me a case that seems to be an unusual shape and size. Immediately, I find myself curious of what could possibly be within the case.

Each hunter and huntress rushes out the room and in single file we approach the train, question after question is thrown at me by the press. My name shouted repeatedly as I grow closer to the train and as soon as I enter it, a wash of relief runs through my veins. It is as if I have just escaped a life threatening danger.

And just as I have done after arriving at each capitol city and finishing the meal, I rush to my room to discover what is within the case. The door closes behind me and I rush to open my case, not paying much attention to the fact that my bedding has been changed so that it too is black with scarlet, elven symbols upon it.

I open the case to reveal scarlet silk material covering what is within the case. I move the scarlet silk to reveal a strange looking black weapon with something to attach it to something such as a belt or armour or a bag. I take it out the case and press a scarlet button and the weapon opens up into a bow.

The string is scarlet whilst most of the bow itself is black. I draw back the bow and a black and red arrow appears.

What on earth? My mind wonders silently as I stare at the deadly arrow. *The technology they have now, I've never seen anything like this in previous games, its-its beautiful, its perfect, its deadly.*

I press the button a second time and the bow folds itself back into the same unusual shape. The scarlet string seems to change so that it can hook onto something. I look in the case that holds my armour a second time and realise that there is a black belt that I hadn't noticed before. A belt that could hold the bow along with several throwing knives. *Goddess knows what I'll receive in the final Capitol City,* I think to myself.

I pack away the bow and place it back in the case before resting it gently against the case with my armour and the bag with supplies. Slowly, the world is preparing me for the hunt and something tells me that they're preparing for something else as well. Something that burns greatly in my gut.

*   *   *

The sun gently rests on my cheek as I awake, yesterday went pretty quickly but nothing really interesting happened. Most the time, I and Callum were followed by cameras when we were together. But throughout the mindless chatter, something seems to be growing in my heart, I feel an unusual need to keep Callum alive at all costs and no matter how much I push it to one side, it seems to be growing.

Could this be a true friendship growing?

This is something I've never experienced in my life and because of how strange it feels, I don't quite understand it.

I lay there, lost in thought when Levi knocks on the door and enters, causing me to jump and my thoughts to deteriorate.

"Good morning," he says with a smile, "are you ready for the final capitol city?"

I nod, "I guess" I sigh.

"Today you receive your final weapons before we begin travelling to the arena," Levi explains but I already know, soon I shall be fulfilling the destiny chosen by the makers. "Lets get you ready," he says with a smile and I nod. He claps his hands and the two girls enter my room. Swiftly, they change my clothes into a short black lace dress with scarlet red beneath it. The bottom of the dress appears to be torn but I guess its to do with the look Levi has been trying to give me. "Remember, I want her to look dangerous yet sexy and beautiful"

The girls nod and begin rushing to do my makeup, with eye shadow they cause my eyes to seem darker and violent yet with a little stuff they call lipstick, they cause my lips to become a rosy red colour, and in general I look beautiful yet dangerous.

The girls create two braids in my hair on either side of my head before placing a black and red circlet on my head. Upon my wrists they place black cuffs and upon my finger they place a ring in the shape of a rose.

A red rose is placed above my left breast with black entwined within it.

"Perfect, you look stunning," Levi says with a large grin on his face, "I'm sure you're taking the world by storm"

I smile softly, but my heart seems to hurt as I begin thinking about Callum, "Thank you" I whisper weakly through the pain in my heart.

"Now, stand straight and hold your head up high, be proud of who you are and show just how deadly you can be," Levi says.

Immediately, I stand up straight and hold up my head in a way that shows an unforgiving woman, a powerful and proud huntress. I step out of my room and approach the dining room where Callum seems to be sat opposite Innocence, talking.

Innocence is dressed in a beautiful, short yellow dress that rests beautifully on her breasts. Her hair has been curled and put into a side ponytail with a sunflower holding it in place. She stands and the dress seems to puff out slightly. Her makeup has been done to make her look beautiful, innocent and young. Her dress seems to compliment her fiery red hair and her small build whilst her peach lips seem to have been defined even further by her makeup.

"Morning," Innocence says with a beautiful grin on her face.

"Morning," I reply, with a soft welcoming smile.

"You look absolutely gorgeous," Callum blurts before he cups his mouth with both of his hands in order to stop himself from talking even further. I giggle shyly at his words and feel my cheeks burn as they turn bright red.

"Aw," Innocence says with a slight giggle, "you two seem so cute together," its her words that bring me back into the world of the living and out of the spell Callum's eyes seem to cast upon me.

"No we don't!" I snap in a fierce voice that could cause even the strongest of men to cower before forcing myself to calm down, I sigh. "Innocence, I must say you look stunning"

"Thank you," she whispers, her voice quivers slightly in fear.

"I'm sorry, I didn't mean to snap," I mutter quietly, feeling ashamed.

"I never knew such a voice could come from you, you sounded so fierce, so angry, it was like a burning flame, one that's completely out of control, like a forest fire," Innocence replies.

"Nor did I, I think I scared myself with it," I reply.

114

Its as if something's changing inside of me, how am I becoming so aggravated so easily, I think to myself.

"It doesn't matter, its already in the past," Callum says with a warm, comforting smile.

"That it is," Innocence says, a smile growing on her face, "I thank you for your compliment"

"It's alright," I reply, a warm smile growing on my face once more.

"I'd have to say you look amazing," Innocence says.

"Thank you," I reply, my smile growing.

"Well now that you've both kissed and made up, how about we have some breakfast, I don't want to be eating anymore of that crap they keep serving us," Callum says.

"I feel kind of sorry for you," I say as I sit beside him, unable to stop my hand from brushing against his, sending waves of pleasure throughout my body, warmth filling me and relaxing me, "the food they serve you must taste disgusting"

"It tastes like its fresh cow crap!" Callum says and I can't stop myself from laughing.

I grab some freshly made toast coated in chocolate spread, Belgian chocolate to be exact. I take a bite and the smooth chocolate spreads throughout my mouth, sending my taste buds wild. They seem to dance on my tongue as the luscious chocolate spreads further in my mouth.

The pleasure it sends throughout my mouth relaxes me, calming me. I look to Innocence to see her pupils have grown larger, she finishes her first slice and grabs another as if it is some sort of drug she has suddenly become addicted to.

*   *   *

Finally, we arrive at the final capitol city. We enter the building and it's the same as before. Socialising, eating, receiving our votes.

"Devotion, you received 746 votes from one of the largest capitol cities, you should be proud," the maker says yet something about his voice says that he is slowly growing angry yet I am unsure of what he is becoming angry with.

The rest seems to have become a usual routine. We are given cases, mine is a small square case this time and it's the smallest compared to the others. Silently, I dread the games that seem to be gaining closer with each passing day. Just as the previous days, I rush to my room and open the black case to reveal several silver throwing knives, that glisten in the light with a deadly shimmer.

I close the case and sigh, the knives seemed like normal throwing knives but something tells me that they're not. Gently I rest it with the other cases and lay on my bed, willing myself to sleep.

*   *   *

The morning soon rises and I find myself having to drag my body out of bed. I change and approach the door, finding that I already miss my bed. The feeling of dread grows in my stomach even further. I stand there for a moment, staring at the door before I open it.

Immediately, I move towards the dining room and grab an apple before I sit down. It isn't long before Callum arrives and we sit there in silence, alone.

"So, I've been thinking about the games," he begins.

"So have I," I reply

"Have you thought about who you're going to hunt down first?" Callum asks, dread growing in his voice.

"No," I whisper, silently hoping that I won't be the one to hunt and kill him.

"Have you thought of strategies?"

"Yea, a little," I mutter

"Good luck, I hope you become the Champion at the end of this"

"Good luck to yourself, I hope you survive"

"Can I ask something?" Callum asks.

"Sure"

"All of this, was this friendship real?" Callum asks solemnly, his voice filled with a range of emotions.

"I think it was, this friendship, I would like to believe it is in fact real," I whisper.

"Then, if I do survive, will we remain friends?"

"I hope so," I reply.

"So do I, I've never had so much fun in my life," Callum says, his voice holding a small hint of joy yet the rest seems to be filled with dread.

"Nor have I, I believe that this is a true friendship and I hope you survive the games so that our friendship may continue," I say.

"So do I"

"So, will you attempt to survive this?" I ask, my voice filled with so much emotion that it sounds as if its coming from a stranger. My body begins shaking as strange emotions, some of which I don't recognise, flood my veins.

"I will"

"Promise?"

"Promise," Callum confirms with the same warm smile that sends a rush of emotions throughout my body and warms my heart.

"Thank you," I whisper breathlessly.

CHAPTER 6

Let The Games Begin

T he day finally arrives, the train comes to a sudden halt and there's a knock on my door before Levi enters. "It's time to prepare you for the games," he says, solemnly, "its been beautiful watching such a friendship blossom but now that friendship shall die a painful death, such a shame," he claps his hands and the two girls enter. "You know how to style her hair for today, I want you to quickly change her into her armour and prepare her for the games. There shall be no makeup so I expect today to be much quicker"

The girls nod before they grab the case that holds my armour and open it. The door shuts and Levi stands and watches carefully as the first of the girls takes out my armour whilst the second begins undressing me.

"You must be quick, we don't have long remember," Levi says and the girls continue to rush.

My training clothes are thrown on the floor, and my bra is removed before they slip on the black armour, ensuring its perfect. The armour seems to support my boobs brilliantly. My boots are put on by one of the girls whilst the second ties most of my hair into a ponytail before she creates a braid on either side of my head and leaves them so that they hang down with my fringe.

It is then she places the circlet on my forehead.

"Stand," Levi commands and I do as he says. The girls rush as they wrap the belt around my waist, place the knives in the suitable pockets and hook the bow on to the belt. My jacket is put on and my backpack sits perfectly on my shoulders. Levi approaches me and cups my face in his hands. "You look stunning, I have never seen such a beautiful yet skilled huntress, I wish you all the luck possible in the games"

"Thank you," I whisper.

"How is your leg?"

"I feel no pain and its mostly healed"

"Good," Levi pauses for a moment, "you have done me proud"

"Thank you," I whisper a second time, feeling everything rush from my body as emotions flood through my veins, taking my breath and causing my heart to hammer in my chest. I take in a deep breath and force myself to remain calm.

"You have not only done myself proud but you have made your mother the proudest woman in the world," Levi says as he steps away from me.

"Wait! You know my mother!" I say quickly, unable to walk away but quickly the girls begin to rush me out of the room. Pushing me towards the door with a strength I wouldn't expect to come from girls with such builds. I find myself unable to fight back and enter the room once more.

"Go, you don't have much time left," Levi calls.

Finally, I manage to begin walking away, finding myself in disbelief as I approach my fellow hunters and huntresses as well as our trainers.

Levi knows my mother, a young, innocent voice whispers in my mind.

Devote approaches me, "I know we have not grown that close and not been together that long but you have done everything perfectly, I have never been so proud of a hunter or huntress. I'm sure you will do me proud in the games"

"Thank you," I say in a strong voice, whilst I attempt to control myself so that I don't ask questions.

"Good luck, huntress," Devote says with a warm, comforting smile and I can't help but return it.

"Good luck, Devotion," Fusion says as he places his hand on my shoulder in an unusual caring manner.

"Thank you both, you have taught me so much, I thank you for everything you have done for me," I reply.

"It has been an honour," Devote says.

"It truly has," Fusion agrees.

The doors open and I glance over my shoulder at the bright light as it enters the train.

"Good bye," Devote whispers, sadness growing in her eyes.

"Good bye," I whisper before I turn and follow the others out of the train in a single file line, as the twelfth candidate, I'm last to leave the train and enter the bright world, where the sun seems to be shining unusually bright.

We approach a private jet and it takes off, leaving our trainers, the press and the sleeping prisoners behind as we shall be the first to be placed in the arena so that we have time to scatter and wait upon their arrival.

Upon our ears they place an ear piece so that if anything happens or goes wrong they can tell us and we can fix it. It's a way of them keeping in contact with us.

It doesn't seem to take very long until we arrive in the arena. One by one, we leave the jet in single file before we begin scattering. No one knows where the prisoners will land.

I glance around the arena, to see it appears to be like a jungle or a forest with plenty of places to climb. In the distance I see a mountain and not far from where we have been dropped off and not far from where I stand I see the ocean and a beautiful beach. I watch as my fellow hunters and huntresses scatter in either groups or on their own.

Innocence grabs my hand and pulls, "Come on! We need to move!" She says quickly, I nod and begin to run with Conquer to my right and Innocence to my left. We immediately run for the trees and I begin climbing one, finding that I would prefer to run in the trees and climb rather than run on the ground.

"What are you doing?" Conquer asks.

"Remaining hidden for when the prey arrives," I reply.

"Good plan," Conquer replies.

"Thank you," I reply before I crouch on the branch and wait. Waiting for the gun shot sound to alert us that the prisoners have arrived and the games have begun.

Silently, I wonder whether I could keep Callum alive but I push the thoughts to one side no matter how much it hurts my heart. I know I can't risk such a thing, it could endanger us both even further. Conquer sits on the floor below me and Innocence joins me in the tree.

"So what's the plan?" She asks.

"We gather some water so that we can survive, then we begin the hunt," I reply.

"Sounds like a pretty good plan to me, lets go," she says with a smile, her voice filled with excitement.

* * *

We're in the process of gathering water from a nearby stream when the gun shot fires and we all know the hunt has begun. Instantly, I place the cap back on my bottle and allow the chemicals to clean it whilst I begin running through the trees, climbing them and running along their branches. Their leaves give me shelter and hide my shadow perfectly as I begin, listening and searching for my first kill.

Soon, I catch the glimpse of a prisoner and begin to run towards him, each step I take being silent, precise and swift. I move in on my prey, unhook the bow from my belt and it unfolds from a gentle touch on the scarlet button.

I crouch as the dark coloured male begins to approach me, I draw back the scarlet string and the arrow begins to form just as I see his face. It's Callum. I sigh and relax my muscles and with no control over my mouth, I whisper "Callum"

He looks up in the trees and stops, somehow he has heard my whisper, "What are you doing? You could have killed me there and then," he says before glancing over his shoulder as a group of three large males emerge from the bushes, "crap!"

"What?" I ask quietly, before I draw back the string and the arrow begins to form. Swiftly, I aim as the males begin to charge towards Callum. I fire the arrow at the middle male that seems to be the leader and it embeds itself in between his eyes. His body collapses to the floor but the other two continue, as if they're oblivious to their friends death. The bow folds once more and I hook it to my belt as quickly as I possibly can.

Unable to control my body, my instincts take hold. I jump from the tree and land directly in front of Callum. Quickly, I turn before I begin charging towards the males. I grab one of the knives and jump off the ground with perfect timing. I manage to flip my body at just the right time so that I slash his throat whilst in mid air and by the time I land on my feet, the males body has collapsed to the floor.

In a perfect and precise movement, I spin around and throw the knife at the last remaining male prisoner. The knife embeds itself in the back of his neck and his body hit's the floor.

I move to retrieve my knife and notice that several small blades seem to have appeared from the body of the knife. My hand brushes against a small button and the small blades return into the original blade, causing it to look like a normal knife once more.

I place the knife in my belt and approach Callum.

His eyes are wide in shock as he stares at me, "They're not joking when they say hunters and huntresses are killing machines," he says, his voice shaky.

"Look, you've got to run, hunters and huntresses are all over the place, make sure you're somewhere fairly safe," I say, ignoring the fact that he's just spoken.

"Why did you do that?" Callum asks, he seems breathless if not exhausted.

"A life for a life," is the answer I give, "now go! Run!" I command and swiftly he moves, remaining hidden in the shadows whilst I must move in the opposite direction, running towards what could be my prey. I need the most amount of kills and so far, I've killed three.

I rush in the direction Callum has run from but I see no prisoners and no hunters or huntresses around and my gut tells me that the other prisoners have managed to escape being slaughtered. I continue cautiously, my instincts seem to have taken over completely, I am no longer a girl, I am a huntress.

I listen for movement as I step further into the forest but I hear nothing but bird calls and animals in the trees. The sun beats down mercilessly on my pale skin and the world around me seems to have become unusually slow.

The scent of prisoners seems to be dying quickly in the area, so that it no longer lingers and it is harder to find them and even so, I continue forth.

Soon, the shade begins calling my name and I climb the trees to find some sort of shelter from the burning sun. I move quickly in the trees, their leaves providing me some relief, the breeze running through my hair. Each step I take remains completely silent to any of those whom could be below.

"Listen to me, Devotion isn't going to be the Champion," Frost's words stab through my body and grab my attention. I pause and hide within the leaves before watching her tower over a small group.

"She got the most votes, so she has the best weapons," a familiar male voice says but I struggle to put his voice to a face.

"Yes, but its only because she put on a pathetic little act and got the world to believe she was slowly becoming friends with that stupid little prisoner, that's why she got the votes," Frost replies in the usual snotty voice she tends to speak in, "she's pathetic, she can't fight and she's not even that good with a bow"

I gulp as I listen to her words, *Doesn't she realise that by saying such words, she sounds pathetic and people will lose interest in her? She sounds childish!* I think to myself. I force myself not to sigh before I continue to move silently in the trees. Keeping myself completely hidden.

*   *   *

Eventually, I catch a glimpse of a small group of prisoners. I know taking them all on at once is too risky for any type of injury to occur and so I wait patiently. Waiting for one to separate from the group so that one by one, I may take them down.

Twilight begins to settle into place as the light brought by the sun fleas the violence of the arena and the moon takes its place. I wait as the prisoners struggle to keep the embers of the fire lit yet keep the smoke and light at bay.

"It's getting pretty cold," a female voice mutters quietly.

"We'll go gather some more wood," a male replies.

"Please don't leave me alone," she begs.

"You won't be alone okay, and we won't be far. If anything happens, scream," the males voice replies.

Safety in numbers, that's what they're sticking by, I think to myself. Carefully, I follow the small group through the dark and continue to wait patiently. Every step I take is silent, my gaze never leaving the group as my eyes adapt to the dark. I listen for any possible danger that could be approaching me as I watch, as I hunt.

All of my senses seem to tingle as everything seems to become more defined. Finally, two prisoners out of the group separate without realising, both of them muttering a short conversation that I take no notice of what it is they're really saying as I unclip the bow.

Quietly, I squat on the tree, unfold the bow and aim. I fire the first arrow and swiftly, I aim the second arrow so that the second prisoner doesn't have time to scream and alert the others that a hunter or huntress is nearby.

The arrows fade within the bodies of the prisoners as they fall to the floor, its this time, I actually pay attention to the bodies as they seem to glow slightly before they seem to disappear into a fountain of ash. I turn and approach the group once more as they seem to regroup.

"Where are Josh and Candy?" The female voice asks.

"They've either been killed or wondered off to be on their own, remember the hunters and huntresses are incredibly skilled. They're either dead or separated," the same male voice says.

"He's right," a young female voice says.

I realise that it will be a while until the next time they will separate and so, I chose to rest and wait, gaining strength once more.

"You're doing very well, Devotion," Devotes voice enters my ear through the ear piece, "so far you're tied on the amount of kills commit. Many of the hunters and huntresses haven't even made a kill yet. Innocence and Conquer have started working as a team and so they're sharing the kills at the minute and they're tied with you, keep up the good work and don't forget you have spells—" I nod as if in response to her words, "—I'll be in contact as often as possible to give you advise but otherwise, you have to follow any orders you're given, remember this"

I nod a second time and her voice fades into nothingness. Leaving me with the words spoken by the prisoners below that are not of interest to me and my thoughts.

* * *

Gradually, I drift into a deep sleep and at the first ray of sunlight, I'm awoken the following morning. Three of the prisoners below are deep in sleep whilst two others are on watch, waiting patiently. They both seem very alert as they wait, listening and looking for any movement. I remain completely still for a while and watch them, as if I'm studying them in a sense.

Suddenly, the sound of clumsy footsteps catch both mine and the prisoners attention. I glance down at first to see them looking in the direction of the noise before I too look yet all that I see is an injured prisoner running for her life, staggering weakly.

Put her out of her misery, a voice in my mind commands but I ignore it. I know the makers will want entertainment and they'll be getting what they want from the slow hunt I find myself conducting.

The two prisoners begin rushing to wake the others and begin running, all of them relying on safety in numbers. I run along the trees and begin jumping from branch to branch, moving between the trees. Following them yet remaining hidden and silent in the shadows cast by the leaves.

I need to be quick, I could lose some prey, they may not even notice me up here, I think to myself.

In the swift movement, holding elven grace within it, I unclip the bow from my belt and press the button, allowing it to unfold.

I pick up the pace as I leap through the trees until I'm only slightly ahead of the group. I draw back the scarlet red string and the arrow appears. Swiftly, I aim, knowing that I don't have much time.

I take in a large breath through my nose and exhale through my mouth as I fire the arrow. Swiftly, it embeds itself in the young females skull and her blood begins to soak her dark brown hair. The blood stains, her deathly white face as her body falls to the floor, her eyes wide with fear.

The fear still lingering there as her body just falls to the floor lifelessly. A slightly older female screams, her voice carrying fear in the purest form known. Somehow, the fear seems to emanate from her body and into mine, giving me even further strength and power.

I know I must continue killing, I know I need the kills in order to become one of the champions but a part of me screams that this is wrong, that this is a way of control.

I turn and continue running, as the others change direction, I need to follow them, to scare them. To give the makers the entertainment they want.

Leaping from branch to branch, the shadows keeping me hidden from my prey. Each step I take is as equally silent and precise as the last. I take several deep gulps of air as I run, listening carefully to my heartbeat as it pounds in my chest and keeping my breathing steady as a way of stopping any possible cramps from lack of oxygen.

Suddenly, my prey come to a stop, each of them completely knackered after running for what must have been several hours in the merciless heat.

I only have one kill, later I must take another kill otherwise I'll begin falling behind, I think as I silently watch the prisoners.

They pant for breath and collapse on the floor, "I think we lost whomever the hunter or huntress was that killed Lilly," says one of the males but through the leaves, I can't quite see who is talking.

Later, I'll fight, I need energy, I think to myself. Carefully, I take off the backpack and take out an energy bar before eating. I need high energy levels for when it comes to hunting them further.

Four now remain, out of this group I have killed three and yesterday, I managed to kill three of those males. That leaves me with six kills over all, hopefully by the end of my pursuit, I shall have ten kills.

Silently, I hope that six kills over two days will assist me in taking the lead of the games and becoming one of the champions. I hope that it will work in my favour later on.

Focus, grab ten kills over two or three days, that's what you need to do but don't risk injury. Remember injuries prove to be fatal, even for huntresses. I force myself to remember the deaths of hunters and huntresses from previous games, remembering how they became injured or accidentally ate something poisonous. I know how dangerous and fatal it can be, even for one trained for such things.

I lean back against the tree branch and a sudden memory flashes before my eyes. The girl outside the train, how she looked at me, how she fled, it all replays in my mind.

I realise I've closed my eyes and when I open them, the day seems to have flown past me. I glance through the leaves and listen yet I can't hear the prisoners anymore.

I've seem to have lost my prey.

"I swear I heard something, you have to believe me," the familiar voice speaks and I realise that it isn't that I've lost my prey, its that they've gone to investigate a noise.

I sit up and look around as they return with wood and begin to build a small fire.

"I'm starving," a male voice complains.

"So am I," a second male complains.

"Well go find us something to eat, if not you can quit complaining because I'll bet everyone is fucking hungry!" A third male snaps.

"He's right, we can't just stand and complain about it, we need to find food ourselves," the female agrees, her voice sounding much calmer than the male.

"Fine, I'll go see what I can scavenge," the first male replies.

"Why don't you wait until morning?" The female asks.

"Because I'm too hungry to wait until morning!" The male growls angrily before I hear his footsteps storm away.

Carefully, I throw my backpack over my shoulders and begin following the male. He seems to storm away quite far from the group before he begins looking in the bushes for food.

He starts picking berries when I press the button to unfold the bow, draw back the string and the black and red arrow begins to form. I aim and fire just as the sound of footsteps grow closer. His body seems to explode in a fountain of ash just as the group emerge once more.

"Jack!" The female shouts as I quickly flea into the shadows.

"Jack!" Another male echoes.

The female crouches near the settling ashes and picks them up in her hand, "Ashes, they are ashes," she says, "I think he's dead"

"There are twelve hunters and huntresses, its not safe to separate because of the possibility of being picked off as they travel. They're more experienced in fighting and weapons than any of us," a male says.

"Either, he's wandered even further or he's gone," the second male agrees.

"Do you want to continue further and search for him or do you want to set up camp for a bit?" The female asks, her voice shaky with fear.

"Lets continue for a bit before we set up camp, you never know, we might find him along the way," the second males voice agrees.

*   *   *

I follow them until they set up camp, they seem to be sticking together now as if they're joint at the hip. I can sense the fear they feel lingering in the air, it seems to feed me, bring me more energy and I don't quite understand why. I wait patiently but it seems unlikely that they're going to separate.

Eventually, I find myself falling to sleep. The girl they called Lilly seems to haunt my dreams, the fear in her eyes remaining in my mind, I find myself constantly seeing it in my dreams as I travel through the arena. Every so often, I seem to see her run between the trees in the corner of my eye but when I look at her she seems to disappear instantly.

The games have just begun and already I've managed to kill seven people in two days. I know it will assist me in becoming a champion.

In my dreams, I wander through the arena, without caution or fear yet I feel as though I'm being watched. Like someone is following me. Suddenly, a white figure runs across my path in front of me, catching my attention. Instantly, I know its Lilly yet I don't understand how I know its her or why she seems to be following me in my dreams.

I pause and stare in front of me, my eyes search for Lilly when I see her a second time in the corner of my eye. I glance in the direction before the radiant woman, glowing a radiant white dress stands in front of me. It's definitely the girl they called Lilly just as I suspected.

The fear no longer in her eyes, instead something else lingers there, something I don't quite understand. Her facial expression seems emotionless if not numb as she stares at me.

"Once half human, half elf, now the blood still remains in her veins along with other things. She is no longer human nor is she elf, none know of what she is, she doesn't know of who she is. Does she agree with what they do? No. Will she agree with them when the truth is discovered? This is unknown. Something's to be found, something's to be uncovered. No longer is she mortal. Soon she shall see. Second sight was gifted to thee. The reason unknown for now but shall be uncovered," she says, in an emotionless tone. Her voice sounds much older than her years, it seems to be filled with a wisdom I've never quite bore witness to.

"What do you mean?" I whisper, my voice shaking with fear.

"Second sight was gifted to thee so that the truth she may see," Lilly replies before she suddenly disappears.

"Wait! Come back! Tell me what you meant! Come back!" I shout, my voice quivering with emotion. My body trembling in fear. "Please! Come back!" I beg.

Suddenly, the sunrise awakens me and I glance around to see that I'm still laid on the branch and not on the ground.

It was just a dream. Nothing more. I think to myself, in an attempt to comfort my mind but something in my gut tells me that it was more than just an ordinary nightmare, it was more than any dream I've ever experienced. There's something about her message that lingers in my mind when suddenly, the woman from outside the train flashes in front of my eyes along with the creature killed outside the prison.

What are they? I wonder.

*   *   *

Time passes and I realise that they're not going to separate now. I grab my bow and come to a quick and irrational decision but I know it's the most I can do.

Silently, I climb from the trees and remain hidden in the bushes, the bow fully built up and ready to be wield as the deadly weapon it is. I draw back the string and with great concentration, I aim the arrow at one of the males, not paying much more attention to anything else but my senses. I fire the arrow and it embeds itself in his throat.

The female screams just as I run out of the bushes, with a swift graceful movement, I grab one of the throwing knives out of the pocket on my belt and throw it at the second male as he begins to run. It lands in his back and he falls down to the floor.

I spin and grab a second knife, just as the female begins to try and run away. With perfect precision, I throw the knife and it lands in the back of her head and this time I see the blades spread out just after entering the woman's body. I approach her body and retrieve the knife, wiping the blood off the blade and onto my thigh before placing it back in my belt once more.

The bow folds and I clip it back onto my belt before I go to retrieve the second knife when I find that the male is still alive.

I take out the knife and roll his body onto his back, "I hope you're fucking happy with what you are, a little fucking killing machine! A cold hearted killing freak! An unwanted killer in society!" He snaps, his tone filled with disgust and hatred. His eyes burning like an endless blaze with hunger, anger and hatred. Hatred directed towards me.

"I cannot help what I am for it is your kin that have created me, it is your kin that created us as killing machines and so it is yourself that you should hate," I spit, my voice spiteful and angry. With the same knife that embed itself in his back, I mercilessly slice through his throat but this time the small blades don't seem to spring out of the main blade.

The light of the morning sun reflects on the blood, shining the eminence of death into my sensitive eyes.

Carefully, I wipe away the blood on the same thigh before I force myself to stand and return to the trees. The shadows cast by the leaves masking my presence once more as I continue the hunt.

*   *   *

The night soon arrives, and I find myself with no further kills. As I rest against the tree branch, Callum begins to haunt my mind. The silver light radiating from the moon dances enchantingly on the floor of the forest, through the leaves.

Tonight seems to be becoming bitterly cold.

I wonder if he's still alive, if he's okay. I hope he's okay. I wonder how well he's surviving, has he eaten? I bet he's cold tonight. I hope he's not dead, my mind swirls with thoughts of him shivering from the cold, starving and alone or possibly even dead. I try to force the thoughts to one side, push them out of my head, but I can't.

Stabbing pains grow in my heart as I think about him. Each possible scenario playing in my mind.

If he's dead, I hope it was quick and painless the thoughts send immediate sharp painful stabs through my chest and ice cold tears begin to stream down my face.

"Please let him be okay," I whisper quietly, not caring if the entire world hears my words or not. In my heart, I truly hope that he is still alive and well.

Eventually, I drift off to sleep.

CHAPTER 7

Compulsion Of The Heart

"Good morning hunters and huntresses," the familiar male voice echoes through my ear piece. I jolt up into a sitting position, startled by the sudden wakeup call just as dawn arrives. The sound of the makers voice rattles my ear drums until I'm wide awake and ready to continue hunting. "You're each doing well, some better than others I must admit but this is expected in all games," he pauses for a moment, "now you all must be wondering why I have awoken you all like this, well here is the first slight change made to this years games"

I gulp down a breath of air, unsure of what to expect him to say.

"Somewhere in the area you have been sleeping, you will hear an unusual beeping noise and find a small parcel, this parcel is from your parents. It has not been signed but shall have a small message and a few things that may assist you in your hunt depending on what your parents think it is that you need," the maker continues, there is a short pause and I capture the sound of beeping coming from underneath the tree, "that is all for today, happy hunting"

Swiftly, I climb out of the tree, grab the parcel before returning to my branch. This will be the first proper connection I will have ever had with my parents.

Shakily, I open the parcel, my body trembling with both excitement and fear. *What if they're not proud of me? What if they hate me because of what I am? Like the prisoner said, I'm a killing machine, how can a parent be proud of such a thing?* I wonder as I lift the envelope and open it.

> *Dearest Devotion,*
>
> *At first, I was unsure of what to write in this letter, with having no contact with you until <u>recently</u> I have never truly known you even though I wish I had.*
>
> *To begin, I must say, I have never been so proud, I feel as if I'm the proudest mother in the world. You're no killing machine, you are a <u>devoted</u> young girl just as I was at your age, and you must remember that there are more important things than the games.*
>
> *You must stay true to your heart, follow it no matter where it leads you because in the end, your heart knows your destiny more than I or anyone else. I know you must feel ashamed and <u>sick</u> of what they have put you through but you must follow it until the end. Only then shall you have your freedom, just as <u>I</u> received mine at your age.*

> *Be cautious in the arena, for you never know what could be behind the next tree or around the corner. You can't risk being reckless. Let your instincts take hold at times for they are you're greatest ally.*
>
> *The makers have great interest in you, remember this. Be cautious, listen to your dreams, heed the warnings in your visions.*
>
> *And of all else, remember the scales.*

I stare at the letter, feeling nothing but confused before something occurs to me, *some of the letters are underlined and some words and sentences are as well.* I glance in the parcel to see a spell book, a note pad and of course a pen. *A secret message!* I realise.

I grab the pen and note pad before I begin trying to crack the code. *Recently, devote, s-I-c-c-u-l-e-t, have great interest in you. Devote is my trainer, I met her recently but could these letters actually be on word. Sicculet. Remember the scales!* I can't help but feel incredibly confused and my temples throb painfully as I attempt to decipher the hidden message but it doesn't seem to make any sense. All I can think about are the beautiful, enchanting scales of the unusual creature outside the train and the one that was killed outside of the prison. I had never seen anything like them in my entire life. Could they be what my parents are talking about in the letter?

I push the thoughts to one side, I don't have time to be figuring things out if I'm going to become a champion. *If Callum's still alive then I'll find out from him if I find him* I think to myself before stuffing everything into my bag and forcing myself to return to hunting. *My mother must have thought it would be useful but its distracting for the time being* my thoughts keep returning to the letter yet I force them to one side.

I must remain focused, the makers, they're trying to distract us. I saw them doing these sorts of things in previous games. If I'm going to be a champion, I can't be distracted.

The rancid smell of body odour invades my nose as I run along the tree branches. A shimmer of light grabs my attention and I climb from the tree to see fresh blood reflecting the light. I rub the liquid between my fingers and thumb. *Someone's injured and they must be close, they couldn't have gone very far at all* I think before climbing the trees once more and following the trail of blood below me. The coppery smell seems to linger in the air, gaining stronger as I run in the direction of the droplets of blood below me. The droplets grow larger the further I go and an unfamiliar smell mixes with the scent of blood and body odor.

Suddenly, a large injured male comes into view and I watch him from above for a moment as he attempts to clean a large gash in his leg with a leaf and some water from a large shaded spring that he is sat beside.

Using the large shadows cast by the trees, I silently approach him. I don't quite understand what's happening, my instincts seem to be pulling me closer to him.

He turns and looks at me, but something seems to replace the fear I would imagine to be in his eyes. Instead, I see what can only be described as relief.

"You seem to be in a lot of pain," I say as he winces. "Your leg is badly injured, how did this happen to you?"

"A trap, I stepped in a trap" he replies in a deep, hoarse voice. He seems startled by my words and my unusual concern for his well being. Why do I seem to care all of sudden? This isn't right.

Cautiously, I step closer to him and crouch by his side. Something in my gut tells me that he isn't going to try and harm me. I look at the wound closely, to see more than one gash, its as if he's stepped in a bear trap, one of those traps that are triggered by stepping on them. Yellow puss oozes from the injury, showing that it is clearly infected.

"Your injury is infected, I'd be surprised if gangrene hasn't settled in already, you could lose your leg," I mutter quietly.

"I'll lose my life not my leg," he replies, his voice shaky "aren't you going to kill me?"

"I'm supposed to," I mutter as I look at him.

"Then do what you're supposed to do," he mutters quietly, his eyes begging me to show him mercy and rid him of the agonising pain he clearly feels.

I gulp, "This is your choice, you realize this, don't you?" I reply.

"Then I choose to die," he says, his voice pleading with me. I nod and something else seems to take hold of me, something deeper inside of me, something I never knew existed. The strange compassion I seem to hold in my heart has triggered another instinct, an unfamiliar instinct. Gently, I touch his warm forehead to feel just how much of a fever he has, its then I realize just how ill he is. I sigh and with a grace much greater than any other elf I have ever witnessed, a powerful radiant white light seems to radiate from my hand, growing larger with every passing second.

"I shall make this quick," I whisper, more comforting myself than my enemy. The light jolts from my hand, pushing me away from my enemy and into the spring as it enters his body. His veins glow brighter and brighter as it grows within his body. He looks to me and smiles with relief and happiness clear in his eyes. All of his troubles seem to have left him almost instantly.

I watch, unable to look away as the light begins to pierce through his skin in cracks and the flesh around the light seems to go black as if it is burning. Silently, I wonder if such a thing is painful for him or if it is finally a relief, a way of releasing all the bad things that have occurred in his life.

The light gains brighter and brighter, the rancid smell of burning flesh invades my nose. It is at that moment, in a blinding flash of light, his body completely deteriorates without a single trace remaining.

I glance around the area, the cold spring water cools my skin and brings relief from the merciless sun. Confused and startled, I don't quite understand what has just occurred but I know that whatever it was, it came from me.

How? How did I do that? I wonder, *I didn't concentrate, I didn't think of magic, it was impulse, it was instinct, my body working on auto drive. How can I be capable of such a thing?* I think about the genetic modification, the experiments conducted upon me when I was merely a child.

I attempt to push the memory, of what has just occurred, to one side but it replays in my mind constantly, as if it is happening over and over again. No matter how much I try to forget it, I can't. As if I'm reliving the scene. I step out of the spring and begin walking within the shadows of the trees until eventually I step out into the sun, my body shaking in shock even though somehow it remains taking every step with caution.

It's the words spoken through my earpiece that finally brings me back to the realm of the living, "Darkness is no longer classed as a hunter. The hunter or huntress to kill him will be rewarded his kills along with ten extras due to him becoming cannibalistic. You are ordered to hunt him immediately, forget what you're doing at this moment, and find him" the makers voice commands.

I pause for a moment and wait for further information but I don't receive it from the maker, instead Devotes voice echoes through the ear piece, "Devotion, he's close to you, if you continue in the direction you're going, you'll come to a small clearing in the forest, he's there," she says.

I nod, "Okay," I whisper before returning to the tree branches and running in the direction I'd been walking. Silently, I wonder how this is happening so quickly? In previous games, it seems to have taken longer but then, I'm already losing track of how many days we have been in the arena.

I leap from tree to tree until I hear a loud shout echo through the trees, followed by a scream. I run in the direction of the noises before I spot a small trap.

It's one of Innocence's traps my mind realises and I wait, patiently. Soon, Darkness appears out of the shadows and begins walking in the direction of Innocence's trap. I hide within the shadows cast by the leaves and wait.

Suddenly, I spot Innocence below, hiding in a bush nearby.

Darkness walks with caution, his sword in his hand, his skin and armour both soaked in blood. I glance back to Innocence to see her watching me, she smiles and nods as if she knows something I don't. I look back to Darkness as he steps in the trap. It moves quickly, the rope wrapping around his ankle and pulling him up, leaving him hanging helplessly from the tree by his ankle. His sword falls to the floor, giving off a slight clattering sound as it hits a large log below him and he squirms angrily. Growling with pure rage and aggression.

With a sudden, unusual impulse, I jump from the shadows cast by the leaves and down from directly above him. My hand touches his unusually warm body as I fall to the ground and land on my feet. As I fall, a horrid sharp pain burns in the palm of my hand, it feels as if something is ripping through my skin. Something sharp and hot.

I glance to my left just as his blood splatters across my face, soaking my hair. His body slices into two where my hand has touched him whilst a sword slices through the remaining part of his body that hangs from the tree. More blood covers my bare skin, it feels warm as it touches me.

I look past the severed corpse to see Conquer behind it, looking down at me, his build towering above me.

"That better be a shared kill!" Conquer says, his voice filled with annoyance.

"I think it should be, it was Innocence who created the trap" I say.

"I know!" He snaps.

Innocence approaches us with a smile, "don't worry, I saw her in the tree, I knew what she would do and I encouraged it" she says.

"Congratulations to Conquer, Innocence and Devotion, you brought down Darkness together and as you wanted, the kills have been shared between you," the makers voice says through the earpiece.

"Devotion, you're at fifteen kills now, you're in the lead but don't let this go to your head, stay focused" Devotes voice says through the earpiece.

I nod in response and look to Innocence and Conquer. "How did you do that? I don't see a weapon in your hand," Conquer says.

I shrug, "Maybe I'm just faster than you," I reply.

"Would that really matter? A throwing knife doesn't cut like that," Conquer replies, his voice snappy and cold, its as if he believes I've been given some special weapon that they haven't seen before and they want it.

"And? It doesn't matter does it? You don't need to know about how I hunt," I reply.

"I just think its strange," Conquer replies.

"Well you can think its strange all you want, the longer we're stood here talking the faster the others will get ahead of each of us and I don't know about you but I want to be a champion," I reply.

"More like you want to find Callum and make sure he's still alive," Conquer replies, his eyebrows raising at me.

"So what if I want to make sure my friends alive? He is my friend after all, is that so wrong?" I reply.

"In the games its wrong! He is the enemy! In the arena he isn't your friend! He is your enemy! Your supposed to hunt him not help him! The enemy can't be your friend!" Conquer replies.

"Believe what you want to believe," I mutter, "we have work to do anyway"

"Are you splitting off again?" Innocence asks.

I nod, "yes" I mutter, "I think I work better on my own"

"Good luck," Innocence replies.

"Good luck to yourselves," I reply before I separate from them both and continue forth. A part of my heart screaming at me to find Callum, to make sure he's okay, to keep him alive and the longer I'm away from him, the stronger that compulsion, that piece of my heart becomes.

*   *   *

The night came quickly, flooding the arena in darkness, the strands of silver light dancing on the forest floor being the only source of light. Yet my eyes adapt to such a scene.

I watch the strands of silver light dance elegantly, as if it is a ballet dancer upon a glorious stage, between the leaves. My mind is preoccupied with thoughts of Callum. *Was it all just an illusion? Was the friendship a lie? I want to believe it was real, I want to believe that it is still very real* I think, silently. My mind floods with memories of the short time I spent with him, something about him screams to me. It talks to my heart in a way I have never truly known.

My eyes slowly become heavy with sleep and gradually I begin to feel lost. My back rests against the cold bark of the tree, my jacket wrapped around me in order to keep me warm in the cold night.

Yet, I don't care that its cold, so cold that I shiver and goose bumps rise on my skin. Even though I'm wrapped up in my jacket, I just don't seem to care. My only thoughts are about Callum and the unusual warmth he seems to bring to me. The strange physical warmth that seems to radiate from his body and enter mine

And the strange feelings he brings to my heart. The mark he seems to have left burns brightly within my body. How he has caused me to feel such unusual emotions is unclear to me. I don't quite understand how he has made me feel such things and I certainly don't understand why I feel such a desperation inside of me to find him. A desperation to be in his arms once more.

"Please let him be okay," I whisper quietly, hoping that if there is a God or Goddess, that they may hear my prayer and answer it.

Suddenly, the world seems to go black and all of a sudden, I feel as if I'm floating. Drifting away from the arena, a place of death and fear to a new place, a happier place. A place that seems to hold a motherly love.

My body feels as if its been wrapped in a quilt of hope and joy, love and passion. I open my eyes, realising that they were shut and find myself in somewhere new.

I find myself, laid on the sand, the sea gently caressing my skin. My hand reaches out further, the touch of the cold sea waves as is engulfs my arm seems to comfort me somehow.

"Child, please sit up and let me see your face," a motherly female voice says, her voice soft and comforting, and filled with what I could only describe as love. Instantly, from the sound of her beautiful melodic voice, I sit up to see a woman appear from behind the trees at the far end of the beach.

As she grows closer, I recognise her emerald green eyes and long black hair that falls down her back. Yet there are things that are different, like the way her hair moves lightly so that it appears as if each strand is a separate feather swaying gracefully in the wind, it appears completely weightless yet the movements it makes in the wind is slow. Her pale skin seems even paler than I remember and her ears have a much larger point, not like an elf's. They're longer and curve around slightly.

She wears beautiful silver armour just like the armour I've been wearing in the arena. I glance down at my body to see that I'm still wearing the armour and her armour looks almost exact only its silver and not black and the symbols are not scarlet on hers but they're emerald green. She wears the same boots only in silver and not black with emerald green symbols and not scarlet. Her circlet is just like mine only again it is silver with an emerald gem in the centre.

She crouches in front of me before she begins to speak, "you're as beautiful as I remember"

"Devote?" I whisper softly, feeling engulfed in a cocoon of emotions.

"I am not Devote but I have taken her form so that I may not scare you," she replies in a comforting voice.

"Who are you?" I blurt before I can stop my mouth from speaking the words in such a rude manner.

"I am Gaia," she replies and instantly, I recognise her name. I recognise it from books I've read in the past, books on religion.

"Gaia? Goddess of the earth," I whisper, wondering whether this is a dream or some sort of vision.

"Yes child," she replies

"Why-why are you here?"

"You are my daughter, just as all those whom inhabit the earth are my children, from elves to sicculets, even though the humans changed you, you are still my children"

"The sicculets?" Immediately, I recognise the word from the hidden message.

"Yes, these are the children you are destined to see, prophesised to save. They're interested in you, they wish for freedom" she replies, the words remaining in my mind but my heart is else where.

"Do you know of Callum?" I ask.

"Yes, and I know of the emotions stirring within you" she replies, her voice seems to become even more comforting, even softer than it was before.

"Is he okay? Is he still alive?" The words rush from my mouth, my heart pounding painfully against my rib cage.

A comforting, loving smile grows on her face and she nods, "he is safe for now, he is still alive" she replies.

"Are you protecting him?" I ask.

"I shall protect him until it falls upon you to do so,"

"When will that rest upon my shoulders?" I ask.

"Soon, as it is not long until you will both find each other but when that comes, so shall a change within you, a change that has already begun but shall soon complete"

"What do you mean a change?"

"In your heart you know of what I speak," she replies, she seems to be talking in nothing more than riddles that I can't quite understand. I want her to answer me clearly, not leave me with even further questions. My heart begs for answers but something tells me I shall not receive these answers for a long time. She stands and turns as she begins to walk away, when suddenly she stops and glances over her shoulder at me, "Callum has never been one for agreeing with violence and hatred," she says before she continues walking and fades into a strange turquoise light that seems to separate and enter the plants, trees and seas.

My eyes fly open and my body is suddenly alert.

I glance around for any signs that what just happened was in fact a dream and not something more but I see nothing. *Right, it was just a dream and you need to get hunting, now!* I think to myself. I shake my head, forcing myself to awake properly before I grab an energy bar and continue searching the island for my next victim.

*   *   *

Soon, I grow sick of running along the tree branches, and decide to walk on the ground for a while. The soft mud feels strange under my feet as it moulds to my boots with every step I take. My steps remain silent but after a while of travelling in the merciless heat, my guard begins to drop slightly and I begin to feel very hungry.

Wait just a little longer, I continue to push myself.

I step with caution through the shadows as I attempt to escape the sun and find relief. Finally, I enter a small shaded clearly, the leaves above, provide plenty of shadows whilst the trees that surround it arch over. Caution enters every movement I make. Every step I take is as silent as the last, and every time I make a step, I am cautious of any twigs that I may step upon.

The foul smell of body odour invades my nose. Their foul smell causes me to want to vomit. My nose wrinkles in disgust from the scent. The smell of sweat, filth and grease, grows stronger and over powers the scent of the damp soil, flowers and the trees that surround me.

I know that the enemy is close.

Suddenly, the sound of a twig snapping, echoes throughout the small clearing, the source of the sound coming from behind me. Instinctively, I spin around and unclip my bow from my belt, pressing the button for it to unfold. Yet for some unknown reason, my movements seem unusually sluggish, something I've never truly experienced.

My bow is knocked out of my hand and I'm pushed to the floor. Fear floods my body as I stare at the largely built male that towers over me. His dark greasy hair clings to his sun burnt face. His brown eyes burning with insanity. He doesn't care if he dies for killing me, his mind is set on what he wants to do and that is in fact, kill.

My mind suddenly hit's the realisation that death is upon me and once I realise this, all fear fleas from my body. I am no longer afraid. Silently, I welcome it.

I shall no doubt be the first huntress to die in this years games, and I shall follow Darkness. My death shall no doubt be replayed in front of the Champions and just as previous years, they shall either laugh or cry about it.

It is then, just as I welcome death and come to terms with my fate, the male is knocked from his feet by another male. Instantly, I recognise his dark skin and dreadlocks as he flies past me and proceeds in attacking the male that had attacked me. His muscles clench angrily and appear to grow larger before my very eyes and an animalistic growl escapes his lips.

For a moment, I'm completely stunned by what has just occurred. I watch as the males fight across the clearing and I know I must do something. Anything. I must save my rescuer.

I scramble to my feet but for some reason I leave my bow as instinct takes hold of me. My attacker manages to kick off my rescuer and proceeds in attacking him. Punching his face repeatedly before he grasps his hands around my rescuers throat. It is the first of the blows that strengthens the deadly instinct within me.

I draw out one of the throwing knives from my belt and gently kiss it. I concentrate on the magic, allowing it to fill my entire body and surround me. I throw the knife whilst concentrating on the magic as I wield it, not allowing my concentration to quiver. A white light begins to radiate from my body and surround the knife as it flies through the air.

The knife hit's the male in the shoulder and he falls to the side, his body stills for a moment, his eyes roll into the back of his head. Suddenly, his body begins to convulse as if he is having an epileptic fit. I stand there, staring at the scene that begins to take place in front of me, unsure of what I have done and what is about to occur but as it begins happening, I seem to instinctively know what he is seeing and feeling.

Blood begins to pour from his eyes like tears. He lets out a blood curdling scream as the magic begins to force him to relive the terrifying, horrific moments of every last one of his victims. Instinctively, I seem to know now that he was a serial killer before he was caught and convicted, that is why he was here in the games. The memories flash in front of my eyes quickly, too quickly for me to gain much information from them. I force myself to look past the flashes and watch the male. Through his face, I can see that he is experiencing every last detail of what appears to be their deaths, in their perspectives.

Feeling their pain and fear, hatred and disgust.

Blood begins to pore from his ears, and nose. I watch as his teeth become stained with blood before it begins trickling out of his mouth, staining his lips.

He lets out one final scream before his body relaxes. Swiftly, I recover the knife and back away from the body, unable to look away from him.

The ground begins to shake as it opens up around his body, his eyes glance around the clearing but it seems as if he is unable to move. The opening in the ground begins to glow an orange tinge, and flames begin to pierce through.

"Have fun in hell," I mutter quietly as rotting hands begin to rise from the illuminating orange and red flames. An extreme heat blasts from the ground and gently touches my body.

"No! No! No!" He screams, his voice quivering in fear as he realises his fate. The hands begin to grab his body firmly, the rotting flesh burning from the heat, the agonising screams rising from the ground. Fear and pain echo in the screams as they surround us, the sound bouncing off the trees that surround the shaded clearing.

The hands pull him into the ground, his face masked in fear as he continues to scream. Finally, the flames engulf him, and a final scream escapes his lips, a scream filled with pure agony before the ground closes leaving no trace of what has just occurred.

A beautiful woman appears before me, her long hair a fiery auburn colour, her eyes glowing like the embers of fire and her skin a ghostly white colour. She hovers above the floor, flames seem to engulf her legs from the knee downwards. Her long black and red dress clings to her body perfectly but only just covers her breasts.

"Thank you, we will be having much fun with this one for he has committed many heinous crimes in his life," she says in a cruel tone, her smile gleaming brightly on her blood red lips. Her eyes seem to glow even brighter with joy and excitement, "we thank you for the pleasure you have given us," she continues.

"You can do that sort of thing?" Callum asks as the fierce apparition fades into nothingness, and the immense heat that surrounds us begins to cool once more.

"Apparently so," I reply as I turn to face him, the light around us seems to grow darker as every trace of magic fades.

"How?" He asks, his voice quiet and his face seems startled by what he has just witnessed.

I tuck the lose hairs behind my ears to reveal the point, "I concentrate" I reply.

"You're an elf?" He replies, clearly he has never noticed the point in my ears before as his voice sounds slightly shocked at such a discovery. "No wonder," he whispers.

"Yea, didn't you know?" I ask. He shakes his head in response, "Because of my heritage, I can wield magic"

"No wonder you seem so fare, but it never occurred to me," he replies.

Stay alert at all times! My mind commands, *I must stay alert! I can't let my guard down, I can't allow myself to fall for the illusion of safety here, its too dangerous*

"Look, err I need to return to hunting," I mutter quietly.

"Then hunt me, its another kill on to the scoreboard for you," Callum replies.

"No!" I snap, a sharp pain stabbing through my heart like someone has just stabbed me with an ice cold blade. My voice sounds angry and fierce because of the pain.

"Why?" He asks softly, the warmth radiating from his body once more and entering mine.

"Because you're my friend and I don't hurt my friends," I reply

"Then it wasn't an illusion, was it?" Callum replies, his smile soft and comforting.

"No," I whisper breathlessly, "why?" I ask after a moment of silence.

"Why what?" Callum replies.

"Why did you save me?" I ask as I pick up my bow, press the button to fold it up and clip it to my belt.

"A life for a life, right?" Callum replies.

I smile, surprised that he remembered what I said when I saved him, "A life for a life" I reply.

He returns my smile, "Do you want to work together? As a team?" He asks. I pause for a moment, unsure of whether I should trust Callum or not. I gulp nervously, as my thoughts become chaotic and wild.

Can I trust him? I don't really know much about him. Is he a murderer? What if he tries something? What if he betrays me? I don't know him that well! I know nothing of his past. I think whilst my heart screams at me to create an alliance with him.

Suddenly, I hear a high pitch squeal through my earpiece and I let out a small cry and my eardrum hurts under the sound. "Devotion! Devotion!" I hear Devotes voice say, her voice filled with panic. "It's Devote, listen to me, I'm your mother, I gave birth to you seventeen years ago and if the makers hadn't taken you away, you would have experienced a completely different life. I swear. Now listen to me! Follow your heart! Listen to your dreams and visions, they shall lead your way! You can trust Callum, I've known him for a good two years, I never thought I would see what I've witnessed but I know now and I'm happy. Good luck and follow your heart no matter what for it shall guide your way!" I hear a sudden commotion in the background and it goes off. I can no longer hear anything from Devote.

PIXIE BIRKITT

"Devote! Devote!" I repeatedly say before I say a word burning within me, "Mum!"

"Are you okay, Devotion?" Callum asks.

I compose myself once more before I speak again, "I'm fine, as you were saying about being allies?"

"Yea, well do you want to become allies?" Callum replies

"What do you mean? Is this the enemy turning into an ally?" I reply, my smile suddenly gleaming and my voice joyful as I pretend what just happened didn't happen.

"I guess you could say I already was an ally," Callum says, his smile gleaming as much as mine. We both begin laughing and once we calm down, Callum speaks again, "so do you want to work together?"

I lift my hand, and nod respectfully, "Allies?" I say.

He takes my hand and pulls me in closer so that our bodies are almost touching, the warmth and pleasure runs through my body, becoming even more powerful, "Allies" he agrees.

*   *   *

I return to the trees and Callum follows only he seems unusually clumsy and off balance as he attempts to follow me. Many times I have had to catch him so that he doesn't fall.

"Maybe you would be best on the ground," I say but he shakes his head.

"I'll stay up here with you," he insists.

"But you're not as balanced as I am up here," I reply.

"Can we sit for a moment?" He asks. I nod and we sit down on the branch, "look if we find a large group of the enemy, I'll try to intercept and separate them," he says after a while.

"How will you do that? You could get hurt," I reply.

"I'll either try to enter the group, or I'll make a load of noise down below, try and get them to separate to investigate, then you take them down one by one," Callum replies.

It's a good plan, but for some reason I'm not happy about it, I don't like the idea of the possibility of him becoming injured, finally I sigh "fine, but be careful," I reply, reluctantly.

"Okay, I'll return to the ground and we'll see what we can find, you need to stay in my sight so you can send me a sign when we get close to them,"

"Okay, what will be the secret sign?" I reply.

He clenches his hand into a fist and slams the side of his fist onto the palm of his other hand before moving it down his fingers and then wrapping his hand around his fist, "That'll work won't it?" He asks.

"I think it will," I reply with a soft smile, "I might go a head a little but if I see anything, I'll raise back and give you the sign," I continue.

He nods, "okay" he replies.

"So, shall we continue?" I ask.

"In a minute, I need a break"

"Would you like something to eat?"

"Yes please, I haven't eaten properly in days"

"What have you been eating?" I ask as I pull an energy bar out of my bag.

"Berries, ones I know are safe to eat," he replies as he takes the bar out of my hand, "thank you"

"No problem, we're friends and allies, we should assist each other where possible," I reply. A warm smile grows on his face and his eyes lighten up, its as if a heavy weight has lifted from his shoulders. Slowly his eyes change to the beautiful hypnotic green and I look away, feeling my cheeks burn in embarrassment. I hide my face with my fringe and giggle.

"What?" He asks.

"Nothing," I reply.

"Okay," he says in a voice that says he's becoming suspicious of my thoughts, "well I tell you one thing, I feel so much more relaxed right now"

"Is it because you feel safer with me around?" I ask.

He chuckles, "I guess you could say that" he replies, his voice relaxed and he sounds as if he's happy.

"So, shall we continue?" I ask once he finishes the energy bar.

"I think we shall," he replies, handing me the rubbish which I place back in my bag.

I consider whether I should ask him about the sicculets but then, it occurs to me that we need to hunt. I promise myself that I'll ask him later.

* * *

Time passes quickly and sunset is close when we finally find a group of three prisoners. All of them trying to survive. I quickly run back to Callum, remaining in the trees and once he's in view. I give him the sign.

He nods in response and begins to run towards the group. I follow him in the trees, leaping from branch to branch. I arrive before he does.

I crouch and wait patiently, hidden by the shadows cast by the trees and the leaves. Soon, I hear the shuffling in the bushes and catch a glimpse of Callum before he begins to cause even further noise out of sight.

I watch as the prisoners become scared but it seems doubtful that they will separate being such a small group. They begin to panic, their heads jolting to each side as they search for a cause of the noise.

"It's a hunter isn't it?" A woman panics and another nods in agreement. "We're dead," she whispers. The noise suddenly comes from behind them and they turn their backs to me, giving me the advantage I need.

I drop down from the tree and unfold the bow, draw back the string and aim at one of the women. I shoot and it kills her almost instantly as the arrow pierces straight through her throat.

The original woman to panic, screams at the top of her lungs as I fold the bow and instinct takes hold once more. I immerge from the shadows and bushes I've been hiding within and run towards the two remaining prisoners.

I pass the only male of the group and lift up my hand. Pain surges through the palm of my hand as I pass him. I stop for a moment, spin on the balls of my feet, jump over the males body as it collapses to the floor, blood splatters on my body as I spin in my jump and land on the floor in front of the female.

My speed is incredible as I move whilst the woman seems to be in shock before me. I grab a throwing knife from my belt and in one swift movement, I throw the knife and it embeds itself directly above her heart.

She falls to the floor, her body limp and I'm unsure of whether she is dead but I know that if she isn't dead now she will be soon. To be sure, I take out the knife from her chest and slice the blade through her throat. Blood splatters on my hands and up my bare arms, covering me in the woman's blood.

I sigh, wiping away a tear as I feel the pity grow inside of me. I feel as if I've been turned into a savage.

"Are we done?" Callum asks, his voice coming from behind me.

"Yea," I mutter, solemnly "would you mind if we find somewhere I can wash away this blood?"

"Of course not," Callum replies.

I turn to retrieve a knife from the males body yet I find none. *I must have used the same knife* I think to myself before we begin walking in a random direction in silence.

It's quite a while until Callum speaks again, "When you killed that male, you didn't use a knife yet you managed to slit his throat, how did you do that?"

"I used the same throwing knife as on the female," I mutter.

"No you didn't, you didn't use a knife and you retrieved the blade from your belt after you killed the male and before you killed the female," Callum replies.

"I don't know, I'm sure I used a knife," I reply, my voice quiet.

"It was just an observation," he says, solemnly. Clearly he thinks he's offended me.

"It's fine, I just didn't notice anything in my attack"

"I tell you now, you're a brilliant and sufficient killer"

"I don't know whether that's an insult or a compliment," I mutter

"I would have thought you would take it as a compliment as you are a huntress," Callum replies.

"I guess"

"What's wrong?" Callum asks, just as we approach a small stream. When I ignore his question, he grabs my shoulders and forces me to stop walking and look at him, "what's wrong?"

"It doesn't matter, its stupid" I reply before I lean in closer and whisper in his ear, "and it could get us both killed if I said what it was"

I pull away and he nods, his eyes filled with realisation, "Okay," he replies.

"Now, I'm just going to get cleaned up," I say before I step passed him and walk towards the stream before I begin washing away the dry blood from my arms with the ice cold water. My fingers begin to feel numb from the temperature but I don't care, all I can feel is the desperation to get rid of the blood.

"Are you okay?" Callum asks, clearly observing how quickly I'm scrubbing at the blood, trying to remove it.

"I'm fine," I reply quietly. Trying to rid myself of the cluster of emotions that are building up inside of me.

This doesn't feel right, all of this, the arena, the killing, none of it feels right. I've been brought up with this as my future, this is what I've been trained to do, why doesn't it feel right? I think to myself, feeling the emotions grow larger.

I notice that the stream has little scuttle fish leaping out of the water and swimming gracefully yet none of them are particularly appealing to the eyes. I take my hands out of the water, knowing that the scent of blood will have drawn them to the stream. The appearance of rotting flesh and bones sends shivers down my spine.

I remember what I'd read, not long ago, about the scuttle fish. I remember how they had originated when humans had begun experimenting with genetics, and radiation on animals and there own kin. Through their experimentation, they had created elves, a kin that could manipulate the world around them through what they called magic. They had also created scuttle fish.

A dangerous creature that buries into the skin of its victims and begins eating the victim from the inside out.

Suddenly, the sound of movement catches my attention just as two males step out of the shadows, approaching the stream, completely oblivious to Callum and I. When they spot us, they seem to grow aggressive as they approach us.

"Callum, you dirty bastard, get your fucking ass here now! I'm going to fucking slice you up!" Shouts one of them, his voice burning with anger.

I glance to Callum, a million questions burning in my eyes. He shrugs.

The aggressive, largely built, pale males continue to approach us. One has shaggy, long greasy brown hair that clings to his face whilst the other has short blond hair. Both of them are a lot larger than Callum in build and I remember these two were lifting weights in the training room.

CHAPTER 8

The Change

Their brown eyes burn with anger, aggression and hatred, all of which is clearly directed at Callum, as they gain closer to us. Clearly, neither of them have noticed me. The first male, with dark brown hair, clenches his jaw angrily. "Fucking animal freak!" He spits before he proceeds in attacking Callum.

Callum growls aggressively before he begins to defend himself. Blocking several of the males punches. He catches one of the males punches and twists his hand so that the sound of breaking bone echoes throughout the area.

Immediately, something inside of me grows even stronger, something protective and a new instinct appears inside of me. The instinct to protect, no matter what. Not the same deadly instinct, this one is different. It's protective yet loving and nurturing, passionate and stronger than anything I've ever known.

The male punches Callum across the face and his body falls to the floor. For a moment, Callum seems completely stunned by what has just happened. He clenches his jaw and continues to growl angrily yet something in the unusual animalistic growl, that seems to escape Callum, speaks of protection and love.

Before the male can continue his attack upon Callum, I find myself standing proud and strong. I hold my head high as an unusual strength begins to grow within me and surround me.

Something begins to stir in the environment, growing larger and stronger. The gentle breeze suddenly changes into gale force winds. The current of the small stream becomes stronger and the amount of water in the stream grows larger until it floods around my feet. An immense heat surrounds me, causing sweat to drip down my forehead and the earth trembles beneath my feet slightly.

Yet the prisoners don't seem to notice, not until the scuttle fish begin to leap out of the stream and attack the male whom is in the process of attacking Callum. The wind causes my hair to whip around wildly, hitting my face slightly.

The prisoner begins to panic, shouting and screaming in agony as the scuttle fish begin to dig into his skin.

Suddenly, I remember a page written in the book I had read about scuttle fish. How it had spoken about the spells that could manipulate scuttle fish. All of them needed incantations in order to be cast yet this didn't need an incantation.

I watch as the scuttle fish begin to eat the prisoner from the inside out, he screams an agonising and fearful scream as they attack his organs and eat through the fat, muscle and flesh.

The prisoner is distraught as the process continues, as their venom begins to flood his veins, causing a deadly burning sensation throughout his body. I recall everything from the book, everything on scuttle fish. How their venom causes absolute agony and then, the final stage begins taking place within the prisoner. His skin blisters from the heat caused by the venom as it passes through his body.

He falls to the floor. His body stiffens as his muscles spasm so quickly that he can't move. He becomes completely paralysed.

Finally it happens, the scuttle fish eat through his flesh and enter the stream once more. Their rotting appearance is now bloated with food. Whilst the prisoner is barely alive, the venom continues to pass through his body, continuing to cause him immense pain before it reaches his heart and finally kills him.

Before it finally reaches his heart and kills him. Leaving his corpse mutilated and blistered. I turn my attention to Callum's second attacker.

He has started trying to run away but something has control over me and I am unsure of the magic that is at work but then I see what is to be his fate. He stops and turns to face us, his body stiffening, his lips turning an ice cold blue and his skin taking a slight icy tinge to it.

His skin begins to blister as an orange glow surrounds him with an unstoppable heat. The wind moves towards him as if its blasting through my body, vines from the trees wrap around him, ensuring he is in place as the wind grows stronger. The vines wrap his legs in place and the inside of his body appears to be growing colder. He begins to shake violently.

Suddenly, the wind grows so powerful that, with the help of the other elements, it rips the enemy in two. His torso falling to the ground whilst his legs remain standing.

The orange glow fades, and the vines release his body and return to where they were. The wind calms until it is a soft, relieving breeze once more and ice seems to melt from the body of the prisoner. The stream calms once more and finally returns to normal. The scuttle fish flea back to their homes, full from their perfect meal.

I approach Callum with caution to see if he is okay when he stands and looks into my eyes.

"I've never seen an elf wield magic like that, the magic you wield, its not like anything I've ever seen. You don't need incantations like most I've met," Callum says, his voice sounding unusually strong considering what has just occurred.

"They changed us," I whisper.

"Your eyes, they seem different," Callum comments as he stares into them even further.

"What do you mean?" I ask.

"They're not the same emerald green colour, blues have appeared within your eyes, deep sea blue shades are mixing into the emerald green," Callum replies.

There's a sudden movement yet again and another male charges out of the shadows, "You fucking bastard!" He shouts, "You fucking killed them you fucking bastard! I'm going to fucking kill you!"

It's just like out of my vision. I feel the agonising pain build in the palm of my hand as the radiant white blade grows from within it. Impulses take hold of me, causing me to spin and throw the knife.

His skin breaks in areas, the white glow blasts through his body leaving only ash as his remains.

The sun finally sets, leaving us in the darkness of the night and I realise that I have become even more of an efficient killer. The soothing, night breeze caresses my cheek, comforting me slightly.

I don't want to be a killer I think.

"We should find somewhere to sleep," Callum says.

I nod, "I've found the trees are quite nice to sleep in," I reply.

"I don't think I can do heights when I'm asleep," Callum replies.

"Don't worry, in a tree you'll be safe and I'll be there," I reply as I grab an energy bar out of my backpack and begin to eat, "want one?"

"If you don't mind," he says. I take out a second bar and hand it to him before searching for the perfect tree to sleep in.

*　　*　　*

Finally, we find somewhere to rest and just as I'm getting comfortable, Callum begins to speak, "So erm, what's it like to be a huntress then?"

"It's not as awesome as everyone makes it out to be," I reply.

"What do you mean?" Callum asks.

"At birth we are taken from our parents and from the moment we can walk, we are trained. Trained to fight and kill, and whilst this is happening, we must survive the experiments which ends up killing a lot of our friends, the people we consider family. In these experiments, they try to alter our DNA even further, trying to create the perfect hunters and huntresses, trying to make us stronger. Then, when we turn ten years of age, if we have survived the experiments, the numbers that have been our names are replaced with new names. These names are given to us depending on our personalities and our appearances. After that, we try desperately to prove ourselves so that we will be one of the twelve chosen. From being a small child, we discover that we must do whatever it takes in order to survive and eventually, we do exactly that. We do everything we can in order to survive," I explain.

"Sounds," Callum pauses for a moment, "horrible, it's a horrible childhood, how could they do all that to children?"

"Its not exactly a secret, its known to most of the outside world, I thought everyone knew what they did in the training centres," I reply.

"To be honest with you, I never really had any interest in the games so I wouldn't really know about this sort of thing,"

"I don't blame you for not being interested, watching criminals suffer as they are hunted by young adults doesn't seem to suit your style if I must be honest. You seem more of a book person to me,"

"I am exactly that, I'd prefer to read a good book than watch TV"

"As would I," I agree.

"You seem to know more about me than most people, you know that right?" Callum says after a moment of silence.

I shrug, "I guess I'm just better at reading people than most," I reply. Silently, I wonder whether I should ask Callum the questions that burn inside of me.

What was the crime you committed? Why are so many prisoners after killing you? Is it to do with the crime you committed? What or who are the sicculets? Is the code right and are the sicculets interested in me? Are the sicculets related to the scaled people I saw twice whilst travelling? Questions circle my mind, I want to ask all of them but then something occurs to me, the cameras will no doubt be on us right now and I'm not sure if its risky to mention any of the questions. It would only take one, a single slip up, and it could kill both of us.

A shiver runs down my spine at the thought of Callum's death.

"Are you cold?" Callum asks and instantly I nod, not wanting to bring anymore attention to the questions burning in my mind. With great effort, I manage to push the questions to one side and I begin thinking about Devote. Silently, I wonder whether she is in fact my mother or was it some sort of cruel change in the games in order to distract me.

"Just a little," I finally say, once I know I'm capable of controlling my voice. Callum moves closer in the strange branches that seem to have formed the perfect bed for us. I feel the sudden spark of please and warmth enter my body, and all of my worries disappear as he puts his arm around me and brings me closer until he's cuddling me.

"This should help us both stay warm," he replies with a soft and warm yet shy smile.

I giggle and nod, "It should definitely help us stay warm," I reply before cuddling into his chest, hiding my cheeks as they begin to burn bright red with embarrassment. I close my eyes and allow the element of air to take me away, allowing me to drift away into the dream world and soon, I fall asleep.

* * *

The day passes quickly and we come across no prisoners throughout our travels. It's when night falls that we begin to have proper conversations.

"So, what's it like in the training centre?" Callum asks.

"It's strict most the time, we have strict time tables that we follow, normally I would be the first up and in the training centre, practising my aim. At some point in the day we would be separated depending on our kin, elves would be practising magic and humans would be practising making traps or something along those lines. The education tended to revolve around the most recent history of how elves were created among other things but it was different. I will admit that I miss the training centre, it was home to us," I explain.

"Sounds weird," Callum replies.

"What's it like in the outside world?" I ask.

"Painful, and I don't know what is safe to tell you and what isn't"

I glance up at the sky to witness the beautiful twinkling stars through the leaves, "I've always wondered what they looks like when you're not looking at them through a window," I say.

"What are you talking about?" Callum asks.

"The stars, they're even more beautiful when you're not looking at them through a window,"

"I guess they are, I never really paid much attention to it. I guess when you're in the outside world, you take things like that for granted"

"I don't understand how you can't pay attention to something so beautiful," I reply before looking from the sky and back to his face, strands of silver light illuminate his dark skin.

"I guess when you've witnessed such beauty all of your life, you don't really pay much attention to it after a while," Callum replies.

"I guess that makes sense,"

"So didn't they ever let you outside of the training centre?"

"They did, but not at night time, we weren't aloud to go very far, it was mainly what the education team called school trips"

"Wow, such a thing must have been so boring. I can't imagine a life like that," Callum comments.

"You're always busy and you never really run out of things to do," I explain.

"So I guess you don't have time to get bored," Callum says.

"No not really," I reply with a soft smile, "but you do get time to wonder things"

"Like what?" Callum asks.

"Like what the stars look like when you're not looking at them through a window or what the outside world is like for other people, why people commit crimes and if what is in the books are true, if love does actually exist?" I reply.

"I don't know, the stars are beautiful looking at them through a window and not through a window, the outside world is dull and boring, different people feel compulsion to commit crimes for different reasons and I've only witnessed true love a few times," he replies.

"Have you ever been in love?" I ask.

"I don't know, I've never been one to understand emotions but I don't think so, I think at the minute I feel as if I am closer to love than I have ever been"

"With who?"

Callum shakes his head and touches his nose slightly, "That's a secret, plus I doubt she feels the same way"

"Why's that?"

"I don't know, but anyway, I just have to wait and see what happens so that I can find out if she does feel the same way," Callum replies.

I sigh, "I guess you do have to wait and find out," I reply and just like yesterday, he wraps his arms around me and holds me closer, his warmth radiating into my body, removing the chills of the night. Happiness and pleasure fills my body along with comfort, helping me drift off to sleep in a warm cocoon of emotions.

I smile as I fall asleep, unsure why I feel so happy to be laid in his arms but I do feel this happy and I don't really want to question it.

*   *   *

The next morning arrives but before the sun has chance to rise, we awaken to an announcement, "Hello Hunters, Huntresses and prisoners, good morning"

I jolt up into a sitting position just as Callum does the same, I glance to him, feeling confused, "Can you hear this as well?" I ask, unsure of whether I can hear the announcement through the ear piece and Callum can't.

Callum nods, "Yea, I can," he replies.

"We are sorry to awake you but there has been a few unexpected change to the rules," the voice of the head maker echoes through the trees. "Due to a sudden alliance between a prisoner and a huntress that we expected to break immediately once the huntress killed him which hasn't happened, we have decided on a slight rule change"

"They're talking about our alliance aren't they?" Callum says.

I nod, "Yes," I reply.

"Prisoners can now attack Hunters and Huntresses if they wish and they shall not be killed immediately, I hope you enjoy the change in rules and lets see if you both can truly trust each other. Is your alliance real? Or a lie to keep himself alive?" The makers voice replies.

A silent tear runs down my cheek as I begin to wonder whether in fact our alliance is a lie in order for Callum to keep himself alive with my protection. *I trust Devotes judgement* I think to myself.

"Don't listen to him," Callum says, "a life for a life remember, you saved my life and I saved yours, we look out for each other, right?"

"I hope the makers wrong, I hope our friendship is real, I hope our alliance is real," I reply.

"I never expected to bump into you in the games and remember what was said before we entered the games," Callum says, "we promised that if I survived this that we would return to being friends in the end of it. I won't betray you, I don't hurt friends and I don't believe in violence or hate"

Suddenly, the dream returns to my mind, I remember the words Gaia had said, *"Callum has never been one for agreeing with violence and hatred,"* my mind quotes the words.

"He has never been one for agreeing with violence and hatred," I whisper.

"Huh?" Callum says.

"It was from a dream I had, a dream that spoke of you, it said *'Callum has never been one for agreeing with violence and hatred'* and I believe it to be another vision," I say.

"Your second sight interfering again? Guess its going to mess up the makers plans"

"It might do or it might strengthen their plans"

"Thinking about it, it just might make their plans stronger," Callum agrees.

"Then, we're just going to have to work as a team and prove them wrong," I say.

"Yea, we'll get through this and prove them wrong!" Callum says.

"We will do this," I reply.

"Do you think we should continue or wait and see what comes our way?"

"I think we should continue moving, we don't know what could come if we wait, just remain cautious"

"Do you want to stay in the trees?"

"No, I'll walk on the ground with you, that way we can watch each others backs," I reply.

"I think that's a good idea," Callum agrees.

He begins climbing down the tree whilst I jump, landing perfectly on the soft ground. A loud crack of thunder echoes through the trees and the rain begins to hammer down from the skies, it's a massive relief from the merciless sun and heat. It feels amazing as it falls on my skin, relaxing my muscles slightly as we begin to walk in the rain, the thunder cracks and flashes of lightening hit trees, causing them to fall and burn.

"It's a good thing we're not in the trees, we could end up dead," I say.

"Yea, we just need to step carefully," Callum replies, "we need to be careful in case any burning trees or tree branches or anything like that fall on us. I especially don't fancy being hit by lightening."

*   *   *

We continue walking, each step we take is filled with caution, both of us alert and listening for any little sound.

That's when we hear it, the panicked scream. We hide within the shadows and approach the scream when we see a hunter, one I recognise holding two pistols. I catch a glance of his face to see that it is Burned. His body is completely engulfed in flames caused by a tree that has caught fire or so it seems.

He panics, trying to pat out the flames. He falls to the floor and rolls but it seems as if the flames don't want to go out. Nearby we catch the glimpse of a prisoner as he runs away. Its just like my vision.

I watch as Burned stops moving and flames completely engulf as much as they possibly can, not even the rain is helping in extinguishing the flames.

As soon as the prisoner is out of sight, I rush to Burned and with my coat I try to pat out the flames and eventually they go out, but its too late. He's gone. His body completely scorched until he is unrecognisable.

"My vision," I whisper as I realise what has just occurred, as it finally settles in my mind. I collapse to the floor, my knees feeling weak as if they have turned into jelly. My body shakes violently as the images replay in my mind.

"What do you mean?" Callum asks as he approaches me.

"I saw this when we were travelling to the prison, I saw it through his eyes, I remember," I whisper weakly, my voice filled with sorrow.

Suddenly, another vision appears in front of my eyes, I see a prisoner stood in front of me, smiling wickedly, "Well, well, with the change in rules, the dangerous huntress is now the hunted," he says in an evil voice, the dark brown eyes of the prisoner are all I see as he speaks, everything else seems to have vanished too quickly for me to grab any further information. I can see the hatred, the anger, disgust and lust for blood burning within the dark brown eyes.

The vision fades and I remember his words, noting them as important in my mind. *'Well, well, with the change in rules, the dangerous huntress is now the hunted,'* something in my gut tells me that this is related to Burned's death. Could this prisoner have killed Burned?

"Devotion, are you okay?" Callum asks, his voice filled with concern.

"I'm fine," I whisper, my voice unusually shaky.

"You blanked out for a minute, it was like you weren't here at all," Callum mutters. I look to him and clearly he can see the sadness in my eyes as a single tear of pure sadness runs down my cheek, "come on, lets go," he says as he helps me stand. The warmth that radiates from his body, enters mine, lending me the strength I need.

After a while of silence as we travel, I finally speak, "I grew up with him, just like I grew up with the others. They're like family to me, even the ice queen herself is like a sister to me,"

"Then it is suitable for you to mourn his death, for you it is like the loss of a family member," Callum replies, solemnly.

"If you need to mourn, so be it, I will not think of you any less, I believe you are strong, no matter if you cry and show emotions"

A killer is not supposed to mourn a death, they have attempted to breed a killer and I am not what they have wanted. I am efficient in my kills, powerful in many ways and intelligent but I am not exactly what they want, I think to myself. *Will they kill me off because of this? Are they trying to get me killed because of my alliance with Callum?* Questions swirl around my mind and I search for an answer but I can't find one.

*   *   *

The night soon arrives and we finally find somewhere suitable to sleep but instead of sleeping, we sit there talking.

"So, were you close to Burned?" Callum asks.

"Not particularly, we were both loners but we used to trade books and discuss about them at times but that was rare," I reply.

"You seemed pretty close to Innocence to be a loner,"

"We weren't really that close, not until after the Call Outs, I guess you could say we were friends before hand and she did give me a hug when I managed to survive the final Call Out and she seemed quite pleased about it, so in a sense she was more of a close sister than a friend, but mainly, I've kept to myself all of my life. I guess it was something Innocence liked about me, so in a sense we were kind of friends but more sisters than friends if you understand what I'm saying," I explain.

"I guess, the people from the training centre, the candidates, your fellow hunters and huntresses must be like family to you,"

"They're more than family, most of them mean a lot to me, some of them mean something to me but there are some I care about more than others,"

"Like Innocence?" Callum asks.

"Yea, like Innocence and Conquer, they're closer to me than any of the others, except for Burned, but he's now dead," I reply.

A sound suddenly catches our attention and we both become silent as a group of seven prisoners pass beneath us, laughing and joking.

"Did you see her face? She looked so pissed off and afraid when we brought the bitch down!" Laughs a female prisoner from below us.

"Yea, this is much better than previous games! The hunters and now the hunted! Ha!" A male replies.

Soon their voices and laughter fade into the distance and its then, I dare to speak, my voice nothing more than a whisper, "I wonder who they killed,"

"Could be the ice queen," Callum replies, his voice equally as quiet as mine.

"Doubtful, she would have frozen the lot of them, she's powerful when it comes to magic, I must admit," I reply.

"Well, I doubt she's as powerful as you are with magic, I've seen what you can do. You sent a guy to hell, caused scuttle fish to attack a guy, you used the elements to rip a guy apart and you managed to conjure some sort of glowing radiant white weapon to kill a guy, I doubt she could do that," Callum replies.

"Probably not, but she's still powerful," I reply.

"Clearly, she managed to prove herself and get into the games,"

"Exactly," I reply.

There is a long moment of silence as Callum stares into my eyes and I stare into his. The same comforting warmth fills my body causing me to feel as if a spark has ignited within my heart, something I've never felt before.

The cold night chill doesn't bother me as the warmth fills my body and rids my body of the cold.

"Has anyone ever told you, your eyes are like beautiful radiant emeralds as they seem to stand out in the night and reflect the moons light. I noticed when you were wielding the elements against that prisoner, when you wield fire, its as if you can see the embers of fire through the emeralds and its as if the embers are what causes them to glow like they are now. They glow brightly with life, strength, hope and absolute beauty?" Callum compliments, and even though it is dark, with my ability to see perfectly clear in the dark due to my elven blood, I can see his cheeks burning bright red as he speaks the words.

"I can honestly say, no one has ever told me that especially in such a beautiful manner," I reply, my cheeks also burning bright red in embarrassment and I silently hope, that he can't see it for the darkness of the night that surrounds us.

"Well, I tell you now, it is my honest opinion," Callum replies, his voice sounding slightly shy and a warm smile filled with happiness grows on his face, warming my body further and causing the spark in my heart to grow larger.

I can't help but smile in response as I speak, "Thank you," I whisper softly, my voice quivering slightly as an unusual impulse begins to grow inside of me.

"For what?" He asks innocently.

"The compliment," I pause for a moment, feeling slightly shy and embarrassed, "about my eyes"

"You shouldn't thank me"

"Why?" I ask curiously.

"Because I'm giving you my honest opinion and I mean it when I say it, your eyes are like beautiful emerald stones with a slight sea blue within them. It wasn't there when I first met you but I guess its due to the amount of magic you've been using lately," he pauses for a moment, "I genuinely think that you are the most beautiful woman, elven or human, I have ever laid eyes on"

"Really?"

"It is my honest opinion," he replies. The impulse grows until it takes hold of my body and I end up kissing him on the cheek. Immediately my cheeks begin burning even further and his smile grows, "thank you," he whispers breathlessly.

My heart hammers against my ribs and my breathing becomes faster, "Why thank me?" I ask.

"Because," he pauses as he searches for an answer, "I don't know," there is a long moment of silence before he speaks again, "we should get some sleep"

"We should," I agree. We both lay down and I cuddle into his chest once again before I fall into a light sleep, still listening for any sign of moment below. Silently, I feel terrified that someone will get to him, that someone will kill him and I curse the thought of someone killing Callum.

I can practically hear the world say aw and talk about how cute it was for Callum to say what he said whilst I can practically feel the rage radiating from the makers because of the words spoken and the actions performed for the entire world to see.

*   *   *

I awake to the sound of birds singing now that the rain has finally gone. I look up to the sky to see a beautiful rainbow forming. The storm has finally passed.

I look up to Callum to see that he is already awake. He smiles softly at me and silently, I wonder whether what occurred last night was real or was it just a dream. I hope it was real.

"I've lost count on how many days we've been in the arena," Callum whispers, "but since I've been with you, the days seem much sorter than they originally felt"

"I would have to agree. I've lost count of the days as well, but the days seem a lot shorter and a lot better with you," I admit, my voice little more than a whisper.

And I bet the crowd will be loving this and the makers will slowly be wanting us both dead for what's happening between us I think to myself. I sigh before sitting up.

"We should really continue moving," I mutter.

"We should," Callum agrees, "how many kills do you have now?"

"Twenty two so far," I reply.

"That's a pretty high number," Callum admits, "do you really need more kills?"

"You never know, its better to be safe rather than sorry"

"True," he agrees.

I grab two energy bars out of my bag and rattle my water bottle, "I need to collect more water," I mutter before handing him an energy bar.

"We'll find some somewhere," Callum says.

"Are we going to set off then?" I ask and Callum mutters. We climb from the tree and begin walking and it doesn't take us long to find a familiar spring. It's the same spring I performed the mercy kill.

Have I travelled in a perfect circle? I wonder silently, I shrug. It doesn't really matter, I need water and I need to hunt. I finish my energy bar, fill my water bottle and add the chemicals before putting it back in my bag, allowing the chemicals to do their magic. As I do so, my mind replays the mercy kill I had to perform, I remember the relief in his eyes. The entire memory is crystal clear in my mind.

"Do you want to travel that way?" I ask as I point in a different direction to the one I went in last time.

"Okay," Callum replies.

We continue walking until we enter a large clearing. This is unfamiliar, the trees don't provide shade from the merciless sun and it is much larger than the one I was attacked in. We begin walking across it when I hear the sound of movement surround us, bushes moving and clumsy footsteps in the mud.

I glance around the clearing, to see movement in the shadows. They appear out of the shadows, a group of seven prisoners, quickly they approach us.

Standing with patience and pride, I watch as the enemy surround us both, allowing no escape for either of us. Callum gently brushes my hand, drawing my attention to him, "Why aren't you doing anything?" He whispers quietly.

"Just wait," I whisper in response.

My senses remain completely alert and ready to fight as the prisoners stop in several places with only a slight gap between them, leaving us no way of escape. I wait for a slight aggressive movement and that shall be my signal, the signal to attack.

I don't care that we are out numbered and there is a large chance I could be injured, I will not hold back in my attack if they attack first. I have to do it. If they attack us, I have to attack. I have to protect Callum.

"Well, well, with the change in rules, the dangerous huntress is now the hunted," the leader of the group says. A male prisoner with dark brown eyes that burn with the same blood lust, the same anger, hatred and disgust as in my vision. I recognise the words from my vision and I watch as his smile grows wicked and evil. His short light brown hair clings to his sunburnt face with grease, his jaw is broad and his build is large, clearly from a lot of weight lifting. The large muscles of his arms clench and relax repeatedly. His clothes are torn and soaked in blood and his voice is dark and sinister.

"Is that what you have convinced yourselves to believe? The hunters and huntresses will destroy each of you in the end, you realise this don't you?" I reply, in a strong firm voice that sounds as if it should belong to a stranger. The enemy shivers at my words as if he has suddenly grown incredibly cold before he composes himself once more.

"Please, don't aggravate the situation," Callum pleads in a quiet voice.

"They are determined to kill us, either way they'll try," I whisper.

"You think you're so much better—" the male begins as he steps closer to us and in a swift movement, faster than any human could ever move, I jump over him and land behind him. I turn swiftly and grab him around the neck. Holding him in a lock Fusion taught me when I was training with him in hand to hand combat. The smell of body odour invades my nose as I hold him in place and I force myself to swallow down the puke rising in my throat caused by the rancid scent.

"Would you like to finish your sentence?" I ask, my lips brushing against his ear as I speak in a seductive manner. Suddenly, his body seems to relax slightly from my touch and his breathing becomes heavier. I can practically hear his heart hammer against his chest rapidly.

"I would rather not," he replies breathlessly.

"Come on, I'd like to hear what you were going to say," I reply, my voice filled with sarcasm.

"I'm sure you don't want to hear it," he replies remaining completely stubborn which causes anger to burn inside of me and the same protective instinct to grow inside of me, slowly taking control over my body.

I tighten my grip around his neck, "I'm sure I want to hear it," I growl viciously sounding more like an animal than a human.

"Okay! Okay!" The prisoner practically begs, I release my grip but only enough for him to speak, "You think you're all so much better than us and so special because of your posh weapons and fancy armour," he replies, his voice turning to a plead. Not a single of the other prisoners have dared to move, instead each of them are just staring at the scene between myself and their leader.

"Now who needs posh weapons?" I reply sarcastically as I dig my free hand into his back, automatically I feel the sharp pain of the blade growing from the palm of my hand, "When you can do this!" I snap as the rest of the blade painfully rips through the skin of my palm and stabs the prisoner in the back.

A sudden scream of pure agony escapes the males lips and I glance over his shoulder and at his face as it screws up, revealing the incredible pain flooding his body. I release the head lock and push him off of the long radiant white blade that has grown from the palm of my hand, revealing it to all of the prisoners that surround us. His body falls to the floor in front of me in a massive heap, his body limp and weak.

Swiftly, I turn him over and slice through his throat with the blade. The life in his eyes slowly fades as his skin begins to crack with a bright radiant light before it finally rids every last piece of life from him body. Leaving him a lifeless corpse.

I glance at the palm of my hand to see the unusual glowing blade that has pierced through the skin. A small amount of blood trickles from the palm of my hand before the wound around the blade heals. I notice the blade has gone straight through his skin and left a large stab wound near his heart. His own blood now soaks his clothing.

An orange glow begins to fill the cracks left by the white light and begins to pour from the cracks which reminds me of molten lava. The rancid smell of burning flesh invades my nose and I feel as if I'm going to puke from the smell. The radiant blade retracts into my skin so that it is not longer visible.

With grace in every lethal movement I make, I move towards another of my enemies. The closest of my enemies is a female, she flicks her long, greasy mess of blond hair out of her eyes and tries to escape me, but I'm much faster than she is. I stand in front of her, fierce, angry and protective. She swings her arm in my direction in a feeble attempt to punch me.

I duck out of the way, dodging her blow and in one swift, lethal movement, I move my hand towards her stomach and I notice a strange tingling sensation in the palm of my hand as the radiant white blade grows from within the skin of my palm once more, sending a rush of pain through my arm. It pierces through her skin and muscle with ease.

With another quick movement, I lift my hand up and the blade slices through her body as the blade rips up her stomach and through the centre of her ribcage. I pull back my hand as the woman's warm blood splatters on my skin.

Suddenly, I hear movement behind me, "Devotion! Look out!" Callum shouts as I spin around on the balls of my feet and block an attack with the blade. The males arm slices through the blade and his hand as well as his wrist falls to the floor. Blood splatters on my face, chest and arm. I lick my lips to find blood has fallen upon them and the sweet, coppery taste floods throughout my mouth, sending my instincts wild.

The male attempts to attack me a second time with his remaining hand, and this time I dodge out of the way, using the blade to slice through his elbow, leaving him with two stumps for arms. Then, with a deadly, swift movement, I clench my hand into a fist around the blade and move as if I am about to punch him in the face. My fist meets his face and the blade embeds itself in his brain.

Killing him instantly.

I pull back slightly before I kick him away with my right leg and his limp, lifeless body collapses to the floor once it is off the blade.

I hear the footsteps running behind me, I turn and with my free hand, I grab the blade and pull it out of my skin, sending waves of pain throughout my body. I spin around on the balls of my feet for a second time and with a quick throwing movement, I throw the blade towards the fleeing enemy. The knife embeds itself in the back of the enemies neck before fading.

The body of the enemy falls to the floor and I know he will no doubt be dead by the time he hit's the floor. I glance to Callum, whom is now under the attack of another prisoner. I watch for a short moment as the prisoner hits him in the face repeatedly before I charge towards him.

The painful sharp feeling of the knife piercing through my skin grabs my attention for a moment. I leap over the male but as I do so, I run the blade through the back of the male. I land and turn around in a swift movement to see that the blade has cut straight through the male with ease. His torso falls to one side whilst his legs fall to the opposite side. I glance down at the blade to see that it is much longer than before.

Slowly, it eases back into my skin until it is no longer visible and the wound it has left me bleeds slightly before it heals completely, leaving nothing but a small fierce red line.

I rush to Callum's aid just as the scream of one of the prisoners echoes through the large clearing, I glance over my shoulder to see him trapped in one of Innocence's traps. She appears out of the shadows and stabs the prisoner in the throat before she runs to a second trap and repeats the process.

"Are you okay?" I panic slightly, afraid that he has been seriously injured. Instead his nose is bleeding and looks as if it could be broken, his lip is swollen and split and his eye is swelling up.

"I'm fine, its just a flesh wound," he says in a joking voice yet I can hear the hint of pain in his voice.

Suddenly, something begins inside of me. My body begins to shake violently, and I begin coughing so much so I can barely breath.

"Devotion!" Callum shouts.

"Is she okay?" I hear Innocence ask, her voice coming from behind me.

My body feels as if I am in oven, I feel so hot. Sweat drips down my forehead at first before my entire body becomes completely drenched in sweat. My legs suddenly feel as if all of the bone has been removed from within the skin and I collapse to my knees in front of Callum, my eyes feel as if they're burning from the amount of light cast by the sun. My heart hammers violently against my chest as I struggle even further to breath through the coughing.

"I don't know!" I hear Callum panic in the background.

A ringing sound appears, growing louder with every passing second, until I can't hear the commotion occurring around me. The coughing stops for a moment and I try desperately to catch my breath and grab as much oxygen as I possibly can before the next coughing fit arrives.

The points of my ears begin to burn and feel as if they're being stretched even further so that they point even more. My eardrums feel as if they're going to burst due to how loud the ringing sound has become.

My body fills with panic and fear as I begin thinking the worst of scenarios. *Am I dying?* I wonder repeatedly as I continue struggling for air.

All of sudden, my muscles begin to spasm rapidly and I manage to let out a small scream of agony as the pain floods throughout my body. I fall onto my back, my knees remain bent but my ankles touch the top of my thighs. I close my eyes, trying to escape the burning sensation within them but it doesn't end. They continue burning, causing even further pain.

I open my eyes once more to see Callum, Innocence and Conquer, huddling around me, each of them unsure of what to do. I can see that they're talking but I can't hear them.

The coughing stops a second time, and I breath in as much air as possible but the coughing doesn't return, instead it is replaced by a horrid burning sensation that appears to flood my veins, originating from my heart. Tears, that feel as though they're ice, flood my eyes and run down my cheek. I feel as though I am being stabbed multiple times in my stomach and chest and the pain worsens.

Then, for a short moment, it all stops and I can hear again.

"Devotion what's happening?" I hear Callum ask.

"I don't know," I whisper weakly.

Suddenly, I feel the burning returns but it is upon my skin as if someone is in fact burning me. I glance down at my arms to see a radiant white light piercing through cracks within my skin. I feel burning in my back, the top of my right thigh, on my left hip, on my right breast and on both of my arms especially around the wrist and hand area.

"Am I going to die?" I whisper before the ringing returns in my ears blocking out their answers. My ears feel as though someone is trying to stretch them, my canines feel as if they're growing through my gums even further, causing discomfort.

My eyes continue with the burning sensation and I begin to cough once again.

Finally, my body relaxes and I feel absolutely exhausted when I catch the sound of movement in the distance. Suddenly, a burst of energy floods my body and I jump to my feet.

"Devotion, what's happening?" Callum asks.

I look around and everything seems clearer than before, as if the world has suddenly become high definition for me.

Everything seems unusually bright yet it doesn't bother me, its as if I've become an even better huntress.

I listen and can feel my ears twitch as the sound grows closer. Somehow in my heart, I can sense that it is the enemy, the last prisoner remaining on the island besides Callum.

"Devotion?" Callum says as he gently touches my shoulder. I flinch slightly, his touch seems even warmer than usual.

"Shush!" I whisper, holding my hand up so that my index finger hushes him. I gulp down a breath of air as that same protective instinct begins to take hold.

The prisoner jumps out of the shadows, a smile gleaming on his face before he sees Callum beside me. His jaw clenches angrily and he clenches his fists as if he is preparing to attack but before he gets that chance, I begin to move.

In an unusual, swift and lethal movement, I touch my right thigh with my right hand and spin on the balls of my feet. Suddenly, I can feel something leaving my skin, its as if it is crawling out of me, I throw my right hand towards the prisoner and suddenly I can see vines, with beautiful blooming roses and thorns sticking out of it, wrapped around an anchor just slightly bigger than my hand.

The vines wrap around the enemies neck and anchor helps hold it in place. I pull on the vine and he falls to the floor, helplessly choking against the vines which are ever so slowly tightening around his neck.

I step towards him and hold my left hand on his head, between his eyes and the radiant white blade grows out of the palm of my hand, causing a slow sharp pain as it grows ever so slowly.

Gradually, it pierces through the skin of my enemy. He squirms and tries to free himself but it is no use against the vines. I feel it as the blade pierces through his skull and finally enters his brain. It is then, his body relaxes and he dies.

"Congratulations hunters and huntresses," the makes voice pauses for a moment as his voice echoes through the arena, "and prisoner, you have each done well in this years games, there was a lot of drama and death, it was truly superb," I force myself not to laugh sarcastically at his words, "it was certainly unique," his voice suddenly changes to one that says he isn't impressed, especially with certain things that have occurred in the games between myself and Callum. "Now, it is time for you to come home"

A large craft appears in the sky and the remaining hunters and huntresses gather in the clearing. I glance around to see how many were remaining. Nymph, Burned and Darkness were certainly missing, leaving us with nine remaining hunters and huntresses. But it seemed as if there were less than nine remaining. Suddenly, I realised that Bullet had also gone.

We each enter the craft and it closes behind us. Automatically, I sit beside Callum and Innocence. The same questions burning inside of me and hopefully, I will receive the answers I've been practically begging for.

Once I and Callum receive some privacy from the cameras that is.

CHAPTER 9

The Real Hunt Begins

W e arrive at our destination, the largest capitol city in the world, to discover our scores and whom has become a champion. Callum walks by my side, constantly ensuring that he is close to me and our hands keep brushing against each other, until slowly Callum touches my hand with his finger. I look to him with an encouraging smile as we enter the large hall, filled with journalists, important people, our trainers and people who have paid to be there.

Once we stop in front of the maker whom is standing on a hovering stage in front of us, Callum places his hand in mine and squeezes it before giving me a cheeky but warm and comforting smile.

I return his smile before looking at the maker and the large screen behind him, "Welcome, welcome hunters and huntresses and survivor," the maker begins, "now as always, I shall present the survivor of this years games!" I nod to Callum with an encouraging smile. The cameras are on us once more. "Come up here Callum!" The maker commands in a false tone that gives the illusion that he is cheerful when he isn't. I search the audience, looking for Devote and Fusion but they're nowhere to be seen whilst the other trainers sit and wait, watching us patiently.

Callum takes in a deep breath and approaches the stage, the cameras focusing on myself and on him as he lets go of my hand and continues. Clearly, he's nervous about all the possibilities of what could happen, of how the situation could change. I notice his muscles seem to have grown larger and the clench and relax repeatedly, showing that he feels protective and angry and I know exactly why he feels that way. Callum walks up a strange staircase that appears in front of him and approaches the maker on the hovering stage.

Once he's up there, the maker continues talking, "This young lad is Callum, the survivor of this years games, and now," he pauses for a moment and picks up a piece of rolled up paper with a scarlet ribbon tied around it, "these are your new documents to help you start a new life, with a new name and a home waiting for you, you are now rewarded your freedom!" Callum takes the paper and the maker mutters something to him that we can't quite hear before Callum steps behind him and waits. "Now, you all wish to know the champions of this years games, don't you?"

I continue to search of Devote and Fusion, panic surging through my body, *where are they? What's happened?* I question, my mind panicking as I remember the commotion I heard through my earpiece. *Where are they? What's happened to them?*

The crowd cheers in excitement whilst we remain still, each of us nervous, all hoping to be the champion but only three can be the champions in the end. I glance to Innocence just as Conquer begins to comfort and sooth her, she's shaking nervously again.

"The third champion of this years games are Innocence and Conquer, you joint third and so you are both to be this years third champions, congratulations, your strategies worked! You totalled with fifteen kills overall," The maker says. Innocence and Conquer relax before approaching the stage but the stairs have gone, instead they stand below the stage as both receive crowns and flowers along with a bronze coloured medal and trophy. I notice that their crowns are also a bronze colour.

"The second champion of this years games is Frost with sixteen kills, congratulations Frost!" The maker announces, this time his voice is filled with genuine joy. I glance to Frost as she throws me a wicked smile and flicks her blood soaked, greasy blond hair and approaches the stage. Again she stands below the hovering stage and receives a silver tiara, flowers, a silver medal and a silver trophy.

"The Champion of this years games, with an amazing twenty eight kills, please join us on the stage Devotion!" The maker announces, the genuine joy leaving his voice. The crowd goes absolutely wild as they shout my name as well as Callum's. I paint on a false smile but on the large screen in the background, I can see my eyes are wide.

I hesitate for a moment before I approach the strange stair case and walk up towards the hovering stage. Once I get up there, the maker shakes my hand and removes my black circlet, handing it to me and replaces it with a gold tiara. He gives me a gold medal and a beautiful bunch of blood red roses. "Congratulations!" He says loudly before he turns to me and speaks, his voice much quieter so that no one can hear him, "Get behind me bitch, we have things to discuss"

"Thank you!" I say in a false tone that sounds happy before I nod and approach Callum, I grab his hand and squeeze tightly whilst Callum gently strokes it in an attempt to calm me down but it isn't successful. I feel nervous and afraid of what could happen.

The maker could easily put Callum back into next years games as punishment or he could kill him as soon as we're alone. Silently, I hope that he won't hurt Callum in the slightest but something in my gut tells me that this man, the maker, is sinister and evil.

I gulp down a breath of air, "And now, I shall leave with both the survivor and the Champion in order to discuss things in the way it has been done for years!" The maker says and slowly I become even more nervous.

My entire body surges with panic as the door opens and the stage enters through it. I step closer to Callum as the wall swallows us up, my body shaking in what can only be compared to fear.

We enter a large white room with a massive window that looks out upon the outside world, we step down from the stage once it becomes part of the floor and approach two white sofas opposite each other with a beautiful, multicoloured rug. The sofas are near the large window, allowing us to look out upon the outside world.

The world I wish to explorer so badly.

"Step forward, Devotion!" The maker commands, in an angry and fierce voice. His worn eyes look down upon my body as I step towards the sofas. "Sit down, Callum!" He commands and Callum does just as he is told. My gaze falls on Callum and never leaves his eyes as the maker begins to circle me. He gently brushes my hair from my shoulder revealing my neck. Gently, he caressed the skin of my neck, "Such a beautiful and perfect huntress," he says.

I watch as the jealousy and anger burns in Callum's eyes as he watches the maker touch my neck with grace.

"Does this make you burn with jealousy, Callum?" The maker asks, his voice slick and lustful sending a shiver of disgust down my spine. Callum lets out a little growl that doesn't sound as if it could come from a human. "It does, doesn't it" the maker laughs evilly as his hands slowly goes down my neck line and towards my chest. Callum growls again, this time its much louder than before and clearly it's a warning, "oh wait, yes, I forgot tonight was a full moon"

The maker flinches away from me and begins to circle me once again, "The perfect huntress and I never thought it was possible," he says. "Without needing to use incantations, you can use powerful magic, even more powerful than any elf in this world can. The experiments have changed you, your ears are more pointed and your eyes are no longer the same innocent emerald green that they were when you entered the arena, there are blues mixed within the emerald green and they're fierce and angry,"

"I have some questions that I want answering," I mutter in a fierce and strong voice.

The maker flinches backwards as if I have just hit him in the face with my words, "No! You do not demand answers from me!" He snaps.

"But I have finished your games and become a champion, I have my freedom now," I reply, anger burning inside of me.

"No, you don't. You belong to me and have done since you were born, you are my property!" He snaps.

"I am no ones property," I growl angrily.

"Is that what you think?" He replies, his voice cocky and arrogant. He claps his hands and several officers enter the room, "Give her a taste of my power," the maker commands before he quickly rushes out of the room.

Suddenly, the officers tackle me to the floor whilst they begin beating Callum. It's the very first of the blows that rattles through my body. The protective instinct begins taking hold over my body as I struggle against the officers. I struggle against them and I can feel the magic growing inside of me but it seems as though a shield is keeping it trapped within me.

I listen for a moment and realise that I can hear elven incantations. Magic is at work in order to keep the magic, radiating from inside of me, from bursting out and killing all of them.

I feel the sharp pain caused by the radiant white blade as it pierces through the skin of my palm. In a swift movement, I manage to free myself and embed the blade into one of the officers necks. They try to control me but its little use.

Every movement I make is lethal as I rely on the blade in order to fight my way to Callum. I can still feel the claustrophobic space of the shield as it surrounds me. Blood stains the white floor and sofas as I finally reach the elf that is chanting the incantations.

I move to kill, my movements quick and deadly but then, I feel the sharp pain as something digs into my neck. It feels like a pin has just pricked my neck. I touch the area and pull out a dart just as the world begins to sway and grows confusing. Everything becomes fuzzy and my body becomes weak.

My knees cave and I collapse to the floor in a large heap, my body limp and I can't move. I struggle trying to move but my body is completely paralysed.

The world goes black.

*   *   *

I open my eyes to find myself lying on the sofa, a helpless heap at first but gradually, I begin gaining some strength and the ability to move. "Don't move to quickly, I don't want you falling unconscious on me," the makers voice echoes throughout the room. I glance down at the blood stained material but it doesn't look right. Everything appears far too bright.

My head jolts to look at the maker, "Where's Callum? What have you done with him?" I snap angrily.

"He will be joining us soon," the maker replies.

"Where's Devote and Fusion?" I snap.

"They seem to have run away and vanished from our world," the maker replies and something about his words ring true. I notice a strange white light surrounding me, and I can feel it containing my magic as if it is some kind of wall. "You're so beautiful, just like your mother," he mutters quietly after a moment of silence. He approaches me and kneels on the floor before caressing my cheek. I want to fight him away but my body feels too weak, "so perfect," his second hand gently traces the tattoos that have appeared around my right arm. Beautiful tattoos of vines with roses still in bloom and thorns that wrap around my hand and the entire of my wrist. "And to think, we have tried to create you for over thirty years, the perfect soldier, the true huntress"

"What am I?" I manage to growl through clenched teeth.

"In your blood is a small fraction that is of human genetics, another larger fraction is elven and a smaller fraction, even smaller than that of human, is Sicculet but you are none of these kin. You are Devotion, the perfect warrior, the perfect soldier," the maker pauses for a moment, "the perfect huntress" he pauses a second time and laughs slightly, "The Huntress," he finishes.

I stare at him, pure anger and hatred burning inside of me like an uncontrollable forest fire and I know my eyes are burning with the emotions I feel. The temperature of the room begins to rise and in a sudden burst, two bulbs nearby burst, scattering flickers of light fall to the floor around us.

"Well that field isn't quite keeping your magic contained very well," the maker comments.

"I doubt anything you have can contain me never mind my magic!" I snap.

"Well you better keep it under control!" The maker threatens.

"Or else what?" I growl.

"Or else this!" He snaps, before clapping his hands once. Two guards suddenly enter the room, dragging the body of a beaten man. He lifts his head and at first, I don't recognise him for the swelling and bruising in his face. His lip is split and his right eye is so swollen he can barely open it. I recognise the dreadlocked hair and tribal designs shaved into the hair on the side of his head but at first I can't think where. Not until he stares into my eyes and his hazel eyes lighten up and begin to change colour into a warm lily pad green. The warmth radiating from them causes a smile to grow on my face but for only a moment before I realise exactly what has happened to him.

"Callum!" I gasp, horror running through my veins sending my body ice cold. I shiver in disgust at what they have done.

"Now, if you don't follow my commands—" the guards drop Callum to the floor and the maker crouches beside him. I jump to my feet, trying to get passed the white field and to Callum but I can't, the field is like some sort of wall, forcing me to keep away from Callum and the maker. I want to run to him so desperately, I want to take him away from this place and protect him but I can't, no matter how many times I punch the field with all of my strength—"I will have your poor little lover killed and you will watch every last second of it," the makers voice is dark and sinister as he speaks. He gently takes Callum's chin in his hand and squeezes his cheeks before releasing him once more. "Do you understand what I am saying?"

"Yes!" I growl angrily. "What is it that you want from me?"

"I want you to ensure that the elves and the sicculets know their place, that they will not take what we give them for granted," the maker begins.

"What do you mean?" I ask.

"We give them so much and they take it all for granted—" the maker begins but Callum interrupts him.

"You enslave them! Punish them when they haven't worked as quickly as you want them too! You hurt them! You don't allow them any rights! They don't have a voice!" Callum growls angrily.

"We do everything we can for them but they are ungrateful for what we offer them!" The maker snaps.

"You give them nothing!" Callum snaps.

The maker loses his patience and strikes Callum in the back. Callum falls back on the floor from standing on all fours. I punch the field with all of my strength until eventually, a crack appears.

Repeatedly, I punch the area where the crack is but nothing further happens. Finally, I calm myself and force myself to think clearly.

"May I have some time to think this through, its all a bit much," I mutter.

The maker calms himself and looks back at me with a smile, "Of course, this isn't something you're used to, you had no idea about all of this, its understandable that it may be a bit much for you to take in all at once," he replies.

"May it also be okay to have some privacy with Callum? There are certain things I wish to discuss with him to try and organise my thoughts," I reply.

"He isn't exactly the best person to help you organise your thoughts—" the maker begins but I cut him off

"I trust his judgement," I reply.

The maker nods, "so be it, I just hope we do not have to be drastic with you," he replies. He claps his hands and the wall opens. The field moves around me as the guards escort both of us into another neutral room with a double bed, a TV and shower along with another large window that takes up an entire wall, allowing me to look over the outside world.

As soon as the guards leave and the door closes behind us, I begin questioning, "Why were you put in the arena? What was the crime you committed?" The words rush out of my mouth quickly, rolling off my tongue in a fast but fluid sentence.

Callum approaches the bed and sits down, first he looks to the floor and buries his head in his hands before he looks back to me, his gaze settling on my eyes, "How did I guess that would be the first question you would ask?" He sighs.

"I have dozens more to go but first, tell me, please," I reply.

"Well in order to tell you my crime, I need to explain why I did it and to tell you that, I have to explain some of the outside world to you"

"Then start explaining," I reply.

"You may want to sit down," Callum says. I nod and sit beside him, my eyes never leaving his. "Out there—" he points out the window, "is a lot of pain and suffering and a lot of it could end so easily, out in that world, humans enslave elves and sicculets, their own creations"

"Why?" I ask.

"Because, elves can wield powerful magic and can cause crop to grow larger and quicker with their magic as well as the fact that you only need five elves compared to twenty humans to simply build something like a simple building," Callum explains.

"I guess that makes sense, but what about the sicculets?"

"The sicculets are faster than humans and stronger, perfect for labour work," Callum explains, "because of this the sicculets planned to escape and hundreds of them managed to, they've been hiding in the forests ever since, fighting against the humans, trying to save their people and the elves. Several elves have managed to escape as well but not as many, they assist the sicculets in their fight against humans"

"So what has this got to do with you?"

"I don't agree with the slavery of elves and sicculets, I believe its wrong. A year ago, I witnessed a man shoot an young elf in the foot when they weren't working fast enough for his liking. I don't know why, it was probably because it was a full moon that night but I attacked the man and killed him," Callum explains.

"So you murdered someone and because of that you were put in the arena, you were defending the helpless, why is that so wrong?" I say.

"Because in this world, there is no compassion for elves or sicculets, they're seen as abominations of nature, they were created by accident and found useful for work. People seem to think that they don't have emotions,"

"I have emotions!" I intercept quickly, my voice sharp and fierce once more.

"I know, all creatures have emotions and none should be subjected to such pain and hatred. They are often discriminated against, there are horrible nicknames for them just as there are for coloured people. They call my people all sorts of names for the colour of my skin and they call your people names just as bad as the names they call mine," Callum continues to explain.

"Why? What's wrong with the colour of your skin?" I ask, feeling slightly confused.

"Nothing, but still people see problems with it, its wrong," Callum replies.

"Because you understand it in a sense you defend others who receive equal abuse," I mutter.

"Exactly, your dream was right, I've never been one to agree with violence and hatred but a lot of people out there do agree with it. The makers, they've been trying to create a weapon to bring the war to an end, to bring what they call order out of chaos which means—"

I finish his sentence for him, "Enslaving my people"

Callum nods, "And the sicculets," he replies, "that's how the games started, they were trying to genetically modify the perfect weapon and every year they have measured how powerful that year of candidates have been, and every year they have become stronger and stronger until you arrived,"

"The daughter of Devote, the strongest known huntress," I whisper.

"Yes, the daughter of Devote and her daughter is even stronger than she is, you are the first not to need incantations to cast spells, the first to have tattoos appear upon your body that are clearly enchanted," Callum says as he traces the vines on my hands, "the first able to create weapons through magic," this time he traces the fiery red line on the palm of my hand from where the radiant blades grow out of.

"It hurts when I use the weapons though," I mutter.

"I'll bet, they come straight out of your skin and I've seen them bleeding," Callum replies with a comforting smile.

Suddenly, my dream of Gaia enters my mind once more and I remember the scene once again, her words echoing through my mind.

"You are my daughter, just as all those whom inhabit the earth are my children, from elves to sicculets, even though the humans changed you, you are still my children," the first of her words echo throughout my mind.

"The sicculets?" I remember asking.

"Yes, these are the children you are destined to see, prophesised to save. They're interested in you, they wish for freedom," her voice echoes throughout my mind.

"The sicculets, what are they?" I ask after a moment, once the memory has faded.

"They resemble humans and elves in many ways only their eyes tend to be larger, their bodies are covered in scales, their ears are even longer and more pointed than an elves, kind of like yours only normal elves are slightly smaller and sicculets are slightly bigger," I touch my ears and gently touch the point, they do seem bigger and more pointed than before the arena, "oh and they have a tail!" Callum adds.

Immediately, I remember the strange woman outside the train as we were travelling, the woman that banged her hand against the window and in a sense, we touched hands through it.

"Kind of like the woman I saw outside the train?" I whisper as the pieces begin to fall into place.

"What woman?" Callum asks.

"That doesn't matter, tell me more!" I reply, the words rushing out of my mouth.

"Well the humans long to enslave all elves and sicculets once more and bring the war to an end whilst the sicculets and the elves are fighting for freedom," Callum replies.

"Is there anything else I should know?" I ask as I rush to get my backpack off and begin searching through it for the letter from Devote, my mother.

"Well yes, years ago an elf delivered a prophecy to the sicculets free in the forests that are fighting for freedom," Callum mutters.

I pause, my eyes widen, the dream appearing in my mind once more, "What was the prophecy?" I ask.

"The elf spoke of a child destined to see past the illusion created by humans, one that would still show compassion towards all creatures even those that they are destined to kill and to be the one that shall make the first domino fall, saving them from the slavery and rewarding them the freedom they deserve," Callum replies.

"Yes, these are the children you are destined to see, prophesised to save. They're interested in you, they wish for freedom," Gaia's words echo through my mind a second time.

" *'These are the children you are destined to see, prophesised to save* '" I whisper.

"What was that?" Callum asks.

I grab the letter and place it in front of him, "Look at this," I command and he reads the letter, "it has a secret message in it from Devote to me"

"The sicculets are interested in you?" He replies sounding confused.

Another memory of a dream appears in my mind, the dream of Lilly, again the scene replays in my mind.

"Once half human, half elf, now the blood still remains in her veins along with other things. She is no longer human nor is she elf, none know of what she is, she doesn't know of who she is. Does she agree with what they do? No. Will she agree with them when the truth is discovered? This is unknown. Something's to be found, something's to be uncovered. No longer is she mortal. Soon she shall see. Second sight was gifted to thee. The reason unknown for now but shall be uncovered," Lilly's words replay in my mind, in the same wise voice.

"What do you mean?" I remember whispering the words whilst shaking in fear.

"Second sight was gifted to thee so that the truth she may see," Lilly's response replays in my mind. I repeat the final words as each puzzle piece finds its place.

"What are you talking about?" Callum asks.

"Another dream I had," I reply, "they're replaying in my head,"

"You must be the child spoken of in the prophecy delivered," Callum mutters.

"In the arena, I did perform a mercy kill," I mutter.

"You have compassion towards those you are supposed to kill, I saw you demonstrate that after you killed those prisoners and panicked trying to wash off the blood,"

"Look, how do you know this much about the elves and sicculets?" I ask.

"When I was a child, my mother '*owned*' a young female elf, she taught me about it," he replies, creating air quotations around the word *owned*. "She was more like family than property, she was like my mothers daughter. My mother gave her a wage that she called pocket money and she brought her up from the age of twelve, that was before my mother passed away"

"That was nice of her," I reply.

"My mother was a lovely woman and the girl, Eva, taught me about the elven kin and the sicculets," Callum continues. "It was a shame that she was taken once my mother died, she wasn't in her will because my mother didn't believe she was property and because of that, she was sold automatically to another family"

"That's disgusting!"

"I know"

I sigh and there is a moment of silence as everything finally settles in my mind. "What am I supposed to do?" I ask as I stand and begin to pace the room, "If I fight back and attempt to save my people then they'll kill you," I mutter before I stop and stare out of the window at the large city that stands before me. Beautiful birds build their nests in a tree just outside the window only approximately ten feet below. I notice the change in seasons since we have been in the arena, it is now spring and beautiful blossoms have started growing on the trees.

"Remember what you said to me in the arena when you saved my life and I saved yours, a life for a life, right?" Callum replies, his voice solemn.

I nod, "Yea, that has nothing to do with this," I reply.

"It has everything to do with this," Callum replies, his voice warm and comforting, "think about it like this, I lose my life in order to improve their lives. I die in order to give others happiness and freedom instead of pain and hate"

I turn around to face him to find that he's stood directly behind me. Tears over flow my eyes and run down my cheek, "What are you saying?" I ask, my voice quivering as I speak the words.

"My life would be the perfect sacrifice in order to save their lives," he replies.

"No!" I snap, trying to stop myself from crying, unsuccessfully. "I won't do it! I can't do it! I can't let you die!"

He wraps his arms around me and holds me close to his chest, gently stroking his hand through my hair, "Don't worry, don't cry okay," he whispers softly, his voice soothing to my ears but I can't stop myself from crying. "Hopefully it won't come to it, but you have to think of them as well and the pain they will be going through"

"Can't we just run away and join them, both of us?" I ask, my voice quiet.

"It would be an idea, but how would we get out?" Callum asks.

I glance up at him, the tears finally stop running down my face and a smile grows, "Are you honestly asking me that?" I ask, my voice sounding as if it should have come from a murderous villain.

"I wish I hadn't said anything," Callum replies with a strange smile and happiness in his voice. "So I'm guessing you have a plan?"

"Well, lets just say what they created me for may just work against them," I reply.

*   *   *

I give Callum a quick brief of my plan before we put it into action. Callum pretends to collapse to the floor and I scream at the top of my lungs, "Callum! Callum!" I force myself to cry fake tears. Two guards rush into the room and run towards him. Before the wall can close once more, I place my bow in between the sliding doors in order to stop them closing before I spring into action.

I approach them from behind, my movements swift and completely silent. The radiant blade grows out of the palm of my left hand, sending a short wave of pain up my arm. Without any hesitation, I move gracefully with a deadly motive.

Leaping from the ground, I flip in the air and land on my hands on the back of the first of the guards. The blade embedding itself in the guards neck and before the second guard has time to react, I jump of the back of the first guard and flip over the second. I land on my feet in a crouching position with my back to the guard.

Swiftly, I spin on the balls of my feet, one of my legs is only slightly off the floor as I remain in the crouching position. I can feel a slight sharp pain as the weapon grows even further from the palm of my hand before I use it to slice straight through the second guard.

I stop moving with my back to the guard once more, I glance over my shoulder as the torso of the guard falls off his legs and wink at Callum, "Are you ready?" I ask, motioning my hand towards the door so that the blade points in the direction of our exit.

Callum glances outside the window and nods as the sun begins to set, "As ready as I'll ever be," he replies, his voice unusually hoarse.

"Then, lets go!" I reply with a smile. We run to the door and Callum forces the walls to part even further whilst I recover my bow and we rush as quickly as we can down through the room.

Suddenly, the room swarms with guards and for the first time, I witness Callum truly fighting with all his strength, proving himself to be an efficient and incredible killer just like myself, I find myself completely stunned by his strength as he begins ripping guards apart with his bare hands. An inhuman noise repeatedly escaping his body.

I force myself to return to the fight at hand and just as I do so, I hear the sound of someone approaching me from behind. I spin on the balls of my feet and dodge his arms as he attempts to grab me. Instantly, without a thought, I stab the guard in the stomach and rip it up between his ribs before I kick him off my blade and allow his body to fall to the floor. The radiant white light cracks through his skin as it slowly kills him.

Swiftly, I run up the wall and use it to jump over three enemies that seem to be attempting to corner me. I land on my hands on the shoulders of the middle guard, the blade piercing straight through his shoulder before I push myself off his body and land on the floor.

A second radiant white blade grows from my right palm sending a wave of pain up my arm. I turn and immediately, I find myself duel wielding against the guards. I notice in the one guards hand is a tranquiliser gun and immediately, I slice through his arm, preventing him from using it against me before I stab him in the throat. I rip the blade to the side with ease, freeing it once more before I begin fighting against the second guard.

At first the guard attempts to block me with his gun but the blade passes straight through gun and with my second hand I force the blade through the guards jaw and into his brain. I pull out the blade just before a guard tries to grab me from behind. I grab his wrist, the blade piercing straight through the skin and bone.

A loud agonised groan escapes his lips as the blade goes straight through his wrist. I twist his arm and the blade twists within his wrist. I hold his hand behind his back and with perfect precision, I stab the second blade into his spinal column and rip it up his spine, completely destroying it.

I pull out the blade and kick his limp, lifeless body to the floor. I spin on the balls of my right foot, in a graceful manner like a ballerina on stage. Another guard prepares himself to attack when I use the blades to slice through the guards stomach in the shape of an X. He panics trying to grab his intestines as they fall to the floor before he collapses.

I glance around the room to see that we have managed to kill every last guard that had swarmed the room.

"Now, how do we get out of this goddess forsaken building?" I ask Callum.

He shrugs, "I only know about the way we came in," he replies.

"Do you know how to work that stage?" I ask.

"Not a clue"

Suddenly, I spot a ventilation shaft, "Do you reckon we could get out through that?" I ask, pointing at the shaft about six feet high.

"Its worth a shot, I've seen them do this in old films," Callum replies.

"So have I," I say with a smile.

We approach the shaft, "Let me give you a boost," Callum says before I jump onto his shoulders and into the fairly large shaft. I turn awkwardly in the shaft and hold out my hand for Callum to grab before pulling him into the shaft. Awkwardly, I turn around a second time in the shaft before we begin crawling along it.

Suddenly, we approach a steep incline and I find myself slipping down it before falling down another shaft and through a gate before I land on the path of an alley with no one around.

That's pretty lucky, I think to myself before I look up the shaft.

"Devotion! Are you okay?" Callum calls.

"Yea, I landed in an alley, no ones down here!" I call.

"Okay, coming down!" Callum replies and I step out of the way. I can hear him moving in the shaft as I turn around and spot the guards that are swarming at either end of the alley.

"Callum! There are guards! They're on either side of the alley!" I shout.

I hear him land behind me, "Shit! How did they know?" He mutters.

"Camera's probably," I reply as the guards begin to approach us. I glance over my shoulder to Callum, "stay here," I command in a firm voice as the protective instinct takes hold of me. Slowly, I begin walking to the centre of the alley way. I can feel something growing inside of my body that's almost like a flame burning brighter with every passing second.

It's as if I can feel the change, that I thought had finished, finishing inside of me. "Devotion!" Callum says in concern. I glance down at my hands to see my entire body glowing a radiant white that seems to be growing stronger. The light seems to radiate from my heart as it grows stronger and spreads throughout my entire body.

I look to the guards as they each stop in their tracks and stare at me completely stunned. I feel something begin to crawl from the skin of my back and the light seems to fill that as well. The light suddenly blasts from within my body and knocks several guards off their feet. They scramble to stand again just as another wave of light knocks even more down.

My feet lift from the floor and its as if I can feel the tattoos coming alive within my skin. There's another wave of bright light that seems to leave my body before my feet touch the floor and I'm crouched with one leg straight.

My body alert and prepared to fight, I wait patiently for a moment, my body feeling completely different. Swiftly, I stand and turn before charging towards the guards to my left. The first guard I approach seems mindless as he moves sloppily, trying to punch me in the face. I grab his arm and bend it in such a way that the bone snaps clean in half and rips through the skin.

The guard screams in agony and panic as he stares at the wound. I move to punch him in the side and can only feel a slight tingle as the blades rip through my palm once again and stabs him before I rip it up his side and remove the blade.

I spin around on the balls of my feet, pull out the blade from within my skin and throw it in another guards direction just as he begins scrambling to his feet. I turn a second time and gently touch my thigh before throwing my hand out. The vines grow from around my wrist with an anchor tied at the end. The vines wrap around the neck of another guard, and I pull him to the floor.

The vines automatically start tightening, suffocating him slowly. I throw my second hand forward and a thin silver chain grows from the tattoo around my wrist. The chain seems to have some unusual small white glisten about it that turns scarlet once it slices through the neck of another guard before it wraps around another guards neck. I pull him to the floor and the chain slices through his neck with ease.

I use the chains as if it is a whip, slicing through several guards with one crack upon it. The vines release the guard once he is dead and return to my wrist whilst the anchor returns to my thigh.

Again, I use the chain as if it is a whip and slice through several more guards before it returns to my opposite wrist.

Both the blades grow from the palm of my hand again and I attack the closest guard, slicing through his arm with absolute ease before stabbing him in his left side and ripping it across to the right side. Even more blood splatters on the already dry blood that stain my black armour.

With a swift movement, I leap off the floor and perform a cartwheel in the air, and as I do so, I notice a tranquiliser dart just skim my head. I land firmly on my feet and turn to the side before stabbing another guard in the throat before he has chance to react.

I turn and notice the final guard at the very end of the alley, struggling with a tranquiliser gun. Clearly he's over weight and silently, I wonder how he qualified to be a guard with such an unfit body. I begin to charge in his direction, my palms tingling as the blades grow larger. I skid beneath his open legs and allow both of the blades to slice through his thighs.

His body falls to the floor before me and he rolls himself over just in time for me to drive one of the blades through his jaw and all the way through his skull. His light, muddy brown eyes roll backwards whilst blood soaks his short black hair.

His ridiculous goatee causes me to giggle slightly as he dies by my hands. Slowly, I remove the blade from his skull and leave his worthless body behind along with the rest of them. Something in my gut tells me that he was an abusive man and that he was in fact worthless and deserved the death he received.

Slowly, I begin walking towards the opposite side of the alley where I find all of the guards seem to have been completely ripped apart. I glance around the alley and notice that night has fallen and I can't see Callum anywhere. Instead, a large creature stands at the end of the alley, his body dark and he's at least seven maybe eight foot tall.

I approach the creature with caution and notice the dark fur instead of skin. The creature is stood on its back legs but its back legs have the appearance of long, muscular dogs legs and large paws. The creatures fingers are long and its nails come to a sharp point and the creatures ears are large and pointed like that of a wolves.

The blades remain sticking out the palms of my hands as I approach the creature, unsure of whether the creature will attack me.

I notice the creature is wearing strange dark blue stretchy bottoms like the ones the prisoners wore in the arena.

The creature turns and looks to me and I realise that it has the face of a wolf, but its eyes, its eyes are the same lily pad green as Callum's eyes when he sees me. Suddenly, I realise what this creature is as I remember things I've read in books.

"A werewolf," I whisper in shock, unsure what to believe anymore. I remember the books saying that werewolves were nothing more than mythology.

Suddenly, a memory appears in front of my eyes. *"Does this make you burn with jealousy Callum? It does, doesn't it,"* the makers voice echoes through my mind with his evil laughter, *"oh wait! Yes, I forgot tonight was a full moon"*

The werewolf approaches me, his eyes pleading with me to understand but I find myself taking a step backwards before I realise that he has control over his actions. The blades return to my palms once he has stopped walking towards me. I lift my right hand slowly and hesitate for a moment, before I take my first step towards him. Gradually, I gain more confidence to gain closer to him, feeling no true reason to fear him yet I still find myself shaking nervously.

Eventually, he takes another step towards me and then another. Once he's close enough for me to touch the soft fur of his chest, he bends his neck so that I can touch the side of his face. I can feel something crawling back into the skin of my back and I'm unsure of what it is but I don't dare look away from Callum.

I feel absolute awe as I stare at him, unable to believe what I'm seeing, "They avoided allowing a full moon in the arena didn't they?" I whisper and he nods his head slightly, enough for me to see his response but not too much for my hand to leave the side of his face. "Is this genetic modification?"

He shakes his head in response.

"Is this natural?" I ask and he nods, I glance over my shoulder, "Come on! We better move!" I say and he nods. I step to the side of him and he falls on all fours, "Which way should we go?"

He begins walking forward and I follow him quickly. Knowing that he knows the outside world better than I do. We remain hidden in the shadows of the well lit streets and running down back alleys, both of us knowing that we both appear like freaks, something this world doesn't see often and we know the makers will be looking for us, for me.

So any suspicious reports of an abnormally large dog running mostly on back legs and a girl that appears to be an elf but covered in tattoos and moving freely in the street, could prove to be fatal for Callum.

Finally, we arrive at a large fence that surrounds the city and again, I feel something crawling out of the skin of my back. I glance over my shoulder and notice beautiful, dark blue, purple and sliver wings have grown out of my skin. I move them slightly, almost automatically.

"Do you think you can jump that?" I ask, staring at the eight foot tall wall that stands before us. He nods in response, "Okay then, lets do this," I reply. The wings begin to flutter quickly before my feet begin to lift off the ground. I feel completely off balance as I fly clumsily over the wall whilst Callum jumps. He lands perfectly on all fours whilst I fall on my side, a sharp pain fills my body, mainly in my ribs, shoulder and pelvis.

Callum nuzzles his nose into my neck, "I'm okay," I cough the words before I recover myself and stand, feeling slightly dizzy and staggering slightly. "I should really practice that," I mutter with a smile, "that was so frigging awesome!"

Callum huffs before he stands on his back legs and touches me with his strange, paw like hand as if to tell me that we should continue, "We should really continue," I mutter in agreement and so he returns to all fours and we begin running through towards the forest. I can feel the wings crawl under my skin once more.

"Do you know where the sicculets and the elves are?" I ask as I glance over to Callum as we run to see him shake his head.

That's not very useful, I think.

*   *   *

Eventually, I grow too tired to continue running and I collapse in exhaustion. "I-I can't continue r-running, I'm t-too tired," I stutter, exhaustion echoing in my voice.

Callum turns and nuzzles my neck slightly, his nose wet and his fur is soft as it touches my skin gently.

"I'm sorry, I c-can't," I say, "I'm too tired t-to make a move"

Callum lays beside me on all fours and carefully cuddles into me, his nose buried in my neck and hair. He seems to be acting as if I'm fragile compared to him. I hesitate slightly before putting my arm around him. I can feel the beat of his heart under the palm of my hand.

Within seconds of closing my eyes, I drift to sleep only to find myself waking on the same beach as before when I'd met Gaia. The sea gently caresses my skin as it washes away the dried blood from my black armour.

Immediately, I sit up, recognising the peaceful and loving atmosphere, and the strange forest at the end of the beach.

I relax slightly, remembering how peaceful, kind and loving Gaia was when I met her the last time and just as I expect, her voice seems to appear from nowhere, "Child," she begins and automatically I look to the forest as she appears out of the shadows and begins to approach me, "I have not felt like such a proud mother in a long time,"

Once again, she takes the form of Devote but this time her eyes are the same as what mine have become since the arena. Emerald with a small mix of blue. She approaches me in the same armour as before, a silver version of my own only hers isn't covered in blood.

"Gaia?" I whisper as she crouches before me.

"Yes child," she replies, "for a thousand years, perhaps longer, humans have turned against each other, against myself and the earth and now that shall come to an end," a proud smile grows on her face as she looks down at me.

"What do you mean?" I ask.

"I wish for my children to once again unite as one, to appreciate what they have and no longer take it for granted. To no longer destroy what I have provided for them," Gaia explains, "for many years now, I have watched them destroy themselves and their heritage"

"How can I stop it?"

"You are to free the people created and enslaved by humans, for you shall always be a new kin on your own, they created you as you are, you are neither elf, human or sicculet, you are a unique creature and my daughter,"

"How am I to find them? How can I free them?"

"Do not fret my child, they shall come to you, an army ready to fight beside you, you are the one prophesised to save them and so you shall lead them to freedom"

"How? I don't know how to lead an army,"

Gaia's smile grows larger, "In your heart you know," she replies before she fades from my dream and the rest of the scene follows, leaving me in darkness.

I awake to the sudden sound of movement in the forest. I glance to Callum to see that he is once again in human form. The sunlight flickers on my face when the wind causes the leaves to move.

I move my hand in front of my eyes in order to block out the sun as it causes my eyes to sting. I glance around the clearing as the sound of movement surrounds us.

"Callum!" I snap as I shake him slightly.

"What?" He says sleepily, his eyes opening slightly but its too late. The movement grows closer and I jump to my feet, the blades automatically piercing through the skin of my palm, causing droplets of warm blood to fall to the ground. The killer inside of me awakens once again as the protective instincts slowly begins taking over.

Silently, I'm terrified that the guards have found us and are about to attack, the thought of a threat coming near Callum drives me almost insane. The sound grows even closer until a strange creature steps out of the shadows, and with no control over my body, I find that I can't stop myself, I attack it.

The killer inside of me breaks loose as I leap from the ground and flip over the creature, landing behind it, I spin on the balls of my feet at speed that no human could imitate. I stab the creature through its scales and directly through to its heart from behind.

"Devotion!" Callum shouts in an unusual commanding voice that resembles a wolfs growl.

But its too late, I stab the creature a second time with my other blade, directly through its throat. I remove the blades and its lifeless body falls to the floor before I realise what I have just done.

Staring down at the corpse, I notice its greenie blue scales, its unusual tail and its ears as well as the fact that it resembles a human. Immediately, I realise what I have just killed, "A sicculet," I gasp my voice little more than a whisper.

The palms of my hands tingle as the blades return inside of my skin and the wounds, remaining from the blades, heal almost instantly. I collapse to my knees as the creatures blood soaks the earth, its unusual sweet coppery scent invades my nose.

Several more rush from within the shadows as a single tear falls down my cheek. "What have you done?" A female voice snaps, I glance up as a female sicculet steps in front of me. Her scales are a dark blue colour and her eyes are a turquoise colour.

"I-I'm s-so sorry," I whisper, "I didn't m-mean to, I was s-startled"

"Its understandable, all you know is death," another female voice appears as a familiar sicculet steps forward, I recognise her from outside the train. "She is a huntress after all, she's been trained to kill since she was a small child, you can't expect anything else when she's startled by something that could possibly be dangerous,"

"I'm sorry, I didn't mean to, I thought he could have been a guard and immediately, I attacked. I'm sorry, I should have paused," I mutter quietly.

"Don't apologise, its natural for you to protect and defend," the sicculet says as she crouches beside me, she glances over her shoulder and growls the next words between grit teeth, "this is something everyone should know!" She turns to face me once more, "Come on child, lets get you home"

"Home?" I whisper.

"Our home, rest until then, we shall take you there," she replies.

"Will I be safe there? I did just kill one of your kin after all" I say.

"You will be more than safe there child," the sicculet comforts, "now rest, we'll take you there"

"I'll walk," I insist before she leads myself and Callum through the forest.

*   *   *

Sunset arrives just as we enter the home of the free sicculets and elves. Their home seems to be based in the centre of the forest, well hidden from the humans due to the trees and magic at work.

I glance around their home as we arrive to see strange creatures flying above us that seem to resemble humans only with wings. The small houses seem to be made of some strange black substance that resembles stone yet is held above the ground by trees, bridges connect the buildings above with strange white lights lightening up the bridges. The houses seem to emanate some sort of strange enchanting glow, bright enough to notice it but dim enough to keep their home hidden within the forest.

As I follow the kind female sicculet and her warriors, I notice people rushing out of their homes on the ground and in the trees. They fall to their knees, tears streaming down their faces as I pass them. Smiles grow on the sicculets and elves as they cry in what seems to be joy.

Passers by immediately drop to their knees and bow their heads in a respectful manner. The trees in this area of the forest seem much larger than the others I passed. They are taller and look a lot stronger.

Finally, we arrive at a large castle like home in the trees. At the bottom of the house, the sicculet in front of me steps to one side and the warriors separate so that they're more spread out as another begins walking down stone steps that seem to be appearing in front of her, magically.

Her beautiful scale skin seems to radiate a silver glow around her as it reflects the suns light and her eyes glow an enchanting grey colour that reminds me of the moon. Her long silver hair falls down her back in an unusually graceful manner as it also covers her naked breasts. Her figure is petite and she looks quite fragile yet something in my gut tells me she is far from fragile.

Somehow, she seems to resemble the moon itself.

Following her steps a young male elf. His skin is fare and flawless and his eyes remind me of autumn leaves. His shaggy dark red hair also seems to remind me of autumn. His build seems fairly large and muscular and his shoulders are quite broad. His appearance seems to look quite intimidating as he towers over me from the steps as he approaches us and even though he appears intimidating and dangerous, his eyes speak of love, hope, passion and freedom

"Welcome," the female sicculet says once she is stood in front of me. "Devotion, is that your name?"

I nod, "Yes," I reply, my voice seems to hold strength along with a strange hint of something that I have nothing that I can quite compare it to.

"Are you the huntress from the arena?" The sicculet asks.

Again, I nod, "Yes"

"Then, I welcome you to our home and I hope you feel welcome," she replies.

"May I ask your name?" I ask.

"Meredith," the sicculet replies, "I am the female leader of our home, one of those whom organised our escape"

"Hello Meredith," I reply with a soft smile and a small curtsy.

"There are a few people waiting for you, if you will follow me," the male elf says in a deep, hoarse voice.

I glance to Callum and he nods in encouragement, I take his hand in mine, "Okay," I say before he turns and begins to walk up the steps once more. The female sicculet steps out of my way and I follow him up the steps with Callum by my side. I gulp a breath of air, my body shaking nervously.

Who could be waiting for me? I wonder silently as the elf leads us across the bridge and to a building that appears both powerful and intimidating with large, black and grey stone instead of brick and a soft oak wooden door with unusual elven symbols carved within it. These symbols I don't quite recognise but something about them appears to be both enchanting and terrifying.

He knocks on the door, "She's here," he says before opening the door and when I see who it is waiting for me, I release Callum's hand and run into the room before wrapping my arms around her, tears streaming down my face.

"Devote!" I cry as she wraps her arms around me.

"Devotion," she whispers as she holds me in her arms. I feel another arm wrap around me and hold me tightly. The sound of two strong heart beats enters my ears as a comforting warmth surrounds me, warming my body even further as I feel myself being wrapped into a blanket of love and protection.

"Devotion," a familiar male voice says, he sounds relieved to know that I'm still alive and well.

Instantly, my mind puts a name to the voice, *Fusion!* My mind screams repeatedly. Even more tears run down my face as relief runs throughout my entire body, *They're alive! They're alive! They're okay! They did escape!* My mind screams in relief.

"Fusion! Devote!" I cry as I feel my body finally relax. Finally, it registers in my mind that they're both safe and well. The other arm releases me and I step back from Devote to look at her face to see that she too has been crying. I look to Fusion and without a thought, I wrap my arms around his waist, suddenly I feel like a small child in the loving arms of a protective father. A father that would never wish any sort of harm to come towards me. Yet, I know there is no avoiding the harm that could come my way. His arms wrap around me as he holds me closer, his arms locked tightly around me as if he is afraid to let me go, as if he is a father desperate to protect his little girl from the evil within this cruel world we live in. "You're both okay! You did escape! You're still alive!" My eyes burn from the amount of tears that seem to be spilling down my cheeks.

My heart seems to slowly start repairing inside of my chest and its now that I realise that it has been broken all a long. Suddenly, it fills with warmth and love especially when Callum touches my shoulder. I pull away from Fusion and look to Callum, pleasure surging through my body from his touch.

I throw my arms around him and hold him close to me, something inside of me seems to be growing larger with every passing moment. I look to Fusion and Devote but I don't let go of Callum. He wraps his arm around me protectively as Fusion and Devote take hands. All of a sudden, I feel as if, somehow I have suddenly become treasured and wanted even though I'm different from all of them.

They seem to genuinely care.

"Mum," the word escapes my lips before I can stop myself from saying it.

Devote smiles and tears begin falling down her cheeks once again, she nods, "Yes," she says her voice sounding joyful yet holding a hint of sadness and loss, "I'm your mum"

Silently, I wonder if she wishes she could go back in time and take back the years where she was never able to see me.

"And I'm your dad," Fusion says and for the first time, I see several tears running down his face and for only a short moment does the intimidating, powerful look in his eyes seem to fade and be replaced by pride, love and hope.

"Dad," I whisper before suddenly, my knees feel weak and I collapse. Callum manages to catch me before I hit the floor but I feel so overwhelmed.

"Devotion!" Devote shouts as my knees give way.

Callum helps me to a seat and I put my head between my knees for moment before I look up to the ceiling, even more tears streaming down my face. "This is a lot for her to take in," Callum mutters as his hand gently caresses my cheek.

I look into his eyes and he smiles the same warm, comforting smile that seems to make all of the evil in the world vanish for a second and I can't help but return his smile, with a soft, shy smile of my own.

"I'll bet, she's like us, she never knew who her mum was until recently and she discovers I'm her dad, it must be a lot to take in," Fusion replies. I glance at the door and realise that the male elf has gone and the door is shut.

"Devote, how long have you known Callum?" I ask after managing to pull myself together.

"Many years, I've known him since he was a child through his mother, she was a lovely woman who had worked with my stylist when I'd been preparing for the games, we kept in touch until she unfortunately passed away," Devote replies.

"Did you know that he's—" I don't even manage to finish my question when Devote answers.

"Yes"

For a moment, I just stare into the distance outside the room and its then I feel the calling. A pull on my heart, that slowly grows so that it feels like a physical pull. I watch as the sun finally sets, plummeting the world into darkness.

Swiftly, I slam my hands on the seat before I push myself up and approach the door, "Devotion! Where are you going?" Devote asks but I don't respond.

I can hear Callum and Fusion as they follow me out of the room. Suddenly, I begin to run, each of my foot steps light and silent as I do so before I jump from the bridge.

The wings crawl out of my skin and automatically I begin to fly, sloppily but only a small amount before I grab a large thick branch and dangle for a moment before I swing myself around and release so that I land on the branch with perfect grace. I swiftly climb the tree, ignoring Devotes shouts as she tries to grab my attention.

Finally, I rest on a branch and stare up at the moon, anticipating the new horizon that is to come. Silently, I hope that it will bring me a plan, a way to help the sicculets and the elves gain their freedom.

"Gaia," I whisper as I rest my head against the tree, "please guide my way. Show me what I need to do"

I sigh as I close my eyes, allowing time to pass me swiftly.

*   *   *

Eventually, I fall asleep and when I open my eyes, I find myself in a dream, stood in front of a camera, beside the maker. "Devotion is going to make an oath to me today, an oath swearing herself to fight for our cause against the sicculets," the maker says in a slick tone. I hold my head higher, keeping my expression blank of emotions as I wait patiently. "Go on Devotion, say the words," the maker encourages before he hisses, "remember, your family have and will betray you, as will Callum"

I gulp a breath of air, unable to believe what is happening around me. None of this seems to make sense. Why would I swear an oath to the maker? "I swear an oath," I turn my gaze from the camera and to the maker, "to follow my heart and do what's right by the goddess and the earth," slowly I lift my hand so that the palm of my hand is not far from the makers cheek and before he has time to notice, the blade grows through the palm of my hand and stabs straight through makers cheek. Blood runs down the palm of my hand from the injury caused by the blades growing from within my skin and a single drop of blood hits the floor. The scent of the makers blood mixed with my own seems to send my instincts wild and the killer inside of me awakens once more. Swiftly, I turn my back on the camera and the second blade grows through the palm of my free hand and I stab it through his jaw before I remove the blades and look back to the camera. "And what you wanted me to do maker, is not right by my heart, the goddess or the earth. Its so good to see you return to the dark"

Suddenly, the room fills with guards as they surround me and a wicked smile grows on my face as the killer inside of me rises and prepares to fight.

I open my eyes and flinch back from the tree as dusk arrives, something in my gut tells me what I need to do. Swiftly, I climb from the tree and swing on the final branch before I land on the bridge.

I approach the building where I was reunited with Fusion and Devote. I kick the door open without a thought and before they can swarm around me, I grab some paper and a pen before I empty my backpack on the floor and stuff the paper and pen in the bag before I turn away and leave the building once again.

"Devotion! What are you doing?" Devote demands to know her voice strong and commanding but no longer does it cause me to feel as if I should be cowering. No longer does it cause the hairs on the back of my neck to stand on ends.

I jump over the bridge and land on my feet in a crouched position before I begin leaving the home of the free behind.

"Where is she going?" I can hear Devote ask.

"Callum follow her!" Fusion commands. I stop under a large tree and begin to climb it. Once I've found somewhere suitable, I begin to write as quickly as I can.

> *Dear Conquer,*
>
> *I know you must be having fun with your freedom but you must pay attention to what I am about to tell you. I don't know if you know but the humans, they enslave sicculets and my kin. I need your help, I want to bring this to an end. I'm returning to the city and I'm putting an end to the maker.*
>
> *I hope you are as good a friend as I remember and I hope that you will assist me in this, for I believe that you are still my brother and that means that means that they're enslaving your kin and family also. I ask that you shall assist me in this, brother.*
>
> *Yours faithfully,*
> *Devotion*

I glance at my ankle as I fold the letter and the image of a burning, pure black phoenix rises from beneath my skin. "Ensure this letter gets to Conquer no matter what," I command in a strong, firm voice and the phoenix gives me a quick nod before it takes the letter in its claws and begins flying away.

Immediately, I begin writing the second letter as quickly as I can.

Dear Innocence,

 I know you must be having fun with your freedom but you must pay attention to what I am about to tell you. I am unsure whether you know but the humans, they enslave my kin, they force them to do all sorts of things. Elves don't have rights in this world, they're seen as property. They also enslave these things called sicculets. I know you've never heard of them, I hadn't until we left the games but they're so kind and they too are seen as property. As am I. For I am seen as the property of the game makers.

 This isn't right and I need your help to put a stop to this. I'm returning to the city and I'm going to put a stop to the maker once and for all, something I believe you will agree should have been done a long time ago.

 I hope you are as good a friend as I remember and I hope you will assist in my kin gaining their freedom. Sister, please help me.

       Yours faithfully,
       Devotion

I glance to my opposite ankle as I fold the paper this time and a fairy crawls out of my skin. "Ensure this gets to Innocence as soon as possible, no matter what the cost it must get to her," I command.

The fairy nods, "Yes ma'am," she replies before she grabs the letter and flies off as quickly as she possibly can.

Swiftly, I begin running between the trees with an impeccable speed as I approach the city once more. *I can do this! I can do this!* My mind encourages and once I arrive at the city wall, I fly over it once again it's a clumsy flight.

CHAPTER 10

A Voice For
The Voiceless

Immediately, I approach the first main road with cameras on it before I stand in the middle of the road and spread my arms out, "Hey assholes!" I pause and smile, "I'm right here! I'm not hiding anymore! So come and fucking get me!" I shout at the top of my lungs as cars begin to swerve in order to miss me. Silently, I remember some of the words used by the prisoners in the games and wonder whether using them will gain even further attention from the city.

"Are you mad? Get out of the road! You stupid cow!" A passer by shouts.

"Yes, I am mad! I am Devotion after all!" I say with a wicked smile. "So come on you fucking assholes! Come and get me!" I shout.

Suddenly, traffic stops driving past me and instantly, I know that they've closed off the road. Guards surround me, "I'm not going to fight you! I'm handing myself in!" I snap.

Several guards approach me and stand either side of me, ensuring that I can't run away. Each guard is armed with tranquiliser guns this time. Slowly, we walk through the maze they call a city and to a large building I don't recognise. The building is white and appears to be a large office block from the outside but when we enter the lobby of the building it appears to be more of a hotel than an office block.

The room has been designed and styled to look as if it should have been in china nearly a hundred years ago with a fake waterfall behind the desk and several statues that resemble beautiful women, all of them Chinese, are on either side of the desk.

A life for a life, my mind reminds me, giving me a slight touch of hope.

"Devotion is here," a male guard says in an emotionless voice. I wait patiently as the male behind the desk types in my name. His long, slick black hair tied in a ponytail and his hazel eyes seem fierce and angry as he looks down his nose at me. His skin appears to be a flawless brown colour that also appears as if it is almost hitting an unusual tangy orange colour, and silently, I wonder whether this unusual colour is his natural skin colour or some sort of make up or fake tan. His eyes appear to be emphasised by a thin line of black eyeliner and a small hint of gold in areas, drawing attention to them.

His full lips glisten with lip gloss as he talks, "Go straight up, the maker is waiting for you,"

The guards lead me towards a glass lift which looks out onto the city and press the number thirteen button. *Number thirteen, unlucky for some* I think to myself as a slight smile begins growing on my lips once more.

Very unlucky for some, my thoughts continue as the lift shoots off the ground at an incredible speed and jolts to a stop at floor thirteen. I can't help but feel physically sick. Dizzily, I stagger out of the lift.

"How the hell do you not feel sick after that?" I question, the world spinning around me.

A gentle hand from an elven male guard touches my shoulder, "You get used to it," he says in a comforting voice, a soft smile on his face. "Don't worry about it," he says before he helps me stand properly and allows me to recover myself.

"You shouldn't be so fucking nice towards her! She's killed loads of fucking people!" Another male guard snaps.

"Don't listen to him," the elven male replies in a quiet voice, "he's human, he doesn't quite understand how we feel"

I nod in agreement, something in my gut tells me he has a vague idea of the reason why I'm here. Slowly, we walk down the neutral coloured corridor and to a white door. The snappy human guard opens it, "Get the fuck in!" He commands and I do as I am told. As I pass him, I hear him mutter several words under his breath, "Fucking freak"

I sigh, forcing myself not to attack him for the insult he has thrown at me. I must remain as calm as I possibly can.

The door slams shut behind me after two guards take their places either side of it. One guard being the kind elven male. "So, it seems you have finally come to your senses after your little escape, have you seen how barbaric the sicculets and elves truly are?" The maker says.

I say nothing, my facial expression completely emotionless.

"Are you going to fight beside us in this war and bring it to an end?" The maker asks.

"If I must," I reply, my voice strong yet emotionless.

"Then I must need your oath," the maker pauses for a moment, "on national TV" he finishes.

Then my dream was right, I realise silently yet I don't allow it to affect my act, *thank you Gaia,* my mind whispers.

"Fine," I say, my voice remaining emotionless.

"Would tonight be okay for you?" The maker asks.

Tonight would be perfect, my mind whispers wickedly.

"Tonight would be fine," I reply.

"Good," the maker replies, his voice slick and evil as he quickly circles me, "sit down, and relax until then," he commands. I sit down on the pure white sofa and look out of the large window that takes up an entire wall and notice the same fairy that crawled out of the tattoo on my leg hiding with a message, a reply. I notice a window on the left wall is slightly open.

Perfect for messages, a perfect way to get my reply, my mind whispers.

"May I have some paper to write on?" I ask.

"Of course," the maker claps his hands once and a young female elf rushes into the room, she glances at me and all hope seems to flood from her sky blue eyes, "paper!" The maker commands, she spins and her deep auburn red hair moves gracefully as the fare young elf rushes out of the room. Swiftly, she returns with paper and a pen and gives it to me.

"Thank you," I say in a polite tone but she doesn't respond, instead the anger and hatred that burns in her eyes causes the hairs on the back of my neck to stand on ends.

"I shall go and make the arrangements," the maker says before he rushes out of the room, his evil smile gleaming brightly. I wait a moment before I motion to the fairy, giving her a little sign to tell her about the window before I rush to it.

"Innocence has sent you a reply on behalf of Conquer and herself," the fairy whispers before she hands me the letter from the window.

"Stay there," I whisper quietly before I rush away, I hide the letter among the paper as I read it.

> *Devotion, tell us where you are and we'll be there as soon as possible. It is about time that the maker got what he deserved, the games must come to an end. We deserved a normal childhood and parents that loved us and he stole that from us in order to train us and turn us into killing machines and the elves, they deserve freedom just as we do. What are they doing about you? You said in your letter that you are depicted as property also, do you not have the freedom they promised us?*
>
> *I hope to receive your reply soon. We will be with you as soon as we possibly can and we shall help you in this fight sister, as we have always done, we shall work together as the family we have always been,*
>
> *Innocence & Conquer*

Swiftly, I hide the note before I begin rushing to reply.

> *Innocence, I'm in a building in the city. I think it's the makers base but I'm not quite sure, tonight he is trying to make me give him my oath, swearing*

that I shall fight against my own kin. I don't have my freedom, in a sense, I still belong to the company. They have broken their promise to the elven hunters and huntresses, caging them and taking away their freedom even further. They're trying to force me to do things against what is in my heart.

Tonight on national TV, I must swear an oath but it will not be to him I shall swear it to. Please get here by tonight and assist me in this fight. I have a feeling this is going to be hard and I may try to free even further sicculets and elves whilst we are fighting if you will help me with this also.

Devotion.

Swiftly, I fold the paper and hand it to the fairy outside the window whilst the phoenix becomes a part of my skin once more. I glance over my shoulder at the guards and notice that they're both elven and both of them wink at me as if to tell me that the know of what I have just done and that they won't speak a word of it. Something in my gut tells me that they're both on my side and they will both assist me in what is to happen next. Its as if all of the elven guards know of why I am here. Silently, I wonder whether the goddess has somehow communicated with them all, possibly through dreams, in order to tell them of what is to happen.

"Please ensure it gets to Innocence as soon as possible," I whisper quietly.

"I will," the fairy replies before she rushes off once more to deliver my message. I watch as she appears to move at impossible speeds. Speeds I know that not even I could reach.

I really need to name her, I think to myself with a cocky smile growing on my face.

Callum

I have to trust in what she's doing, she knows what she's doing and I know she wouldn't betray us, I trust her my mind swirls with thoughts as I try to encourage myself, encourage my belief in her but I can't help but doubt what she is doing. Are the sicculets right? Has she changed sides? Has she betrayed us? Is she against us?

"Why else would she return to the city?" A female sicculet snaps, it's the same sicculet that began shouting at Devotion when she killed the male warrior because she'd been startled.

And she'd been protecting me, my mind whispers softly. *Is that what she's doing? Protecting me at the price of everything else? I hope not.* My thoughts pause for a moment, *A life for a life* my mind gasps.

"I'm sure Devotion wouldn't betray us, she has passion and hope, her heart is filled with love for all creatures and no matter how much the makers have tried to erase her passion and love, it has remained in her heart no matter what, just as it has in my heart. She is like me in many ways," Devote continues to defend Devotions actions, "you should have faith in her decision"

"She isn't the leader you all seem to believe she is! She is not the child from the prophecy! She will not bring us our freedom!" The sicculet growls angrily.

Its her words that cause me to stand and slam my hands on the large wooden table that appears to be made out of an unusual, soft wood. Instantly, I realise that the unusual strength that remains in my body after the full moon, has caused a large dent in the wood where the palms of my hands lay on the table. "I trust her! She has compassion and love! She proved that in the games did she not! She kept me alive even though it meant risking her life! How do you know that is not what she is doing now! Risking her life to save all of us!" I growl, my voice sounding more like an unusual animal than a humans.

"What would you know? Of course your going to trust her! You and her are in love with each other! Of course you trust her actions and will stick by them!" The sicculet snaps.

"People! People!" A young female sicculet says, trying the get everyone's attention but its little use.

"I know she won't betray us! She's too kind hearted! Too loving to do such a thing! She would only betray us if she knew something worse would happen! You never know! I know she will be doing what's best!" Devote snaps.

"She may have had another vision! Another dream!" I growl, anger boiling inside of me causing me to feel as if I'm about to explode, "She is gifted with second sight after all!"

Suddenly, I remember something that Devotion had said to me, something out of her dreams, *"Second sight was gifted to thee so that the truth she may see,"* I remember how she'd had flash backs to her dreams. Their messages seem to mean something now, something more than they had before.

"Second sight was gifted to thee so that the truth she may see," I whisper as a realisation suddenly hits me, "she must have seen a truth,"

"Shut the fuck up!" A young male sicculet finally shouts, grabbing everyone's attention. We all look to the young male and female sicculets that have been trying desperately to grab our attention.

"There's an emergency announcement that has appeared on the TV, its on repeat so you all better come and see it!" The female says, her sky blue hair shimmering in the dim light.

"Now!" The male growls, his hazel brown eyes burning with anger and frustration.

"Its about Devotion!" The female explains when everyone remains in their places. I rush out of the room and in front of the TV just as it begins the announcement again.

The maker stands in front of the camera, his smile twisting evilly and his eyes boiling with pride, "Devotion has returned and she has finally witnessed how barbaric the sicculets and elves are, tonight she will swear an oath to our people saying that she shall fight for us so that we can bring order out of chaos once more. Please prepare yourselves for tonight because at nine o'clock, Miss Devotion will submit herself to us,"

I collapse to my knees, unable to believe what I have just seen. *She's betrayed us, she's betrayed me* I realise. The realisation of her betrayal sends a sharp pain through my heart and tears running down my face.

"I hope you all enjoy what you see," the maker laughs evilly.

Devotion

Finally, the time arrives and I know what to do. Innocence's last letter has informed me that she will arrive ten minutes before the announcement along with Conquer but they will be hidden in the small crowd that shall gather in the same hall where we were crowned champions.

Several enslaved elves clean the dried blood on my armour and place my black circlet on my forehead once more. I know that there is no point in cleaning the blood off my armour as it will soon be replaced with fresh blood. The maker soon approaches me and smiles. "You're doing the right thing," he says, "after all, I am sure you have realised that your dear mother Devote would have had the strength to save you from the games, to stop everything that has happened to you but she didn't. Instead, she left you, she betrayed you, as did your precious father, Fusion. They both could have saved you," I know what the maker is doing, he's trying to lead, me away from my path. From the Goddess and the light to darkness and the evil within him. To turn to him and away from my people.

The clock strikes nine o'clock and I am called in front of the small crowd and the cameras. I take in a deep breath and centre myself.

"Welcome, welcome all to Devotions oath," the maker begins, his voice slick and filled with hatred. I catch a glance of Innocence and Conquer stood in the centre of the crowd, both waiting patiently.

Conquer winks in my direction and smiles in excitement.

"Devotion has realised just how barbaric and chaotic the sicculets and elves are, she has realised that they are not like her because of the training she received as she was growing up and even though elven blood fills her veins, she has realised she is unlike any elf in the outside world," the maker begins, the camera settling on his face as he stands beside me. "Devotion is going to make an oath to me today, an oath swearing herself to fight for our cause against the sicculets," the maker says in a slick tone.

Immediately, I hold my head up high in pride whilst keeping my expression blank of any possible emotions as I wait patiently, trying not to give away the act I have created.

"Go on Devotion, say the words," the maker encourages before he hisses the next words, exactly like he had in my dream, "remember, your family have and will betray you, as will Callum"

I stare directly at the camera as it zooms in on my face, "I swear an oath," I turn my gaze to the maker, "to follow my heart and do what's right by the goddess and the earth and not assist in the greed and evil held by humans such as the maker whom have turned their back to the light in order to cause evil and chaos," and just like out of my dream, I slowly lift my hand so that the palm of my hand is not far from the makers cheek and before he has time to notice and react, the blade suddenly grows from the palm of my hand. Warm blood trickles down my wrist and falls to the floor as the blade goes straight through the cheek of the maker.

I turn my back to the cameras and the second blade grows through the palm of my free hand and I stab it through his jaw. This time, unlike my dream, I whisper a few words into the makers ear, my lips brushing against it lightly, "Don't ever expect me to go against what's in my heart,"

I remove the blades from the maker and turn to face the camera as the room floods with guards and the audience begin to scream. The makers body falls to the floor as I speak in a strong confident voice, my voice seems so powerful that it causes the entire room to go silent for a moment, "And what you wanted me to do maker, is not right by my heart, the goddess or the earth. Its so good to see you return to the dark," I pause for a split second before I continue speaking, "finally you return to where you belong, in the darkness of hell, I hope you fear the dark," a deadly smile grows on my face as the killer inside of me begins to break loose once again.

Innocence suddenly locks all of the doors trapping the audience inside as Conquer unfolds his sword and begins to attack.

The guards surround me and the first of them try to shoot tranquilliser darts in my direction but I jump out of the way. Swiftly, I run towards the male guard just as both of the elven guards also begin to attack their fellow guards. With the blades, I slice through his arm so that he can't shoot anymore tranquiliser darts in my direction.

I catch the sound of another gun firing and I flip over the male, swiftly using him as a shield whilst he panics. The dart ends up hitting his chest just as I stab him in the back with one of the blades.

Swiftly, I move, using the corpse of the guard as a shield as I approach the next guard. I drop the corpse as flip over the guard, landing on his shoulders, the blades digging into his shoulders before I push myself off him and land on the floor in front of another guard.

Before the guard can shoot me with a tranquiliser dart, I stab the guard in between the eyes with one of the blades whilst with the other I slice through another guards throat. I remove the blade from the skull of the guard before I turn and use the blades to slice through another guards stomach.

In a swift movement, I crouch just as a dart flies above my head. On the ball of my left foot I spin whilst with I stretch out my right leg so that I trip several of the guards that surround me. They fall to the floor and with a lethal movement, I slice another guards throat.

I take out one of the blades from the palm of my hands and spin on the balls of my feet, throwing the blade at a guard as he scrambles to stand, the blade embeds itself in the neck of the guard and he falls to the floor once again.

Suddenly, a guard grabs me from behind, leaving my arms stuck by my sides. I struggle against his strength but its little use he has me trapped. The vines begin to crawl out of my skin and wrap around the guards body, trapping him as well. Quickly, they wrap around his throat and begin to squeeze. Suffocating him.

He suddenly drops me and begins to struggle against the vines as they grow tighter. I pull him to the ground with the vines and then, with an incredible strength I've never known before, I use the vines to throw the guard up in the air and towards the entrance of the room where the stage had gone. His body smashes through the wall with an immense force, revealing the white room, the sofa still stained with blood. The vines release him as he flies through the air.

"Welcome to the dark!" I growl as the blade enters my skin once more and the chains crawl from beneath my skin. I wrap the chain around my hand once, the white glow has returned to the chain but as soon as I begin attacking the guards, killing them one by one, the glow slowly turns scarlet red.

At first I use the chains as if they are some sort of whip, causing them to slash through the guards, whilst the vines wrap around several of the audiences necks, suffocating them before I use it to throw them into and through walls.

Finally, it is just myself, the two guards, Innocence and Conquer remaining. I stand in front of the camera and put on a wicked smile filled with hope. "Here's an announcement for the entire world from me and you all better be listening, this is just the start, I shall not rest until my people are free. A new horizon is on the way, and this world will soon change.

Everything will change. Is this understood?" I pause for a moment and my smile grows larger, "Welcome to the new horizon that's to come and I hope you enjoy the ride!" I turn to Innocence, Conquer and the two guards as I unhook the bow and unfold it, "Ready guys?"

"I'm ready, I don't know about you guys!" Conquer says, his voice sounding excited and a smile growing on his face.

"I'm as ready as I'll ever be," Innocence says with a shy smile.

The guards look to each other and remove their white helmets and take out two pistols from the pistol holders around their thighs, "We're ready," says the male guard.

"Then, lets do this," I say, the killer rising even further inside of me. Excitement running through my veins along with adrenaline, I'm prepared to kill now, even more so than I was in the games. Something has changed inside of me. I'm no longer the girl I was, I'm stronger, faster, more passionate and loving and on top of it all, I'm more devoted to this cause than I have been devoted to anything in the past.

Innocence approaches the door and unlocks it. The first to leave the building is Conquer, whilst the guards look at me in confusion, "Go ahead," I encourage, "I'll be right behind you,"

Swiftly they leave the building. Innocence looks to me and I nod in encouragement for her to leave before me and she nods before she rushes out the building, leaving the door unlocked.

"Sicculets and Elves, enjoy the view because this is for you, I am a voice for the voiceless, and his life is for another life," I say in front of the camera before a large gust of wind fills the room, causing my hair to lift from my shoulders and rise into the air, moving wildly. The temperature slowly begins to grow as a white light begins to fill the room.

The gust of wind picks up paper off the floor and leaves as I begin to leave the building. I walk slowly as the temperature continues to rise. At first it causes droplets of sweat to rise on my forehead and before I step out of the building, the heat has risen to the point where I feel as if I'm being cooked alive.

Once I'm out of the building, it bursts into flames which seem to grow larger as I walk away and when I get far enough for it not to harm any of us, the building explodes. Flames engulf it and walls collapse. We watch from the shadows as people struggle trying to put out the fire with strange vehicles that seem to carry hose pipes filled with water.

We travel through the shadows of the streets, moving towards the giant wall again but as we travel, I notice a female sicculet with two children running around her feet, trying to serve her 'master'.

But it seems she's not serving him fast enough, he throws orders after orders at her, snapping the orders angrily. I watch for a moment before he slaps her across the face. Swiftly, I draw back the scarlet string of my bow, aim the arrow and fire. The arrow pierces through his throat, his body falls to the floor and the sicculets gaze falls on me.

"Come on if you want your freedom," I say with a smile.

She smiles, hope glistening in her violet eyes as she picks up the youngest child and grabs the hand of her second child. She begins running, following Innocence before I begin following her. We come to the wall and without a thought, the chain crawls out of my skin and all of a sudden, its as if someone has taken control of my body. I use the chain as a whip and crack it on the wall before it returns to my skin as the wall crumbles to the floor.

"You're seriously getting the hand of this magic stuff," Innocence compliments.

"No time for comments, lets go!" I say as I run towards the forest and enter its shadows once more.

CHAPTER 11

Betrayal?

We arrive at the home of the free and immediately I run to the bridge near my parents home, I leap and the wings crawl from my skin, fluttering just enough to allow me to grab on to the bridge and jump over. With a strong voice, my words echo throughout the trees, "A voice!" I shout with a large smile on my face, feeling proud of what I have started.

I have created a voice that won't end.

I knock on the door of my parents home and open the door but when I open it, Callum stares at me with a blank expression whilst Devote shakes her head, "What's wrong? What's going on?" I say, a sharp pain stabbing through my heart.

"We know of your betrayal," Fusion says, his voice emotionless, "we saw the announcement"

"My betrayal?" I ask, feeling confused as pain begins to flood my body, the enchanting warmth that normally floods my body when I'm around Callum is nowhere to be seen, instead it is replaced by ice that seem to fill my veins, causing immense pain throughout my entire body.

"We saw the announcement from the maker, we know you made an oath with him, to fight against the freedom of sicculets and elves," Fusion replies.

I back out of the door, feeling the ice spread through my veins as my heart pounds in my chest. "I didn't make an oath with the maker," I whisper, my voice choking on the words.

"Not according to the maker, he announced that you will be fighting along side him," Fusion replies, his voice suddenly as cold as ice.

"No, I never made an oath, I'm not fighting along side him, I swear!" I reply.

"Stop with the lies!" Callum snaps angrily, his voice cold and heartless.

"I'm not lying," I say, my voice pleading.

"We saw it! You made an oath! You betrayed us!" Callum snaps.

"No! I didn't!" Tears begin streaming down my face as the stabbing pain continues to stab straight through my heart, growing more and more painful with every passing moment. "I would never betray you!" Soon it grows too much to take, no longer can I handle the pain growing in my heart, my eyes sting with even more tears as they continue to run down my cheeks. "I thought you would know that!" I mutter, before I shout angrily, no longer able to take the pain, "I would never betray you! Ever! But do you know what? You can go through this war without me!"

The wings crawl from the skin of my back once more, the pain spreading throughout my entire body. Callum looks up from ground and too my face, his eyes suddenly fill with pain and I know he's seen the honesty in my eyes, along with the pain caused by him.

"Devotion," he says in a calm, comforting voice but its too late. I turn my back on all of them and my wings automatically begin to move. I leap from the bridge and at first I fall before I begin to fly. I shoot up towards the sky, "Devotion!" I hear him shout in the distance before I begin to fly further into the forest at unusual speed. No longer am I sloppy and clumsy as I fly and I can't help but wonder whether its because of the need I feel in my heart. The need to leave.

Tears continue to stream down my face and in a stiff, rough movement, I wipe them away.

Eventually, I land and climb up a tree so high that I can watch the sunset over the trees.

"Gaia! I've done everything for you! I've done everything you wanted and this is what happens! You cause everyone to hate me! Why? Why would you do this?" I shout to the sky, demanding answers but I receive no answer from her. Tears continue to stream down my face.

They can fight this war on their own! Without me! My mind screams as the pain grows stronger in my body.

Innocence

I climb the stairs that appear, anger in every step I take. I approach Callum and slap him around the face as hard as I can, causing a large red mark to appear on his face in the shape of my hand. "Innocence! Calm down!" Conquer commands but I ignored him.

"What have you done!" I scream at the top of my lungs. I can feel Devotion's heart breaking as sharp little stabs begin to run through my body.

"She betrayed us!" Devote replies.

"Did she? Did she indeed?" I shout before I throw the letters in front of them, "Check the fucking messages and the footage! I think you'll find the makers dead and died at Devotions hands! Devotion made an oath to be a voice for the voiceless! She made an oath to defend and fight for you no matter what and you reward her with this!"

"And how would you know?" Callum mutters, his voice filled with pain and sadness.

"We were there," Conquer says in a calm voice.

"She came to the city to get us and save any sicculets or elves on the way!" I shout, motioning to the two elves and the small family of sicculets below. "She went to kill the maker! She had a plan on how to do it and she went through with it! She killed him! He's dead! She fought for you!" I push Callum with all of my strength and he falls to the floor. "And you treat her like this! After she kept you alive in the games! She risked her life for you and you do this!" I glance around the small village, "She got us to join her to help her fight for you and do you know what, maybe you're too selfish to realise this but she put her life on the line now for you and Callum," I look back to his face, "this is the second time she's put her life on the line for you but you're nothing but a selfish bastard!"

I storm away before I do something stupid due to the anger boiling inside of me. Silently, I wish them all to rot in hell but I know it's the wrong thing to wish for.

Suddenly, a young blue haired sicculet runs up to us before I can get to the stairs. She seems filled with fear and frustration.

"She didn't make an oath to the maker! She killed him! We just saw the feed! We recorded it! Come see!" The sicculet shouts.

"We told you," I snap between clenched teeth, "you better go find Devotion and apologise before its too late because right now, her heart is breaking and fuck knows what she'll do when it finally breaks"

With those words said, I walk away with Conquer not far behind me and eventually I sit down on a patch of dirt below the buildings in the trees.

How dare they treat my sister in such a disgusting manner! I wonder, feeling absolutely disgusted by their actions.

Devotion

I climb down from the tree and sit at the bottom with my back leant against the trunk of the tree. I punch the floor repeatedly, tears streaming down my face as my screams echo through the trees. The pain floods my body as slowly my heart breaks and as it does, something occurs to me. A thought.

An idea.

And it appeals to the killer inside of me. Swiftly, I begin running towards the small home of the free, and when I arrive, I walk straight through.

"Devotion!" Innocence shouts but all I do is pass her.

"Devotion!" Callum shouts from above before he jumps down and lands in front of me. I don't even look at his face, instead I just try to pass him. "Devotion!" He says as he grabs me by my shoulders yet I keep my face hidden behind my hair, "I'm sorry," he says.

My head snaps up and I look at him with a cold expression on my face, "Welcome to the dark, I hope your not afraid," I say, my voice cold and emotionless as my heart finally breaks completely. I step backwards before I remove my jacket from around my waist and throwing it to the floor. Hanging below the bridge is a pure black cloak. I grab it as I pass through and throw it over my shoulders. Using the broach upon it that reminds me of a leaf in the beginning of winter, covered in frost, to keep it in place.

Swiftly, I begin walking away when the breeze caresses my cheek softly and then, I become paralysed, unable to move from my position. With much effort I manage to glance over my shoulder as Callum approaches me, "Let me go!" The killer inside of me forces me to growl the words angrily.

"I'm not doing anything," Callum replies and I can see the honesty in his eyes.

"What do you want?" I growl as he steps in front of me.

"To say sorry, we saw the footage, we know you didn't betray us, we saw you kill the maker," Callum replies, solemnly.

"What would it matter anyway? I'm a traitor in your eyes!" I growl, suddenly sounding more like an animal than a human.

Callum steps back slightly, its as if my words have just slapped him in the face, "I know you're not a traitor," he says, his voice comforting and warm once more.

"Ha!" I say.

"What's happened to you? Your eyes, they've turned black and you've turned into a cold person, this isn't you"

"What would you know? You know nothing! To you I'm a traitor but the truth is I'm nothing more than a cold hearted killer!" I growl. The warmth that radiates from him tries to enter my body once again but I try to fight it away. "You brought the cold killer out of me now deal with consequences!"

"I'm sorry, I really am. I thought you had betrayed us and I felt my heart rip in two but I know the truth now," Callum replies, his voice unusually calm.

I want to strike him down, to punch him, hit him. I want to let out the pain that I feel in my heart but I can't. I can't move. "You don't trust me," I manage to push past the killer inside of me and whisper the words weakly.

"I do," Callum says as he lifts my chin with his hand so that I have to look into his eyes. I continue fighting the warmth that tries to enter my body but its little use, slowly it enters and begins trying to mend my broken heart. "That's my Devotion, a gorgeous girl with emerald green eyes not a cold blooded killer with black eyes," he says after a moment.

Finally, I manage to move and I flinch away from his touch, "I'm not property, I own myself, I am no ones," I mutter as tears begin to burn in my eyes.

"Is that true? Is that really true?" Callum says as he cups my face in his hands and forces me to look at him again but instead of looking in my eyes, he closes his and kisses me passionately.

At first I feel completely shocked as my body fills with pleasure and passion. The warmth in my veins grows stronger and continues to mend my heart. After a quick moment, I close my eyes and begin kissing him back, matching his passion with mine. I feel my body heal under his touch as his arms slip down from my face and to my waist, holding me closer. His arms wrap tightly around me, and my body moulds into his.

I run my hands through his hair as I wrap my arms around his neck. The more he kisses me, the more passionate it becomes. He holds me even closer, the warmth of his body completely surrounding me, comforting me and causing something to stir inside of me.

My heart pounds against my chest, sparks of pleasure run through my body and my breathing becomes much heavier.

Eventually, we both manage to pull away and he rests his forehead on mine, both of us are panting for breath. "Err, I'm sorry to interrupt," Meredith's voice appears from behind us, "but its getting late and soon neither of you will be able to get back in your home, we're closing up shop so to say,"

I smile as I look up to Callum. "We'll be at the stairs in a minute," Callum says with a smile, his voice filled with joy, happiness and warmth. Whilst I'm unsure I can trust my voice to speak.

"Okay, see you both in a moment," Meredith says, "oh and tomorrow morning, we're planning our next move,"

Finally I manage to speak, my voice little more than a whisper, "I already know my next move,"

"Do you?" Meredith asks.

"Yes," I whisper with a smile.

"Care to share it tomorrow?" She asks.

"I think I might be a bit busy putting it into action tomorrow," I reply.

"Well, I hope we'll get to hear it," Meredith replies before she begins to walk away.

Swiftly, Callum moves in for another kiss, holding me as close as he can and he moves in for the second kiss but this time I flinch away.

"Why are you doing this?" I ask.

"What do you mean?" He replies, seeming confused.

"What I mean is, why bother trying to bring me back? Is it to ensure that the elves and the sicculets receive their the freedom of do you truly care?"

"I truly care, I swear to you," he replies before he continues to move into kiss me and this time I allow him to.

I manage to pull away after another long moment of kissing, "We should get to bed," I say breathlessly.

"We should," he says with a smile before he lifts me up and I let out a little squeal before he begins carrying me. Both of us laughing, my heart is now at rest now that I know that he actually cares and that it isn't just some sort of act. "and guess where you'll be sleeping tonight!"

"Where?" I ask, innocently.

"My bed," Callum says as he spins with me still in his arms. He climbs the stairs and enters my parents home before taking me to a small bedroom with a double bed.

* * *

The next morning, I'm up and dressed long before anyone else in the small village. I rush out of the room and once I'm outside, I go in search for Innocence, Conquer, and the two elven guards. I wake them in their extremely small homes by clapping my hands.

"Devotion, what's going on?" Conquer asks, sleepily as he rubs his eyes.

"We have work to do which means us getting to the city before everyone awakes," I whisper.

"What are we doing in the city?" Innocence asks.

"Freeing as many elves and sicculets as possible and bringing them here," I reply.

"Why?" Conquer asks.

But the male guard beats me to the answer, "Miss Devotion seems to be forming an army," he says with a smile.

"Exactly," I say with a smile, "look, I don't your names but what you need to do is intercept the guards and get as many elven guards out of their, get them to join us in the fight for freedom"

"My names Caeli and my partner is Calla," the male replies.

"It's nice knowing your names, now do you understand your part in the plan?" I reply.

"Yes ma'am!" They both reply.

"Shush! People are still asleep and we don't want them waking up," I pause for a moment, "anyway, that's just the beginning of your part of the plan, can you see if you can grab some weapons for us to fight with?"

"We can try," Calla replies with a smile.

"Right, Innocence and Conquer, what we need to do try and gather as many sicculet and elven slaves that are on the streets or in homes," I reply.

"So basically, we're going to steal from peoples homes," Conquer says.

"Basically yea and if the people are in and put up a fight, we fight back, understood?" I reply and they both nod, "Good because we need to start forming an army as best we can and what would help is if we had more weapons, so if you see any weapons in the houses, grab them"

"Understood," Innocence replies.

"So are we ready to go?" I ask as I empty my bag on the floor.

"I think we are," Conquer replies.

"Then, lets do this!" I reply with a large smile on my face. We each get up and leave the village behind, and set off for the city once more.

*   *   *

Finally, we arrive in the city just after the sun has just passed sunrise. We sneak into the city no problem and the elves split off from us whilst we begin with the first house to break in. Innocence picks the lock carefully so that it doesn't make much noise and we enter quickly. I check the ground floor and cellar of the posh house whilst Conquer checks upstairs.

When I open the cellar door, I feel applaud as I stare at the conditions that three sicculets and an elf are living in. I rush down and wake them up in the freezing cold, damp room. "Wake up!" I whisper softly. Each of them look at me sleepily, clearly they're confused, "Do you want your freedom from this place?" I ask and each of their eyes lighten up and suddenly, they're wide awake, "Then come with me. My names Devotion"

They each smile brightly as they quickly get up, "You're the girl from the arena aren't you? The one that swore to save us," a young male sicculet asks.

I smile and nod, "Yea that's me," I whisper, "and that's why I'm here. I made an oath to free you and that's what I'm doing so come on!" I reply. They follow me out of the cellar and into the street where I find Conquer and Innocence waiting.

"How many do we have?" Conquer asks.

"We have three sicculets and one elf, sleeping in damp cold conditions and they each look malnourished," I reply.

"They do don't they," Conquer agrees.

"Wait!" I hear a familiar female voice appear not far from us, I glance over my shoulder to see Meredith has followed us, "So this was your plan"

"Yes, it was and you've come in perfect timing. We're gathering slaves, once we get to a certain number, will you please begin escorting them away from the city and into the forest," I say.

"It'll take me too long to get them home," she replies.

"I'm on about you taking them so far into the forest where they won't be seen and they'll be safe, then every hour or so begin escorting them please," I reply.

"I think that's possible to do," Meredith replies before she begins escorting the first lot of slaves into the forest and somewhere safe.

The beginning of it is easy but soon, people will begin awakening and things will get much harder.

*   *   *

It hasn't taken long but we manage to help several slaves escape by the time the guards arrive. "Stop what you're doing!" A male commands.

"Ignore him Conquer!" I command, "I'll deal with these guys, you keep going!"

He continues helping the slaves escape whilst I take my stand in front of the guards. My palms tingle and warm blood trickles down my finger tips as the blades grow through my palms. I stand before the guards. There's approximately twenty of them stood before me.

"Bring it on!" I say as I stand firmly on the ground as the killer inside of me begins to rise, the deadly instinct grows swiftly, "Come on!" I challenge. The guards begin shooting at me but this time, instead of tranquilisers, they're using the same ultraviolet light we use in weapons in the games. Immediately, I begin dodging them as I charge towards them. I leap from the ground and land directly in front of one of the guards and before they can press the trigger, I stab him with one of the blades. The blade pierces straight through the guards helmet and into his skull with ease. I turn swiftly, before allowing another guard to turn and with the second blade, I stab them in the throat.

Using both corpses as shield either side, for a moment before I take out the blades and leap from the ground, using gravity to my advantage, I flip behind the next guard and stab him from behind before the phoenix and the fairy crawl from my skin and begin attacking the guards, distracting them for a moment. I remove the blade a second time before I stab another guard in the heart. One of the blades returns to my skin as the chains are released from around my wrist.

I wrap the chain around my hand several times before I skid between a guards open legs whilst the fairy keeps him distracted. With the blade I slice through the crotch of the guard before I roll to my feet and drop the chain to the floor. Swiftly, I use it as a whip, against several guards.

The chain slices through the guards with ease, the radiant white glow turning scarlet as the blood soaks the floor. I turn as the blade enters my skin once more and the chain returns through my palm once again.

Suddenly, I come to a stop as the breeze begins to grow around me, sending my hair wild as it turns from a slight breeze into a gale. The sun becomes covered by rain filled clouds. Rain begins to pore from the sky as the fairy joins forces with the phoenix in distracting the guards. I close my eyes and centre myself and when I open them, several pipes in the ground and the near by houses burst and the water begins to form a large tidal wave behind me. I can feel the water by my feet through the armoured boots as it fills the wave further.

I lift my hand and open my fist and as I do so, the wave hurdles towards the guards, knocking them all off their feet. "Do you mind getting me soaked?" The fairy snaps, her form now completely drenched.

A giggle escapes my lips before the killer inside of me rises even further. The instincts grow stronger. The instinct to kill.

The vines grow from my arm and I throw it towards one of the guards, immediately it wraps around his neck and begins tightening, suffocating him slowly. But as I stand there, one of the guards pulls the trigger of his gun and the large bolt of light hurdles towards me. I jump out of the way but I'm not quick enough. I feel the sudden burning sensation in my leg as it skims the skin leaving a deep burn in the calf of my leg. Silently, I wonder how it could be possible for the guard to have used the gun once it had become absolutely soaked but then I realise that it no doubt has some sort of water protect shield around the actual weapon.

As I fall to the floor, something inside of me awakens, something stronger than the killer. I look at the guards and lift my hand before they can pull the trigger again. I clench my hand into a fist instantly and every last guard bursts into flames. The vines return to my skin but the fairy and the phoenix remain with me.

"Shit! Crap! Your pretty badly injured! Look at that burn!" The fairy panics as we both assess the injury. The burn is deep and almost the size of my palm.

I try to get to my feet but the pain in my leg is too much and I collapse back to the floor, a scream releasing from my lips. "Devotion!" Innocence shouts as she runs towards me, "Crap! Your injured!"

"It's just a flesh wound," I mutter quietly, gritting my teeth together to keep control over my voice despite the pain. I want to scream in agony so much but I can't.

"It's more than a flesh wound, Calla and Caeli are back, we'll take the elves and sicculets back, we've helped a large amount of them, a lot have escaped, we have larger numbers now," Innocence says. "Conquer!" She shouts and Conquer runs to us.

"Crap!" He gasps.

"Carry her, we need to leave! Now!" Innocence commands, suddenly turning from an innocent, young huntress and into a strong, powerful leader. Conquer picks me up and begins to run towards the forest once more. "Follow us and run!" Innocence commands and several sicculets soon follow.

Meredith collects the slaves we have assisted in escaping and Conquer carries me as they run towards our home.

*   *   *

Finally, we arrive home with a larger number of sicculets and elves, most of them are clearly willing to fight for their freedom, it burns in their eyes. The magic in the elven eyes seem almost hypnotic once the will to fight joins it and the sicculets appear much more powerful once they reach the home of the free. Callum rushes to myself and Conquer. "Devotion! Where have you been all day?" He asks, his voice filled with worry before his eyes fall on the wound, "What happened? Who did this to you?"

"I'm fine," I mutter, whilst attempting to control my voice and not allowing anyone to know that I am in pure agony.

"We need to get her medical help now!" Meredith intercepts before Callum can speak again. "We'll take her to our doctor!" Meredith says before she leads us to a small, stone hut beneath the trees, in an unusually secluded and dark area of the small village. Callum follows us.

We enter the hut and Conquer places me on a bed. The doctor is an elderly elven woman, her long grey hair is held up in a ponytail and her large grey eyes are worn and old. "Let me see the wound!" She commands as she passes Conquer, she appears to be half the height of Conquer. "It looks quiet serious, child," she says as she begins looking at my wound.

"Is there anything you can do to help the healing process?" Meredith asks, "Maybe speed it up?"

"Unlikely, it will heal at its own pace," the old woman replies before she looks into my eyes, "the best thing for you young Devotion, is rest," she looks back to Meredith, "leave her here and allow her to rest for a few days"

"May I speak with Devotion quickly?" Callum asks, he pauses for a moment, "In private?"

"Of course child," the doctor replies before she scoots everyone out of the hut and leaves, closing the door behind her.

"What happened? Where did you go? Where did all those sicculets and elves come from?" Callum begins bombarding me with questions.

"Innocence, Conquer, Calla, Caeli and myself went back to the city and saved a large amount of slaves and we have weapons now," I explain.

"Why didn't you wake me? I could have helped you!" Callum snaps.

"Because I wouldn't allow you to come harm no matter what! I want to keep you safe!" I plead.

"You can't keep disappearing off like this and not letting me know where you're going, I'm bound to worry and look what happened, I could have helped you," Callum replies sounding much calmer than before as he sits on the edge of the bed.

"It's just a flesh wound,"

"Tell me what happened, please"

"Well, we were freeing loads of slaves and a lot escaped but then the guards got involved. I told Conquer to continue helping the slaves whilst I took on the guards. This time they weren't shooting at me with tranquilisers, they were trying to kill me. I managed to to kill the majority of them before one of them shot at me. I dived out the way and it skimmed my leg, its nothing compared to what it could have been," I explain.

"You shouldn't have taken them all on your own, you should have had Conquer help you," Callum mutters.

"No! We need numbers, I have a plan, trust me! But just because I'm injured doesn't mean it shouldn't go underway. I'll heal soon enough, trust me," I reply.

"I trust you but this doesn't look like its going to—" suddenly, Callum stops mid sentence and his eyes widen as they settle on the wound once more. "What on earth?" He gasps before rushing to the door.

The doctor enters the room once more and gasps. "Impossible! Completely and utterly impossible!" She says. I glance down at the wound and gasp, my hands clamp over my mouth as I watch the burn as it begins healing itself at an unusual speed. No longer can I feel any pain. "At this rate, the wound will be gone in the next hour," the doctor gasps.

"This means she will be fit to continue fighting, right?" Meredith asks.

The doctor shakes her head, "I would still recommend that she rests for a day or two, allow her leg time to fully recover and allow her strength to recover before she fights again," the doctor replies.

"Understood," I mutter unable to look away from the wound as the burnt flesh falls off and is replaced by new, fresh, fiery red skin. I yawn, feeling absolutely exhausted, "may I return to bed now please,"

"Is someone able to carry her to her home?" The doctor asks.

"No need," I say as I sit on the bed, my legs dangling above the floor. I stand and ignore the sharp pain that runs up my leg as I stagger towards the door.

"You shouldn't be walking," the doctor snaps.

"I won't be walking for long," I say as soon as I open the door and exit the hut. The wings crawl from beneath my skin and begin to flutter automatically, I lift from the ground and clumsily land outside my home. Callum runs up the steps and over the bridge as I open the door.

"No! You need to rest," Callum says as he sweeps me off my feet and carries me into the house and to my bed. As soon as my head hit's the pillow, I fall straight to sleep and my dreams begin.

It's the same place as every other time I've seen Gaia only this time I'm stood at the edge of the sea water, the waves hit my ankles as I watch the sunset and before she speaks, I sense her presence nearby, "What do I need to do next? I can't fight for a few days because of my injury," I say softly.

"Your injury shall heal faster than most," Gaia replies, her voice holding the same soft, motherly love as it fills my ears like a song.

"Callum won't allow it," I mutter.

"I know child," she replies, I can hear her footsteps as she approaches me.

"So, what is it you need me to do next?"

"Collect even further numbers, there are more free sicculets and elves hiding in other areas of the forests that surround the cities and none of them know of each other,"

"What do you want me to do?"

"To collect them together as a large army and slowly bring down the cities one by one. I will show you the way to the first home of the free tomorrow, there are several villages close together in one area, bring these together and attack the first city before you bring the army to the village where you live at this moment. Send messages to other villages and send them in the direction of the village you live in and slowly, an army shall form as the slaves become free in different cities," Gaia commands.

"Understood," I mutter, "is that all you want me to do?"

"For now, yes," Gaia replies.

CHAPTER 12

A True War Begins

I awake the next morning, wrapped in Callum's arms. I glance up at him to see if he's asleep. He's awake.

He smiles at me, "Good morning, beautiful," he says, in a warm, loving voice. His eyes sparkle with life and happiness as he looks at me.

"Good morning," I say with a smile before reaching closer to him and kissing him softly. Pleasure and warmth bursts throughout my body and I don't want it to stop. I pull him closer and he holds me tighter.

Slowly, my hand begins to wonder up his t-shirt, the warmth of his chest is beneath my palm of my hand, his heart beat becomes quicker just as mine does, and he becomes breathless just as I do. My second hand pulls at his top, whilst the other begins to venture down and tease him by tracing the line of his trousers.

He suddenly grabs my wrist, stopping me from going any further and pulls away. I look at him, feeling confused. *Doesn't he want this?* I wonder silently.

"Not now, not when your injured, its not right," he says breathlessly.

"Why?" I ask.

"Because I could injure you further," he replies.

"You won't, I know you won't," I whisper before I remember the dream. Remember Gaia's orders. "Shit!" I whisper as I pull away and begin climbing out of bed.

Callum grabs my wrist again, "Where are you going?" He asks.

"There's something I need to do," I mutter.

"You're not doing anything! You need to rest!" Callum replies, his voice slightly raised yet its still filled with warmth and love.

I pull away from him and begin to walk out of the room, "I don't have a choice," I mutter before limping out of the room.

"What do you mean you don't have a choice?" Callum asks as he follows me towards the door. He grabs my shoulders but it doesn't take much of a struggle for me to release myself once more. "What do you mean you don't have a choice?"

I limp out of the door and the wings crawl out of my back, "What I mean is, I don't have a choice," I reply, glancing at him over my shoulder. I climb onto the rope that works as a fence and swiftly leap, the wings flutter and I fly through the air. Rushing through the trees, following the map appearing in my mind to my first destination.

Bird songs fill my ears and the heat of the sun rests on my back. I land on the floor to rest my wings as the fairy and the phoenix crawl out of my skin once again. "Listen to me, I have a message for you both to deliver to other villages of the free out there," I begin and the fairy nods.

"I'll write it down on a note for phoenix," she says with a smile.

"Okay, here's the message, tell them these words exactly; this message is from Devotion, the champion of the most recent games, she wishes for you to follow me to another village filled with free Sicculets and Elves. She is building an army to fight against the humans in order to bring freedom to all Sicculets and Elves and she needs your help," I say.

After a moment of silence, "This message is from Devotion, the champion of the most recent games, she wishes for you to follow me to another village filled with free Sicculets and Elves. She is building an army to fight against the humans in order to bring freedom to all Sicculets and Elves and she needs your help," the fairy says.

"This is the rest of the message okay?" I say and she nods, "Devotion is in the process of bringing down several of the other capitol cities, by the time you all gather and arrive at the village, she will be there with weapons and she will be ready,"

"Devotion is in the process of bringing down several of the other capitol cities, by the time you all gather and arrive at the village, she will be there with weapons and she will be ready," the fairy repeats.

"Good, now go!" I command and both she and the phoenix fly as quickly as they can before I too return flying, using the trees to keep me hidden.

*   *   *

Finally, as the sunsets, I arrive at my destination after flying for the entire day. The village, set to be my destination by Gaia, consists of approximately twenty handcrafted tents. Just as I arrive at the destination, and struggle to come to a stop, the moon rises and the people seem to rise from their tents as if they have just woken up.

Slowly, the entire village awakens and comes to life.

In desperation to stop, I force myself to crash into the floor of the forest, in the centre of the village. A sharp pain surges through my shoulder as I gradually pick myself up off the dirt and dust off the mud.

People swarm around me instantly, clearly none of them understand what I am and I don't really blame them, I don't really know what I am either.

"Is that a fairy? Mommy?" A young child asks, her long strawberry blond hair slightly messy and her blue eyes look tired as she rubs them. Her eyes never look away from me as she stares, curiosity clear in her eyes as she glances to my wings whilst the return to my skin and appear to be a tattoo once more, her eyes suddenly beginning to gleam with hope.

"I don't know," an older, female voice replies. I glance to the little girls hand to see that it is in the hand of a much older woman with the same strawberry blond hair only hers has a touch of grey that has appeared with age. Her hazel brown eyes watch me cautiously, "she certainly looks like one,"

I am not a fairy! I am a huntress! My mind screams in frustration before I force myself to calm down.

Gradually, I stand and glance around at the people that surround me. None of them have pointed ears or scales instead of skin. None of them are unusually fare or have a tail.

They all appear to be human.

The camp is filled with a mixture of human races, their skin colour is different and there seems to be no conflict between

271

them, not like I remember Callum telling me about. Suddenly, I notice something that they all have in common, even their children.

They all have similar tribal tattoos on their forearms, and their tattoos resemble the tattoo I recall being on Callum's forearm.

Can this be some sort of connection they have? A connection they have with Callum? Is this why they've been cast away like this? Suddenly, the realisation hits me, *Are they all werewolves?* I wonder silently.

Swiftly, an old woman approaches me along with another woman behind her that appears to be middle age. The old woman's skin is incredibly pale and her eyes are a dim green colour, worn with age and tired of life. The elderly woman has a hunched back and uses a walking stick in order to give her some sort of support as she limps towards me. Her long grey hair has been tied up into a bun and held into place with chopsticks.

Her companion, the middle aged woman has much darker skin and her hazel eyes resemble Callum's. Her long black hair falls down her back and as she walks, she moves gracefully without causing a sound, and her back remains straight at all times. They both stop in front of me and the elderly woman begins to look at the tattoo of wings on my back even closer. I can feel that the wings are still returning to my skin and she seems to analyse them as they return to being a tattoo.

"What are you?" The elderly woman asks, her voice sounding slightly snappy.

"A messenger," I reply, my voice strong as it is carried by the gentle comforting, night breeze that caresses my cheek softly.

"From who?" The elderly woman asks.

I gulp nervously but force myself to remain looking strong, my back straight and head held high, "Gaia," I reply.

"The Goddess, could this be true?" The middle aged woman asks, her voice sounding much younger than her years.

"Yes, for we know it can be true," the elderly woman replies, "what is your name?"

"Devotion," I reply.

"And what is your message, Devotion?" The elderly woman asks.

"I am unsure, my duty by the goddess is to set the slaves free and ensure that there is equality in this world once more. She sent me here and I do not understand why you have been cast aside by humans," I reply.

The elderly woman lifts up her arm to bare her tattoo, "Can you not see? Are you blind? We are of wolf blood and not of human, of course we shall be cast to one side and gifted little rights," she snaps.

"Then perhaps this is why she has sent me here," I pause for a moment, "do you wish for equality?"

"Of course we wish for equality," a masculine voice shouts.

"Then you may wish for it all you want but it will never happen, not unless you are willing to fight for it, are you willing to fight for your wish?" I reply.

"We are willing to fight," the middle aged woman replies.

"But depending on the fight, will it to be speaking and your human forms could do this, alone probably not but you could still achieve such a goal however this fight has resulted into blood and you can not fight it alone," I reply.

"So you're here to help us?" The young child's mother replies.

"Not just myself, but you don't realise whom you are neighbours with. Close by are several villages of the free that will fight for equality beside you, it just depends if you're willing to help them as well as yourselves," I reply.

"And who do you speak of?" The elderly woman asks.

Suddenly, images begin to flash in front of my eyes to the nearby villages, "Sicculets and elves whom have both escaped the city," I reply. My legs suddenly begin to feel weak and my body feels exhausted. Suddenly, my knees seem to turn to jelly and my body becomes weak before I collapse to the floor and become unconscious.

*   *   *

I open my eyes to see the inside of a tent above me. I glance around and try to sit up but someone restrains me. I look to the middle aged woman's face and she gives me a warm, soft smile. Her eyes glisten and turn from hazel to a similar lily pad green to Callum's eyes.

"For a messenger of Gaia, you are slightly dim at times," she says in a warm voice.

"What's that supposed to mean?" I ask, my voice sounding weary and tired.

"Travelling when injured and not drinking enough" the woman replies.

"I didn't have much of a choice, the goddess told me she wanted me to travel when injured and I must have forgot to drink, it kind of happens when you're determined to do something, you forget things," I reply with a cheeky smile.

"I understand that to an extent," she replies.

"May I ask for your name?"

"Savannah,"

"Are you what I think you are? Are you werewolves?" I pause for a moment, "The elderly woman, she said you were of wolf blood"

"We are werewolves yes, personally I prefer to call us Lycans"

"So you're like," again I pause as I struggle to find the word I wish to use, "my partner, he is a lycan"

"You are consorting with a lycan and yet you're not a lycan," Savannah mutters, "you don't judge him for the beast within him"

"Beast? What beast?" I ask feeling slightly confused, "I've seen him in his other form, he acts like no beast around me but then what I would class as a beast and you would class as a beast maybe two completely different things"

"I class a beast at those whom kill without giving it a second thought," Savannah replies.

"Then you class me as a beast as well," I reply.

"You are no beast," Savannah replies.

"I kill without giving it a second thought, I hold no guilt for those whom I have killed, it doesn't phase me," I reply.

"How?"

"As a child, I was taught how to kill, told I had to kill, I was trained, experimented on, changed. Throughout my childhood, I'd only ever known one thing and that was death. I'd seen children my age die from the experiments, I'd never experienced any sort of parental love or any sort of normal childhood experiences. In the end, there was only one thing we knew and that was death, the humans, they were preparing us for what we call the games. They were preparing us to kill, they tried to wipe all passion and love from us," I explain.

"Then the Goddess saved you?" Savannah guesses.

I shake my head, "Unfortunately no, the Goddess chose me after I went out of my way to protect someone in the games, my partner, a lycan. I kept him alive until the very end," I reply.

"What is his name?"

"Callum," I answer immediately.

"He must certainly be special for him to be consorting with one chosen by the Goddess," Savannah replies. "Now, that is enough chit chat for now, you need to rest and we shall see how you are feeling in the morning," she pauses for a moment before she begins to sing a strange lullaby, "rest your head, now my child, for you own the night, as a wolf you are wild, but there is no reason, for you to fear, as we all know, you are safe here, we are your pack, and she is your Goddess, for the rest of time, you are one, with the earth"

The words echo in my mind along with the melody as slowly, I fall asleep.

Rest your head,
Now my child,
You own the night,
As a wolf you are wild,
But there is no reason,
For you to fear,
As we all know,
You are safe here,
We are your pack,
And she is your Goddess,

For the rest of time,
You are one,
With the earth,
You are one,
With the earth

*　　*　　*

Suddenly, I awaken with flashing images of violence flooding my mind before the small fairy flies into the tent, "Devotion! I sent the messages, they're preparing to make their way to the village!" She says quickly, tripping over the words slightly.

"Good, where's phoenix?" I ask.

"He's here," the fairy replies before the phoenix enters. "We have brought the villages together so that they shall travel together,"

"Okay, good. Phoenix, I need you to do something else for me, whilst fairy, please guide them to the village, phoenix I need you to bring Callum, Innocence and Conquer here," I say my voice filled with urgency and I don't quite understand why I've said the words.

"Okay," the fairy replies before they both rush out of the tent and I force myself to rise. I limp to the exit of the tent to see the sun slowly set and the people rise once more.

The village bustles with life as everyone approaches me, "So what are your plans today?" Asks Savannah.

"Today, I'm going to take you with me to the next village," I reply as I begin to follow the directions to the next village. Everyone begins following me as if it were in their instincts to do so.

*　　*　　*

The night passes quickly, as we find each village and the villagers begin to follow me. Gaia was right about them being close together.

The sunrise soon comes and I settle with those chosen to be the leaders of each village, "Tomorrow at sunset, I suggest that we take actions on the nearest capitol city," I say.

"Sounds like an idea, but how shall we go about it?" Savannah asks.

"Well first, what city is the closest capitol city?" I ask.

"Veniva," Savannah replies.

"Understood, right what we shall do is I shall be the first to intercept the walls before everyone follows and we work our way into the centre, slowly taking over. The guards will be armed but you need to have faith, I'm sure we can do this if we put our minds and our strength into this," I say.

"We do have powerful magic to wield," the male elven leader replies. He has long dark brown hair braided into hoop beads and deep sea blue eyes, his skin is incredibly pale and his skin is almost flawless.

"And between the lycans and ourselves, we have strength and speed," the sicculet leader replies. He has short, shaggy black hair and rose red eyes whilst his scales appear to be more of a scarlet red colour.

"We can't change when we want to—" Savannah begins to explain but the elven leader interrupts her.

"That can soon be amended with a little spell," he says.

"Well, everyone better start getting ready, children will stay here with a few females but we need as many warriors as possible," I say.

"Understood," Savannah says.

"Then let the real war begin," I say with a smile before everyone separates to prepare whilst I rest.

* * *

Sunset arrives and the army gather themselves together, "Are you all ready for what will happen?" I say and I receive a loud yes from the army I have gathered, "I will be honest with you, many of you will die but your deaths will not be in vain for we shall take our freedom and our equality!"

"Yea!" The crowd shouts.

"You know the plan do you not?" I ask.

"Yea!"

"Then, let the real war begin!" I call before I turn and begin creeping in the direction of the capitol city. Soon, it comes into view and I fly over the wall that surrounds it, landing in a crouched position before I swiftly investigate to see whether there any guards around. There aren't, not yet anyway.

Swiftly, I turn and send a blast at the wall, causing it to crumble and allowing the army through. The noise clearly grabs the attention of nearby guards and quickly, they gather.

"Stop what you're doing!" One shouts.

Slowly I turn, "I will break everything and anything until I find what I'm looking for, I will use the threat of my heart," I say quietly before the blades grow from the palms of my hands. Swiftly, I charge towards the large group of guards and using the nearby buildings, I leap from wall to wall until I land behind them. In a quick, lethal movement, I stab the first of the blades into the spine of the first guards before I turn and slice through the second guards throat.

"We need back up immediately, the huntress is here—" a guard begins to say into his headpiece but before he has time to finish what he's saying, I interrupt him by slicing the blade straight through his stomach, his blood splatters on my armour and on my skin, sending the killer inside of me wild.

Another guard goes to use his gun but I slice through his arm causing the gun along with his hand, to fall to the floor before I stab the blade through his jaw. I remove the blade and turn.

I kick the next guard to the floor before slicing both blades through his throat, decapitating his head. The blades return to my skin once every guard is dead on the floor. I glance over my shoulder, "Are you coming or what? More guards will be on the way soon," I say.

Savannah is the first to run to my side, "You're certainly an exceptional killer," she mutters.

I smile, "I've been training to kill since I first learnt how to walk," I reply.

"You can definitely tell," she replies before we begin travelling through the city. Guards begin to surround us as the army travel through the streets.

"Don't hold back!" I shout in a strong voice, the blades ripping through my skin once more. I leap from the ground and land between two guards. With a swift movement, I stab both blades into their sides and slice upwards. I remove the blades as the lycans take on the forms of wolves and begin to attack. Elves seem to be using spells more than hand to hand combat whilst the sicculets begin using their speed and strength against the humans.

I turn on the balls of my feet and slice through a guards throat. His head falls to the floor, *This should be over fairly quickly,* I think to myself as I spin on the balls of my feet a second time, the blades grow out of my hands and i pull them out in order to throw them. I stop and throw the first blade at a guard. The blade pierces straight through his helmet and enters his skull.

I spin again and throw the second blade, killing another guard as it enters through his throat.

Swiftly, I unclip the bow and press the button. It unfolds and I begin shooting several guards with arrows.

Suddenly, I catch a guard approaching Savannah from behind whilst she is in the form of a wolf. She seems unaware of the guard as she attacks another. Quickly, I draw back the string and the scarlet red and black arrow forms. I aim and fire, hitting the guard just above his collar bone as Savannah brings down the other guard. She glances at me and I throw her a smile with a wink before I return to attacking.

Use your strengths to counter your weaknesses, my mind reminds me. I grab one of the throwing knives from my belt and turn as I hear a guard approach me from behind, swiftly I throw it before I press the button on the bow and it folds. I clip it to my belt before the chains crawl from beneath my skin.

I throw the chain at the closest guard and it wraps around his throat before decapitating him. The white glow turns to scarlet as I move it through the air, using it as if it is a whip. I gain closer to a group of lycans that seem to be struggling. I take the chain in both hands before I grab a guard from behind and hold it to his throat.

The smell of burning flesh invades my nose as the chain burns straight through his throat and his head falls to the floor. I drop the chain and in a quick movement, the chain rises in the air and slices through several guards.

The chain wraps around the ankle of one of the guards and I pull him to the floor before the chain begins burning through his skin. He screams in pain as the blade grows through the palm of my spare hand. I approach him and stab him through his left eye.

I look at the blood soaked pavement below us, its like a small stream that consists of nothing but blood. The coppery smell invades my nose as I glance up at the moon as it slowly turns scarlet red.

"A scarlet moon, further blood shall be spilled upon this night," I mutter before I continue further down the streets, leaving the helpless, lifeless corpses of the guards behind as we prepare to fight further for our freedom and our equality. More guards begin to surround us, "Savannah!" I shout and she approaches me. I pull an elf and two sicculets out of the soldiers that follow us, "Come with me," I glance over to the rest, "keep the guards distracted as best you can,"

"Where are we going?" The young elven girl asks. Her chocolate brown hair soaked with blood and her grey eyes twinkle like stars as we begin running down a small ally.

"The capitol building, there we will take this city," I say, my eyes fixed on the building not too far in the distance. We run swiftly towards it, using the shadows of the night to remain hidden from the guards as we approach the large building.

We approach the large wall that had worked as doors when I'd arrived here for the votes from the capitol. Swiftly, I smash my hand into the wall and a small opening, large enough to step through, crumbles to the floor and we enter.

Guards seem to surround us instantly, "Do you really want to try it?" I ask with a wicked smile growing on my face. I can see the fear growing in each of their eyes as my hands rest on my hips, "Do you really want to take me on? Do you dare?"

The first steps forward and takes off his helmet, revealing his pointed ears and his fare skin. He kneels before me and several others repeat his movements. "We want peace," he says softly, his voice echoing the fear he clearly feels.

I know he's afraid that I will kill him.

"What the fuck are you doing?" Another guard snaps.

I approach the other guard and lift my hand, my palm touching his helmet before the blade grows and pierces through his helmet and his skull. Killing him. I turn to look at the guard on his knees as the blade returns to the palm of my hand and the guards body falls to the floor. The elven males body shakes, "As do I, all we want is peace, freedom and equality," I reply, holding out my hand to him. He hesitates for a moment before taking my hand and I pull him to his feet, "fight beside us,"

"No! Elves and sicculets do not deserve equality!" A human guard snaps as the elves stand to their feet once more but before anything more can be said, I move swiftly, stabbing the human through the neck.

"Anyone else want to stand up with an opinion?" I say in a sarcastic yet challenging voice, and after moment of silence, I speak again, "Didn't think so," again I pause, "would you mind showing us the way to the leader of this city?" I ask.

The elf shakes his head whilst the others part, allowing us to pass as he directs us in the direction of the city leader. Two large doors with angels engraved in the oak wood open and the female leader approaches us.

"Please, hand over the city or I will take it by force," I say before she can speak.

PIXIE BIRKITT

"I only did what I thought to be best, and I thought that the games were best," she replies.

"You took us from our parents the day we were born and never allowed us to know them, and then you terminated most of the people we'd grown up with, all we knew was death," I reply.

"I apologise, you are a strong girl, you may take leadership for it seems you see what it is best rather than I," she replies, her voice old with a hint of wisdom and I remember how kind she had seemed to be when I'd first arrived.

"Just don't try to stab me in the back otherwise I will kill you," I reply.

"Understood,"

Why is she giving up her power so easily? I wonder as the elderly lady attempts to limp towards a seat when she collapses to the floor, swiftly I rush to catch her.

When she looks into my eyes, the life seems to be fleeing her eyes, "Do a better job changing this world than I did," she commands, her voice weak. She reaches into her pocket and takes out a small chain with a pentagram and a strange stone dangling from it. "I give you this to ground and protect you in this war, please wear it so that you may bring equality and peace to this world once more,"

"What is it?" I ask in a soft voice

"The stone is a tigers eye crystal, it is good for protection and the pentagram is a symbol of protection," she replies, her voice growing weaker. "Allow it to protect you throughout the rest of this war," I take the necklace into my hand and hold it tightly. She takes in a last breath and exhales slowly, the last piece of life fleeing her eyes.

Gently, the elven male touches my shoulder, "She already knew she was dying, even in this time there is no cure to avoid death," he says softly. "She was never one for fighting but she was a kind leader, if only she wasn't over ruled by so many of the others in this world they deem as perfect,"

I stare into her lifeless eyes, unable to look away from how peaceful she appears to be, "Set up a camera and ensure it goes out to the world," I command softly, "and please ensure she receives a true burial,"

"I shall," the elven male replies before he stands and begins walking away. Next Savannah touches my shoulder gently.

"Death happens to us all, you should know this," she says in a gentle, comforting voice, "this city is now under our control, she passed the leadership to you and I believe that you're a great leader, it seems to be in your blood."

"Thank you," I mutter quietly.

I guess I judged everyone to be like the maker, she seemed so nice perhaps they're not all evil, I think silently as I brush back her hair to witness the point, *she was an elf?*

I look to Savannah, "Did you know she was an elf?" I ask.

Savannah's eyes widen as she looks to the dead woman's ears before she shakes her head. "No, no," she mutters repeatedly, "I thought they didn't allow elves into power," she whispers.

I glance over my shoulder, "Did any of you know?" I ask and each of them look to me in shock and confusion, "This leader was an elf,"

Savannah grabs my shoulder, "No wonder she didn't fight," she whispers, "we must keep this a secret for now"

I nod, looking back at the elven leader unable to look away.

*   *   *

Eventually, Savannah pulls me from the woman's body and brings me into a room with a camera, "We're ready to go live," she says before she steps out of the camera view.

"Hello," I say once the count down has finished, "My name is Devotion and as decreed by the old leader of this city, I am its new ruler and due to this, I create a new law in this city. Everyone is equal, no matter what their race nor their colour, there shall be no slavery and their shall be punishments if anyone is caught with a slave"

I walk out of the view of the camera and take a seat, feeling nervous and slightly nauseous.

I hope that Callum has seen me, that he knows I'm okay. I hope fairy has told him I'm okay and is leading him in this direction, that she's showing him the way. I need him and Conquer and Innocence to go through with the next part of my plan. I need Callum right now, I need his strength. He's my wall, suddenly with that realisation, I finally realise just how much I need him in this fight. In this war.

I can't do this on my own, I finally admit and suddenly, I feel as if a large weight has been lifted from my shoulders.

"Are you okay, child?" Savannah asks, pulling me out of my trail of thought, I look up at her and straight into her soft, green eyes.

She reminds me of Callum so much, I don't understand how but she does. I wonder silently to myself.

"I'm fine," I mutter quietly, almost choking on the words. "I'm fine," I repeat before distancing myself and remaining hidden in my thoughts.

*   *   *

Several days pass and I wait until I get the message I've been waiting for, "Innocence, Conquer and Callum have arrived," says a familiar, comes from behind me, as I stare out of the large window, looking out at the beautiful city. The ruins of the ancient city from the past, still stands proudly in the distance.

I turn from looking out the window to see the beautiful, winter fairy in front of me. "Thank you," I reply in a soft voice before she enters my skin once more. I rush out of the building and to the gates as they arrive. Without thinking, I run towards them as quickly as I can, and once I approach them, I throw my arms around Callum's neck holding him close.

"So this is what you got up to then," Callum says, his voice filled with joy as he wraps his arms around my waist. "You should have been resting,"

"No time for rest," I say, "the next part of my plan must go into action soon,"

"You have this all worked out in your head don't you?" Callum says.

"You can bet on that one!" I say. I grab his hand and begin pulling him into the city, "It's all on lock down for now, to keep the people safe within the walls until this war is over," I say with a joyful smile.

"Not a bad idea," Callum says.

"So what's the next part of the plan?" Innocence asks, her voice sounding professional and to the point.

"A break out," I say with a wicked smile growing on my face.

"Of where?" Innocence asks.

"The training centre," I pause for a moment, "what they don't realise is that they've bred the perfect army, an army that know us and trust us more than any other because we were in their shoes, we know what its like—"

Innocence interrupts me as she realises what I've been thinking, "To escape a living hell, and receive their freedom, of course they won't want it to happen to any other children, they want freedom just like we did, we dreamt of freedom,"

"Just as they are now," I reply.

"When do we set off?" Conquer asks.

"Tonight," I reply, "so rest up because Savannah is preparing our transport and Callum, there's something I need to talk to you about,"

"What is it?" Callum asks, his voice suddenly filled with fear.

"Something we need to discuss in private," I reply. "Come with me," I guide him to the large building that I have called home for the past few days and to the room I've been sleeping in.

"So what do we need to talk about?" Callum asks after a moment of silence.

"The elves know a spell, a spell that effects lycans or werewolves, which ever you prefer to be called," I say.

"And what does this spell do?" Callum asks.

"It makes it so that you can turn whenever you wish to instead of only on a full moon," I explain, "I don't quite know the ins and outs of how it works and how you would call upon the change but the elves will explain that, that is if you wish to go through with it"

"Well, it would make it easier for me to protect you," Callum mutters, "and I won't be entirely useless"

"Your not useless as it is anyway," I reply.

Callum steps towards me and gently holds my upper arms in his hands, "I am because your trying to protect me, as a wolf I can protect you and make sure no harm comes to you," he pauses for a moment, "I'll go through with it so that I can protect you," before I can say anything, he kisses me passionately.

Instinctively, I kiss back, feeling sparks of pleasure flood my body and an unusual, pleasurable warmth begins to run through my veins. He holds me closer, his arms wrap around me even tighter.

The warmth that radiates from his body, enters mine, sending a shiver of pleasure running down my back. He gently touches my neck as he traces the curve of my neck. Instinctively, I begin to undo the buttons on his white shirt and pull it off his body, revealing his warm, dark muscular chest. Gently, I touch his skin lightly with my finger tips.

Gracefully, he pulls off my armour, leaving me almost completely naked in front of him and if it weren't for my pants, I would be naked. The bare skin of my chest touches his as our kiss becomes even more passionate.

I struggle trying to undo his jeans due to my hands shaking nervously. He calms me as he softly combs his hand through my hair in a soothing manner. My muscles suddenly relax under his touch.

His hand drops down from my hair and carefully caresses my neck as he traces the curve of my neck and down to my breast. He caresses my left breast with a soft, teasing touch. His lips leave mine for a moment before he begins kissing my neck, each kiss is as gentle as the last and sends sparks of immense pleasure flying throughout my body.

I fall backwards onto the bed and he carefully follows me. He begins to experiment, playing with my nipple with his tongue and lips before he bites it gently. A quiet moan filled with pleasure and excitement escapes my lips.

Callum looks up at me, a smile growing on his face as he sees the pleasure in my eyes but before he can return to teasing me, I begin kissing him on the lips once more.

Unable to stop myself, I begin clawing and scratching his back like a cat whilst I kiss his neck repeatedly, before I bite him and nibble at his skin. A moan escapes him that sounds more like a wolfs growl than a moan of pleasure from a person.

I stop, suddenly feeling terrified at the thought of him disliking what I was doing. He looks at me, almost as if he can sense my fear. His eyes are the same lily pad green but something deep within them reminds me of a wolf more than usual.

He smiles at me in a comforting manner, "Don't stop," he whispers breathlessly before he returns to kissing my lips passionately once more. Unable to stop myself, I return to clawing his back and he releases another growl of pleasure instead of a moan.

Slowly, his hands begin to explore my body further until he removes my pants, leaving me naked beneath him. With incredible precision and clearly, a lot of practice, he begins to tease me by playing with me down below.

Instinctively, my hand ventures down his pants as pleasure begins to surge even further throughout my body.

He kicks off his pants and crawls in closer, his naked body presses against mine, "Are you sure you want this?" Callum asks softly, whispering the words in my ear, his lips gently touch my ear as he speaks the words.

I nod, "I want to do it with you," I reply breathlessly. In my heart, I know that I want to lose my virginity to him and no one else.

"Are you sure?" He asks.

Again, I nod, "I want my first time to be with you," I whisper.

Slowly, he enters me and at first it hurts as he enters. Once he is inside of me he moves as if he is going to exit me again but he doesn't. Instead, he slowly thrusts back inside of me once more. Clearly, he's afraid of hurting me.

Gradually, the pain eases and pleasure floods my body more so than I have ever known. The deeper he is inside of me, the more I struggle not to scream with pleasure.

Another moan escapes my lips before I bite his neck again. This time I gently lick the skin before sucking it slightly. The sweet taste pf blood enters my mouth and dances on my tongue, teasing and playing with my taste buds.

I wrap my legs around his waist and my hips move to meet his, almost as if it is some kind of instinct. Gently, he wraps his arms around me and holds me closer. He gently kisses my neck before he bites the base of my neck and another quiet moan escapes my lips.

Suddenly, he turns over, forcing me to go on top, leaving everything unpredictable. Instinctively, I move my hips and thighs, I can feel the muscles tightening up and I feel incredibly breathless but I continue. The pleasure I'm feeling is worth everything in this world and more.

His hand finds mine and our fingers entwine together. He begins to growl even more and pleasure is written on his face. Suddenly, I feel something strange that I don't quite understand when Callum's sperm fills me.

I lay on top of him, resting my head on his chest, suddenly feeling light headed and dizzy. His heart pounds in his chest and I can hear every breath he takes. Gradually, I look up at him and he smiles.

"Did you enjoy it?" He asks breathlessly, his voice sounding soft and comforting. I nod in response, "Well I know you climaxed at the end," he says with a small chuckle.

"Did I? How would you know?" I ask curiously, my muscles still tightening to the point where it feels as if they're going to tighten up so much that Callum will be stuck inside of me. Gracefully, I move and he shows me the unusually large wet patch on his body and on the covers.

My cheeks burn in embarrassment as I stare at the wet patch, "Don't worry about it, its normal," Callum tries to comfort me when he realises the embarrassment I feel.

Another fear suddenly hits me, "You did enjoy it, didn't you?" I ask.

"Yea, I enjoyed it a lot. Its definitely the best sex I've ever had," Callum replies.

*　　　*　　　*

I awake two hours before sunset, cuddling up to Callum, my body completely bare. My naked skin touches his. His comforting warmth enters my body.

I nudge Callum slightly to wake him up before I quickly change into my armour, for some reason, I feel afraid at the thought of him seeing my body. I feel as if I should be ashamed of my body because of what I have achieved through using it.

A killing machine is what my body has become and that's something I feel ashamed of.

My armour covers my body once again and I feel confident again. With my armour on, I no longer feel ashamed of my body. Nor do I feel ashamed of the killer within me.

"Wake up Callum," I say softly.

He opens his eyes and looks at me drowsily, a smile seems to automatically grow on his face as soon as his green eyes settle on me and I can't help but return the smile, "Are we starting to get ready?" He asks, his voice tired and drowsy.

"Yup, so we're starting with the spell," I reply, my smile soft and warming.

"What spell?" Callum replies.

"The elven spell that shall allow you to turn whenever you wish to," I reply.

"Oh yea!" Callum replies as he drags himself out of bed and stumbles slightly. Immediately, I catch him before he can fall and he looks at me. His eyes burn with a question and silently, I wonder what this question could be.

"Earlier did we honestly have, erm you know?" He says nervously.

"Sex? Yea, we did," I reply.

"Didn't you say it was your first time? Is that true?" He asks.

I nod, "Yea, its true. I lost my virginity to you," I whisper. He stands there for a moment and gathers himself.

"I can't believe such a beautiful woman was still a virgin," he mutters.

"Yea, well you can't have sex in the training centre," I reply and he laughs as I begin leading him out of the room and down into a large hall lit by candle light. Beautiful black and white candles are scattered around the room as well as a large circle in the centre of the hall. In the middle of the circle of black and white candles is a silver candle.

A young female elf stands in front of the silver candle that is the only candle that no one has lit yet. I step towards the elf and Callum follows. I turn around to look at him, "Are you sure you want to do this?" I ask.

"Yes," he replies.

I step out of his way and he continues walking towards the centre of the circle whilst I remain outside of it. Waiting. Watching.

"Callum, Devotion, I welcome you both to this circle," the young female elf says as she finishes platting her shining silver pigtails. Her moon grey eyes never move from me as she stares. She truly reminds me of the moon but something in my gut tells me that this has occurred since she began casting spells so that werewolves could change whenever they choose to and not under the full moons influence. "Callum, have you decided whether you will go through with this so that you may change as and when you please instead of under the moons influence?" The elf asks, her voice soft, comforting and understanding.

"Yes, I have decided to go through with it," Callum replies.

"You must understand that even though you will be able to change whenever you wish to, you will be physically stronger when it is a full moon, a blue moon and you shall be incredibly powerful when it is a blood moon," the elf explains, "which for some unknown reason, the moon has been a blood moon for quite a while"

"A blood moon has been caused because of the amount of blood spilled recently, it is so that it may be announced to the rest of the world by the Goddess," I whisper, the words coming from my heart for some unknown reason.

"May we begin?" The elf asks and I silently wonder whether she heard what I said.

"Let's begin," Callum insists, his voice quivering slightly in fear. I can practically feel his fear and nervousness radiating from his body.

"Goddess to us you are kind, please allow them to keep a human mind, allow them to use the gift that was given, when is needed in a battle arisen, when the battle begins a wolf shall take their human form, so that they may help end this horrid storm, we need their assistance in this war, so that we may defeat them at their core," the elf says.

I watch as she seems to illuminate and glow like the very moon itself. A radiant silver thread seems to appear around Callum and the elf and immediately the blades grow from the palms of my hands causing an uncomfortable tingling sensation, that closely compares to pins and needles, in the palm of my hand.

The elf lifts her hand at me and shakes her head. Automatically, I seem to relax and the blades return to my skin.

The silver thread begins to cling to Callum wrapping around his body and entering him through his tribal tattoo and his eyes. He lets out a blood curdling cry and falls onto his knees and then on to his side.

"Callum!" I scream at the top of my lungs.

"Do not worry child, for this shall be painful but it is almost over," the goddesses voice surrounds me and fills my ears, *"it shall be a painful process as it is a change in his body but it shall be over soon, do not worry yourself, you have much to do,"*

Callum stands up and looks at his hands and arms, "Do I look different to you?" He asks as he turns around so that I can see him. All of a sudden, his arm muscles appear larger and his build seems to be larger also.

He appears to be much stronger than he did before. "You look stronger," I whisper, unable to bring myself to believe what I'm seeing. His eyes seem to be glowing but soon they begin to return to the way they were before.

He steps towards me and at first I flinch away, "Are you afraid of me?" He asks softly.

I shake my head before I step towards him and wrap my arms around his neck, "I'm not afraid," I whisper softly, "I will never be afraid of you, just cautious at times when I need to be," I pause for a moment, "remember, a huntress should always be on her guard,"

He chuckles, "The day in the library back in the prison," he whispers.

"One of my most cherished memories," I whisper. "Now, are you ready because I need to get a few people together to assist us and some transport,"

"Yea, I'm ready," he replies. I let go and step back before grabbing his hand and leading him into the main entrance of the building where the same elf and two sicculets that came with me before, wait for me, along with Savannah.

Savannah steps forward and seems to be completely mesmerised by Callum and at first I step in front of them and its when both of them speak at the same time, I realise something.

"Mom?" Callum gasps.

"Callum?" Savannah replies.

With no control over my body I grab both Callum and Savannah by the wrist. Suddenly, I see a flash of several detailed images in front of my eyes.

It begins where I see the guards and the maker stood in front of me, "Your son has commit a heinous crime and so you must leave the city immediately, no one will know where you have gone. You're friends and your family will believe you are dead and you are never to return and never to have contact with anyone, understood?" The maker says.

"You can't do this, you can't punish me for my sons supposed sins for you know he is innocent," I say.

"I don't care if he's innocence or not! Your people are not welcome in this world! In our civilisation! You will never be welcome!" The maker snaps. "Take her!" He commands and the guards grab me and take me away.

A cruel disgusting man! My mind screams, *A power hungry evil man!*

The images change and suddenly, I'm in a prison, sat on the edge of a bed. I'm rocking back and forth nervously as I try to find a way to calm myself but I can't. The guard comes in, causing me to jump.

I glance over my shoulder at the door as the guard enters. I stand, "How is she? How is my mother? Is she okay? Is she getting better?" I ask.

"Your mother died this morning at six hundred hours of cervical cancer," the guard replies in an emotionless voice, bringing me no comfort. I feel almost as if I will erupt because of the amount of sadness that is growing inside of me. My eyes burn with tears and my heart feels as if it is being torn apart.

I stand there, unable to breath due to the amount of emotion pumping throughout my body with every beat of my heart.

I open my eyes and gasp as I appear in the room once more. "A vision again?" Innocence asks as she approaches us.

I swallow and nod, unable to trust my voice.

"What happened?" Innocence asks.

"They forced you to leave, he said you weren't welcome in their civilisation didn't they?" I question, my voice quivering as I speak. I turn to look at Callum, "And the guard, he told you she died of cancer, cervical cancer at six hundred hours,"

"How did you know?" Savannah asks just as I begin to gag.

"She had a vision, she saw it," Innocence says.

"Second sight," Callum gasps, "does this mean she can see visions of the past?"

"In your point of view, it appears so," Innocence replies.

"Second sight was gifted to thee so that the truth she may see," the words replay again in my mind. My legs feel weak but I force myself to stand.

"Second sight was gifted to thee so that the truth she may see," I whisper.

"The words from your dream right?" Callum mutters.

"Its so that I can see the truth. Past truths, present truths and future truths," I whisper as I finally begin to understand. After a moment of silence, I speak again, "Anyway, shouldn't we be travelling?" I ask.

Savannah nods as she finally looks away from her son and to me, "You and I shall go collect the transport," she says.

"Okay," I reply. She guides me out of the room and to the horse stables, "Who's this beautiful mare?" I ask as I begin to stroke the nose of a beautiful pure black forest horse.

"She doesn't have a name it appears," Savannah says.

"She's around two years old and no ones ever been able to calm her," a young male sicculet says, his scales are a dark green colour. "She's never been ridden, she's never let anyone near her before,"

"May I try?" I ask.

"Okay? But be careful," the male sicculet says.

I prepare the horse with a saddle before I climb onto her back and the horse begins to walk out of the stables, completely under control. *"Mist,"* a young female voice whispers and instinctively, I know its her. It's the horse. *"My name is Mist"*

"I think I'll be travelling with this beauty," I say.

"Well you've chosen your mode of transport, I'll go get the bikes for the others," Savannah says.

"How are you travelling? And how did you know I'd prefer a horse?" I ask.

"You strike me as an animal person and I'm travelling by foot but before I go, there is something I need to say," Savannah says.

"Say what you need to say," I reply.

"When you told me that you were consorting with a male lycan called Callum, I thought it could have been anyone but it wasn't. You are consorting with my son. You kept him alive in the games and I would like you to know that you have my blessing. I'm sure that I'd prefer Callum to have you instead of any other girls. You are quite the special and unique one and clearly, you care about him deeply, if not love him," she replies.

"Thank you, I care about him quite a lot," I reply.

*   *   *

Finally, the time comes and after a nights journey and a days rest, we're ready to take on the training centre. I stand outside, staring at the large building, remembering how we had trained all our lives, been enclosed by its black walls and large windows. All of us knowing there would be no escape for if we tried, we would be killed.

My entire life had once revolved around this place. The strict training, the strict diet and the strict education. I'd never had any sort of freedom.

I sigh as the memories flood my mind, *They all will be going through the same thing,* I remind myself.

"Are you ready to do this?" Innocence asks as she gently puts her cold hand on my bare shoulder.

"I know I'm ready," Conquer says with a dark, cruel smile growing on his face, clearly from the thought of shedding even more blood.

"Ready," I whisper, squeezing Callum's hand gently. He pulls away and takes the form of a werewolf. I can hear his bones cracking as they break, his muscles ripple as they spasm and change. I look away unable to watch.

Silently, I wonder just how painful it must be to go through such a change yet Callum doesn't make a noise.

Not until the change is finished.

He nuzzles his nose into the palm of my hand, his nose is wet as it touches my skin. Suddenly, he sneezes and horrible snot covers my hand, he moans. "Eww!" I say as I wipe away the snot onto my armour. "I hope that gets replaced by blood," I mutter.

Conquer chuckles, "Sounds like the old Devotion I used to know! The Devotion before the games!" Conquer says.

"So are we going to do this or what?" I say, my voice holding no amusement. I step forward, gaining closer to the only entrance to the training centre. I feel my hand burn slightly as I grow closer to the door. I glance down to see a ball of light beginning to form in my hand. A powerful glow that seems to radiate an intense heat that only causes the skin of my hand to feel as though its slightly burning.

My hand feels as if someone is stubbing out a cigarette on the palm of my hand instead of a burning, glowing white ball. Gracefully, I throw the ball of light at the door and upon impact, the white light spreads so that it covers the entire door before it begins to burn and crumble to the ground.

I stand in a strong position, showing the pride and strength that I hold inside. Guards begin to rush towards the door. Towards me.

The blades grow from the palms of my hands, causing an unusually painful tingling sensation in my hands and arms. Callum and Savannah stand on either side of me, growling viciously at the guards, both of them are prepared to fight until the death. I ignore the pain and continue forth, walking towards the guards with the same pride and strength in my stride.

Conquer and Innocence walk either side of me along with Callum and Savannah. We are all prepared for what is about to come.

I can see the fear in the guards eyes as they watch us, they seem to be unsure of whether they should step out of our way or attack. Using their hesitation to my advantage, I grab the closest guard, the blade rips straight through his arm and due to the blades length, it rips straight through the guards side. I pull out the blade just as I stab the second blade into the guards throat.

With a swift movement, I move towards the second closest guard and in a lethal movement, I stab the blade straight through the throat of the second guard. Swiftly, I spin on the balls of my feet before I slash through the back of another guard.

I glance over my shoulder for a split second as Callum wraps his jaw around the throat of another guard, and clamps down, his teeth digging in causing a pool of blood to gather underneath his body.

Savannah claws another guard, whilst Conquer slices through several guards with his large sword and Innocence uses her speed in hand to hand combat along with a small knife in order to kill them. I watch as she throws several knives at different guards, killing each of them with almost perfect precision.

I turn back to the guards that are now surrounding me, I go to punch the first guard and the blade slices straight through his skull. I pull out the blade and turn around before slicing the blade through another guards throat.

Suddenly, a guard grabs me from behind and tries to restrain me. I use the blade to slice through some of the skin of the guards legs, causing two large gashes in the guards legs but it doesn't seem to have an effect on the guards hold on me. I struggle against his grip but its no use.

Swiftly, I bite into the guards arm, clamping my jaw down as much as I can until the sweet taste of blood fills my lips.

The guards blood. The taste sends my taste buds wild and I can't help but bite even harder.

The guard immediately releases me and I fall to the floor and my jaw relaxes. I land in a crouched position and turn around.

"Fucking hell! You little fucking whore!" The guard shouts angrily.

Unable to control myself, I growl in an inhuman voice. With a movement that seems almost impossible, I move as if I am about to punch him in the stomach but the blade stabs him. I rip through his muscle and flesh causing a deep wound to form and his blood splatters on my face, and soaks my hair.

CHAPTER 13

Break Out

I turn just as a guard tries to punch me. I block his attack before using the blade in my spare arm to slice through the guards arm. I slice through the guards throat. I pull out the blade and turn before throwing the blade with perfect precision. The blade embeds itself in the guards throat, perfectly.

I slice through another guards stomach and another guards throat. Both of their bodies fall to the floor, and I glance around looking for another enemy but all I can see are fallen enemies at my allies feet.

"Are we going to continue?" Asks Innocence with a smile filled with excitement.

Without saying a single word, I begin walking further into the training centre. My mind focussing on my goal, my goal to save my fellows and nothing will cloud my goal. I continue walking down the white corridor that now has slight drops of blood stains whilst the entrance is now completely soaked in blood. The sweet scent fills the room and invades my nose even as I'm walking away, leaving the gruesome scene behind.

With no shame, no fear, only memories, anger, pain and hatred burn inside of me now. My stride grows faster as I begin to approach a security door. Without giving it a single thought, I seem to throw a ball of energy from my body and into the door, causing it to fly open.

I continue forward, every guard that seems to try stepping in my way suddenly flies into mid air, hit's the wall and is knocked unconscious. My focus grows stronger as I approach the training room, wondering whether any trainees will still be in training.

The doors open with an incredible force causing a loud bang to echo throughout the training hall, grabbing everyone's attention. Everyone stares at me for a moment, the trainees appear to be absolutely stunned whilst the guards rush for the weapons.

I enter the room, and approach the centre before I allow the magic inside of me to grow stronger. It builds until it begins to move from my body, and surrounds me. My hair whips around wildly as a powerful wind begins to form around me, and the temperature rises. Droplets of sweat form on my forehead and I feel as if I'm stood in water. I glance down at the floor to see ripples around me as if water has formed around me.

A guard suddenly pulls the trigger of his gun but the glowing ultraviolet bullet doesn't hit me. I lift my hand and the orb of a bullet stops in mid air. I look over my shoulder and without thinking, I glare at the guard that pulled the trigger and instead of hitting me, the glowing orb turns and hit's the guard, causing him to blow up in front of me. His blood coats the white painted walls and stains the floor.

Pieces of his skin stick to the walls at first before it falls to the floor. I look back at the wall in front of me as vines and tree roots begin to crawl and grow up the wall. Flowers blossom upon the roots and vines as they begin to take charge of the training hall.

Several other guards begin to shoot at me but each time, the strange glowing orb like bullet stops in the air but this time they begin to spin around me, going in the same direction as the wind as it begins to form a tornado around me.

I close my eyes for a moment, feeling the magic grow even stronger. I concentrate on it for a moment, allowing the magic in my very core to grow and bloom like a beautiful blood red rose.

I open my eyes and allow the elements and the magic within me to blast through out the room. The glowing orbs that were shot at me suddenly burst into several of the guards, causing them to blow up just like the first guard. Their blood stains the walls and the floor, their skin covers everything around me. The training gear is suddenly dripping with blood.

With a swift movement of my hand, several other guards are knocked off their feet. I lift my hand so that its directly in front of my chest before slowly clenching it into a fist. Five of the guards seem to become stiff, their eyes roll and their muscles begin to spasm violently, causing them to appear as if they're having a fit.

Three other guards begin to cough, their noses, and ears begin to bleed and at first each of them cry normal tears but soon they begin to cry blood. Each of them release an agonising scream before deep gashes begin to appear in their bodies and their pure white uniforms become blood red.

The final guard is suddenly slammed into the wall in front of me. I release my clenched fist and turn my hand so that my palm is facing him. I lift my hand slightly and the guard lifts even higher so that his feet are no longer touching the floor.

Slowly, a radiant white ball of light begins to grow in the hand that is in front of me and once it's the size of a golf ball it flies towards the guard. The ball enters the guard leaving no wounds on him, not until the cracks in his skin begin appearing and a white light begins to glow from within his body, glowing from within the cracks.

The white light begins to change into an orange colour and the smell of burning flesh invades my nose as a strange, glowing liquid that reminds me of lava, begins to ooze from the cracks in his skin. The unusual, thick liquid burns his skin until it goes black as it spreads through his body.

A blood curdling scream escapes the guards lips before the life fleas from his eyes and his lifeless body falls to the floor.

I glance around the room at the young candidates as they stare at me in astonishment. "All of my life, I wished for freedom as I trained just as you have been training, I survived the experiments and they changed me. I became a huntress and then, a champion of the games but what occurred in the games shall haunt me for the rest of my life, would you prefer to have your freedom without having to prove yourself and go through the games or would you prefer the fate you have already been given?" I say, my voice firm and strong. It sounds as if it should have come from someone with much more power and authority than I do.

A young, short female elf steps closer to me, her long curly fiery red hair tied back into a ponytail and her blood red eyes glow as she watches me, suddenly they seem to lighten up with life and hope, "I can't speak for everyone within these walls but I can certainly speak for myself," she says in a strong voice as she stands proudly with her back straight and her head held high. She looks around sixteen almost seventeen. In my heart I know that next year she would be in the games if they continued. Her skin is incredibly pale, almost to the point where she appears to look like a ghost. "I choose freedom, I choose to create my own destiny and not have it chosen and controlled by the makers or the games. I do not wish to be feared by those from the outside world, those from the free world. I wish to be free to be my own person and not be the property of another person. They have already changed me, turned me into a killing machine and a freak and I do not wish to be what they have created any longer. I wish to be who I am, in my heart."

"Then will you join us?" I pause for a moment, "Join us in the fight for freedom?"

"I shall join you, Devotion. My name is Red," the young elf replies.

"Thank you Red and welcome to our fight," I reply.

Several others glance at each other and nod before they step forward and one of them speaks, "We will join you to," he says, tucking a long piece of dark blue stray hair behind his human ear yet I notice something strange about his arms. A small amount of very light blue scales on the back of his arms.

How much have they altered with this years candidates? I wonder silently before glancing down at the tattoos on my arms, *They've changed them nearly as much as they've changed me,* I think just as I realise how altered they've become.

"We will join you also," another group step forward, each of them holding their heads high and standing with their backs straight with pride and strength.

One by one several more groups step forward, each of them saying that they will join us in our fight. Just as I had suspected they would. *They want their freedom, they want to survive, they want to live normal lives and not have to fear for their lives. Just as I and the others wanted. They have the same wish we had and still have. They no longer wish to be property.*

"Conquer, please escort them out of the building whilst I find the others," I command and Conquer does just as I command. He begins escorting them out of the building whilst I continue forth to the sleeping quarters. The first of the quarters is where the ten year olds have been resting and swiftly I begin waking them up one by one.

*   *   *

Eventually, we gather every last candidate out of the training centre and manage to rescue all of the children and babies so that they won't have to be subjected to the torturous experiments and witness the death the rest of us have seen. Unfortunately, many of the children we have rescued have already been subjected to these experiments so that they are now either facing death or becoming something that they never should have become.

Maybe some of them will become like me, I wonder, *then I won't be the only one of my kin I guess.*

We are in the process of leaving when a blood curdling scream escapes Innocence's lips, sending shivers down my spine. She collapses to her knees and curls over on her stomach. Immediately, I run to her and collapse beside her, worry and fear pounding in my veins.

"Innocence! What's wrong?" I say, my voice quivering in fear and panic. The hairs on the back of my neck suddenly standing on ends. The air around us suddenly becomes icy cold. The mud under my knees feels like ice as I kneel there, panicked and afraid.

"I don't know," Innocence cries, the tears run down her face but then, suddenly they seem to evaporate before they can fall to the floor. Then they begin to evaporate off her face, leaving her rosy cheeks completely dry. Innocence begins to cough violently and falls to the floor. She falls onto her side, her head landing on my lap, I try to comfort her by stroking her forehead and combing my hand through her hair, "My wrist! It's burning!" She cries.

Swiftly, I begin rolling up the sleeve of her waterproof jacket to see flames wrapping around her wrist but the flames don't seem to be burning her skin even though they're clinging to her wrist. They don't seem to be burning anything around her either.

"Magic!" I whisper in realisation. The flames die down and seem to settle in her skin as a strange black tribal tattoo of flames. I look down at Innocence's face and smile.

All the experimentation has left her with magic, a human with magic my trail of thoughts pause for a moment, *no! She's no longer human anymore!*

Innocence slowly picks herself up off the floor and stares at the marking, "What is that?" She asks. I realise that the flames resemble a bracelet in a sense in the way they have formed to wrap around her wrist.

"It's magic," I whisper, "you have magic,"

"I-I can't h-have, I'm human," Innocence stutters.

THE HUNTRESS

"You can, the experimentation, its changed us and clearly its given you magic as well," I reply as I stand and offer my hand out to her.

She grabs my hand and I pull her to her feet, "But why has it only appeared now? Why not before?" She asks.

"Maybe Gaia has decided its time for it to appear now, maybe its because you need it now more than you did before, think about it, we're not in the games, we're in the middle of a war. We were trained for the games but we haven't been trained for war and in this war, a few little traps aren't going to help much," I reply.

"So she wants me to have more use and be able to protect myself," Innocence whispers before a smile grows on her face.

"Exactly!" I reply, a smile growing on my face as well. We both realise exactly why she has been gifted with magic so quickly.

"But how do I use it?" Innocence asks as we continue walking towards the capitol of the European Countries.

"Let your killer instincts take hold, using magic should be in your instincts," I say.

"Okay?"

"Concentrate on the flames now, just concentrate on something you want them to do," I explain. Innocence nods and stops walking once again. She closes her eyes as everyone passes us and follows Conquer. Callum stops beside me. I watch Innocence and the concentration in her face before the tree beside her bursts into flames that are pure black. The sudden burst of flames causes me to jump and the hairs on my arms stand on ends as my killer instincts try to take hold and control me but I force it to one side. Smoke rises from the

311

black flames, the smell of burning invades my nose and the flames seem to radiate an immense heat. The smell of burning, the amount of smoke and the immense heat is more than any fire I have seen before.

The black flames seem much more powerful than any fire I've ever seen in my life.

"Innocence! You did it!" I say in excitement, clapping my hands once.

Innocence opens her eyes and the flames begin to die slightly, "I did it!" She says, her voice sounding like a small child as she jumps up and down, her ringlets bobbing up and down. Clapping her hands as she applauds herself.

"Congratulations!" Callum says with a proud smile, "Gaia must be proud of the army you are helping Devotion create and she must want you to be able to create a massive effect in the battle,"

"How far do you think we are from the capitol city of the United European Countries?" I ask.

"A few days journey," Callum replies.

A cruel smile grows on my face, "Oh I can't wait," I mutter.

"I'm guessing you're wondering what Nial's plotting?" Callum asks.

"I'm thinking of as many strategies as I can in order to get to that guy," I reply.

"I doubt he's just going to hand over his power to you,"

"So do I but then he'd be stupid not to," I pause for a moment, "because I will kill him"

"I wouldn't put it past you to do so," Callum says.

"Personally, I think she's looking forward to the possibility of having to kill Nial," Innocence replies, "but then it could always just be a little gut feeling," she giggles slightly at the end of her sentence.

"Well he did give me a bad case of the creeps," I reply.

"I don't quite get that but I know he was creeping you out when you met him," Callum says.

"That's pretty much what I said," I reply with a little laugh.

*   *   *

Eventually, we arrive at a perfect camping area and the werewolves return to their camp in order to retrieve some tents and soon they return. We build up the tents and settle down for the night. Savannah ensured that Callum and myself have a tent to ourselves. "Here," Savannah says as she hands me a long beautiful black dress with a long slit up one side, clearly to make it easier to move in. The dress only has one small sleeve that only goes over the shoulder and has a beautiful pin upon it. The pin is made of a similar black metal to my armour and has a beautiful scarlet symbol that is clearly elven but I don't know what the symbol means.

"Why are you giving me this?" I ask, feeling confused.

"It's a gift from me, something for you to sleep in for now so that you don't have to sleep in your armour and can hopefully get a better nights sleep," Savannah pauses for a moment, "it can't exactly be comfortable to be sleeping in your armour after all"

"Thank you," I reply.

"I made it a few years ago, before everything happened and my family was torn apart by the maker, I used to make things for a living with an elf and I made this and told Callum that if he ever dated a girl I actually approved of then I would give this dress to them," Savannah explains.

"A girl you approve of? You approve of me? How many girls has Callum dated?" I say, feeling slightly overwhelmed by what Savannah is saying.

"He has had quite a few I must admit, and yes I approve of you, you're the first I've ever approved of," Savannah says with a large smile, "go on, get changed into it and we'll see how you look," I turn my back to her and remove the coat before slowly removing my armour and slipping on the dress. I turn around, the dress clings perfectly to my figure, "give me a twirl," she says joy in a her voice. I twirl and she claps, "you look beautiful and it fits you perfectly,"

I curtsy, "Thank you," I reply.

"Now hurry, go let Callum see you in your beautiful dress," Savannah says. I smile softly as I pick up my cloak and put it back on quickly before grabbing my armour and rushing out of the tent.

For the first time in my life, I feel as if I have a family, I feel accepted, I feel as if I belong.

I feel happy.

I approach the tent that I am to share with Callum and as I enter it Callum gasps and smiles at me, his smile strong and warm as he approaches me, "What?" I ask, feeling unusually shy.

"My mom actually approves of you then," he says, his voice mirroring his grin, "I knew she would,"

"Yea, she told me about the dress thing,"

"Yea, it was going to be her sign to me to tell me whether she approved or not," Callum pauses for a moment, "lets just say when I was younger I wasn't the easiest person to talk to so my mom chose to use little signs to tell me things"

"Such as the dress, now I guess it makes more sense," I reply.

"I was like every other teenager, I didn't listen to a single word my mom said so these were her little signs to me and they weren't exactly hard to ignore at times," Callum explains.

"I guess this ones quite easy to over look though,"

"Eh! Well when you know there's a beautiful sexy dress that you could give to a beautiful girl that you find sexually attractive and you know giving her that would no doubt get you laid then yea, you do pay attention to it quite a bit,"

"Get you laid?" I ask, feeling confused.

"Sex," he replies

"Okay then, how can a dress get you sex?"

"In these times, in this world, with most girls all you have to do is get them something beautiful, sexy and unique that not many other girls, if any, will have, they'll give you sex in return, its kind of weird,"

"It sounds weird, the outside world really is messed up and needs a good tidy up," I reply.

Callum touches my forehead with the back of his hand, "Are you feeling okay?" He asks.

"Yea, I feel fine," I reply.

"Did that honestly come from the same girl that said *'sometimes its easier working with mess and chaos than clean and order'*?" He asks.

"Yea, and it is true but still, if a girl will give herself to a man just because he has bought her something, well to me that sounds like prostitution and it needs to come to a stop. A girl should respect her body not defile it in such a manner," I reply.

"I guess your right," Callum replies, "at least your different, you're down to earth, beautiful, intelligent and I must say, in that dress you're absolutely beautiful,"

I smile softly, my cheeks burning in embarrassment from his compliment, "Thank you," I whisper shyly.

"Don't thank me for speaking the truth," Callum replies as he wraps his arms around my waist and pulls me closer. Automatically, I wrap my arms around his neck, I can feel his dreadlocks rest gently on my arms, it feels soft and tickles slightly when he moves his head. The warmth radiates from his body, even more so than usual. The enchanting pleasurable feeling the warmth brings spreads throughout my body, sending my senses wild.

He bends his neck and moves into kiss me, his lips are soft as they touch mine, the beautiful sensation causes my lips to tingle and my body to mould into his. His arms begin to hold me even tighter and in my heart, I know that he doesn't want to let go, no matter what.

He's done so much for me. He went through that painful change in order to protect me and fight in the war so that he too may receive equality.

My heart hammers against my ribs and my stomach seems to flutter. I'm suddenly breathless and excited to know what will happen next. His arms begin to trace my spine gently before he wraps his arms around me once again and holds me tightly. He picks me up and moves me towards the camper bed that has been set up for us.

We stand there for a moment, his tongue enters my mouth and my tongue enters his before I push him onto the bed and climb on top of him. This time its my turn to go wild. I undo the buttons of his clean white shirt and pull it off his body before throwing it in a random direction.

His muscular chest beneath me looks sexy and throws all thoughts out of my mind. Its as if someone else has taken hold of me. Someone who has a better idea of what they're doing than I have.

This must be some sort of instinct.

I begin kissing his neck downwards, I kiss his collar bone and then I begin moving down his chest. I stop for a moment at his nipple and begin to kiss and lick his nipple.

A growl of pleasure escapes his lips and now that I am more familiar with his growls, I smile from the sound of it and continue down his chest. I reach his trouser line and undo his jeans. I pull down his boxers slightly to see his reasonably sized penis. I take his penis in my hand and begin to massage it gently. I move in with my mouth, softly licking it as if it is a lolly pop.

I continue massaging his penis as I lick it and Callum releases another growl of pleasure. I slowly put his penis in my mouth and begin to suck whilst licking the end as best I can and massaging it, ensuring that I squeeze it slightly.

"Oh Goddess!" Callum whispers, "You're amazing Devotion!" He continues before he releases another growl of pleasure.

I continue for a bit longer before I begin kissing his chest again and return to kissing his lips. In a sudden change, he seems to go wild, growling more and more as we kiss and with each growl he seems more like a wolf than a human.

Unable to stop myself, I pull away and look to Callum, "What's wrong?" He asks as he stares at me and as he speaks

I notice that his canines have suddenly grown much longer like they are in his wolf form. I glance at his hands to see his nails have started turning more like claws and his fingers have started growing.

"Callum, you're starting to turn into a wolf," I mutter.

"I am?" He glances at his hands and his eyes widen, "I guess I need to gain more control of this *turning-whenever-I-want* thing, I'm not really used to it,"

"And I'm guessing lycans normally breed with each other in wolf form?"

"Yea, that's what normally happens,"

"Well I'm sorry to tell you this but I'm not having sex with a wolf even if it is you, its wrong and its gross,"

"Yea just a little I guess, I wouldn't really want to have sex with a wolf, even if I am in wolf form at the time, it just isn't my thing,"

"Yea, its not my kind of thing either,"

"But saying that, there is something I would love to try," Callum says.

"And what's that?" I ask curiously.

"What do you think to the idea of having sex whilst flying?" Callum asks, his voice sounding cheeky and cute.

"Might try it some time, but when I've got the hang of flying a bit more and I know I can actually fly with extra weight especially considering well, I'm not the best at flying with just my own weight. I never really realised how heavy I was until I started flying," I reply.

"You don't weigh that much,"

"Oh trust me, when your fighting against gravity it would be nice to be as light as a feather, you have to trust me on this one,"

318

"I guess I wouldn't know, but its certainly something I'd love to try,"

"Me too," I mutter cheekily, "do you want to know something I would like to try?"

"And what would that be?" Callum says in a seductive voice as he grows closer to me.

"I would love to try," I pause for a moment after speaking the words in a seductive voice, "having sex in the ocean," I lick my lips before biting my bottom lip in a seductive manner.

"That sounds like a plan," Callum says.

"Want to try it?" I ask.

"When all this is over?" Callum asks.

"Definitely sounds like a plan,"

"Is it a deal then? Have sex in the ocean when all this is over?" Callum says.

I shoot him a seductive smile, "It's a deal!"

"Definitely!" Callum agrees.

I kiss him passionately on the lips, his tongue enters my mouth once more and my lips tingle. My body floods with pleasure and begs my mind to give myself to him. I force myself to pull away, "Sealed with a kiss," I whisper seductively.

"Someone seems a little horny to me,"

"Could that person be you by any chance?" I ask pointing at the boner that's still on show.

"Well yea, but you seem a little horny to me as well," Callum says and I giggle, "the change is reversed and I'm completely human again,"

"Well maybe I am and if we do, you better not starting changing again," I reply.

"I'll keep it under control,"

"Promise?"

"Promise!" Callum whispers before kissing me softly at first but slowly it grows into a passionate yet loving kiss and slowly we return to what we were doing before.

*   *   *

"Devotion?" Innocence's voice intrudes my dreams. I'm in a beautiful forest, free to go in the direction I chose. The full moon provides large amounts of light that touches the forest floor in thin silver threads that dance along the forest floor. The wind blows through the leaves, carrying whispers and secrets from the night and trees, and bringing a cooling breeze that welcomes all to follow it.

I run freely in the trees, jumping from branch to branch, my bare feet are precise as the bottom of my feet touch the cold, rough branches. The wind blows through my hair, keeping it out of my face, most of the time.

I feel free. I feel safe. I feel happy.

Below the branches that I run along, jump from and land on, I can hear Callum as he pants, running and struggling to keep up with me. I smile cheekily as I catch a peak of Callum running in his human form. *Why isn't he changing into the form of a wolf?* I wonder.

"Devotion?" Innocence's voice intrudes again.

I stop for a moment to glare at the moon and stars, *Go away!* My mind commands.

"Devotion? Wake up!" Innocence commands and my eyes fly open. I stare at her for a moment, "Nice to see you finally wake up,"

"Nice to have awesome dreams shatter," I mutter, grumpily.

"Well someone's grumpy this morning," Innocence mutters and I growl slightly.

"Devotion, we were both trying to wake you up because everyone's packed up and we're going to continue travelling today, we have a long way to go and," Callum pauses for a moment when I realise that we're no longer in a tent and we're moving. I look down to see that Callum is carrying me, "I'm not going to carry you all day so that you can lay in"

"Well I do apologise for being tired but I have been under a lot of stress lately and I've been doing a lot of things so of course I'm going to be tired," I reply, my voice sounding unusually harsh because of how tired I feel.

"Someone is definitely grumpy this morning," Innocence says.

I struggle out of Callum's arms and begin to walk, I glare at Innocence and growl, "I'm tired,"

CHAPTER 14

The United European Countries

Finally, after what feels to have been an eternity, we arrive at the capitol of the United European Countries. I stare at the large wall that separates us from the city and leaves us unable to enter at will. Well leaves everyone else unable to enter at will.

An immense heat suddenly appears in my right hand, the palm of my hand becomes clammy and the centre feels as if someone is stubbing out a cigarette on my palm. I glance down at my hand to see a ball of radiant white flames in my hand, radiating a large amount of light that penetrates through the darkness of the night that engulfs us.

I glance up at the silver moon, knowing that soon it will radiate a scarlet red colour as death occurs.

I take in a deep breath and close my eyes, concentrating and preparing myself. I open my eyes as the killer inside of me begins to grow. I throw my hand forward and the radiant ball of flames shoots through the air, its speed continues to increase as it moves before it hit's the wall and causes a silent explosion with a quick flash of blinding light. I cover my eyes to protect them from the bright flash of light.

Swiftly, I recover myself before we enter the city. "Callum, Innocence, Conquer and Savannah, you're with me! The rest of you, keep the guards off our backs as best as you can!" I command in a strong, firm voice. We begin running, remaining hidden in the shadows of the night through several disgusting dirty alley ways.

Already the agonised screams of pain and death as well as gun shots begin to echo through the city. I stop for a moment and glance over my shoulder, "Goddess to them please be kind, please bring my people peace of mind, upon them allow protection given, bless them throughout the battle arisen, so mote it be," I whisper softly. Small beautiful radiant balls of white light begin to surround me, circling me as I speak the words and once the words have been said, they rush from me and towards the army that have been fighting for me.

I turn and return running as quickly as I can to catch up with the others, "Someone seems a little behind today," Innocence jokes.

"No time for jokes!" I say quickly as several guards come into view. Guards that have spotted us. I skid to a stop and we stand staring at them for a moment, unsure of whether they're going to attack us or not, when the first of the guards takes out his gun.

The killer inside of me rises and without a single thought, I begin to attack. I charge towards them, jumping between the wall to dodge the radiant white bullets. My palms tingle as the blades grow from within my skin. I leap from the ground and land on my hands, on the shoulders of one of the guards, the blades cut through the skin and muscle of his shoulders with ease. The blades come out just as easily as I jump to the floor and land in a crouched position.

I glance over my shoulder as one of the guards becomes engulfed in black flames, *Well done kiddo!* I think to myself as I throw a quick smile in Innocence's direction before I return to fighting.

Swiftly, I spin on the balls of my feet and return to my attack. I move to punch the nearest guard and the blade slices straight through to the back of his head. I spin around to see that there are no more guards to attack already. *Working with skilled killers means less guards for myself to kill,* I realise with a smile. I don't feel too bothered about it, it means things happen a lot faster.

We continue running, each of us knowing our destination. The company building. The centre of the city.

Suddenly, I hear it. The cries of a young child and something inside of me forces me to stop. The sound of the child's scream echoes through my body, sending the instinct inside of me wild. The instinct to protect.

I run off course and into the direction of the child's screams and cries when I find myself in front of a large building. The child is curled over the body of a woman, crying. Cautiously, I step towards the child.

"Devotion!" Callum shouts.

"Devotion! What are you doing?" Innocence shouts her voice sounding slightly snappy but I can't respond. My body seems to have gone into auto drive.

I crouch beside the child and touch her gently. She turns, her golden blond curls bobbing and her deep blue eyes searching me. The sadness buried deep within them.

The girl jumps away from me and begins to step backwards. I approach her cautiously.

"Don't worry, I'm here to help," I say in a comforting voice. Suddenly she begins to run and I find myself following her. Feeling the sudden need to help her.

So much so that I run straight into the building. The doors suddenly slam shut behind me, separating me from Callum and the others. "Devotion!" I hear Callum shout.

I glance around the large room to see that the little girl has vanished. I look back to the door, "Don't worry about me!" I command, "Continue with the mission!"

"Well, well," I hear a familiar voice say, the slight sharp icy tone sends a shiver down my spine, "I've been looking forward to this for far too long".

Slowly, I turn to see Frost stood before me, her armour perfectly polished and something about her seems different. Her lips have turned an icy blue colour and her skin has taken a slight tinge of blue as well. "Frost, what are you doing?" I say.

"What you should be doing, fighting for what's right. Fighting for order," Frost replies, her voice sharper than ever and her eyes burning with hate.

"You're fighting for the slavery of your own people," I reply.

"No! Neither of us are like those mindless savages!" Frost snaps.

"They're not mindless nor are they savages, they're kind people that could offer a lot to the world if they were given the chance!" I snap.

"Well then, we know which side both of us are on," Frost says, her voice suddenly bitchy and sarcastic.

"Yes, we do"

"Well lets see who the best huntress actually is, after all you did have help," Frost says, a crooked smile growing on her face.

"No, I had a strategy," I reply with a small smile growing on my face as well, "let the best huntress win,"

"Yes," Frost replies, "and that huntress is me!" She shouts as she begins to move in for her first blow. Swiftly I dodge her move and the blades grow through the palms of my hands. I move out of her reach as she begins using sharp icicles that seem to be appearing in her hand and throwing them at me as if they're throwing knives.

I dodge each blow. Several times I find myself using the blades in order to smash the icicles into several tiny pieces. The shattered pieces fall to the floor and Frost seems to come to a sudden stop.

"Well it appears you've gotten better since training, but you're still no match for me," she says, her tone seeming to be sharper than all of the icicles she threw at me and that seems to have more of an effect on me than her attempt to kill me.

The blades return to the palms of my hands and disappear and the chain crawls out of my skin and I begin attempting to use it as a whip against her but she seems to dodge it every time. Suddenly, she catches it in her hand as ice begins to crawl up the chains until it focuses on one area.

She pulls against the chain and it snaps, sending an icy sharp pain up my arm and throughout my body. I release a cry of pain as I fall to the floor, cradling my arm. The chain returns to my skin, forming a tattoo once again.

I glance up at Frost, "Look what I've got," she taunts as she dangles the chain in front of me and without a single thought, I cause the chain to begin rising in temperature rapidly. A cry of pain releases from Frosts lips as she throws the chain to the floor and she seems distracted long enough for the vines to crawl from my skin and begin to approach her. "You little bitch!" She shouts angrily. Anger and hatred burn in her eyes as she begins walking towards me, still remaining the little twitch in her stride.

An icicle begins to form in her hand, large enough and sharp enough to be a blade that can be fatal. She towers above me, "I'm going to fucking kill you!" She shouts angrily.

"You should have paid attention," I say in a cocky voice.

She hesitates for a moment, seeming to be confused and that's all the time I need. The vines wrap around her throat and begin to tighten and suffocate her. She drops the icicle to the floor and begins to struggle against the vines, her golden blond hair becoming a large mess as she fights against it.

A second vine grows from the first and wraps around her ankle keeping her in place as the blade grows from my spare hand. With a quick movement, I stab the blade straight through her stomach.

"You were right, I have gotten a lot better since training," I say in a sarcastic voice as the blade grows larger in her stomach.

Blood trickles from the side of her mouth as she speaks in a weak voice, "You always were a bitch!" The vines loosen from around her throat as the life drains from her eyes.

"And I was always the best huntress out of the two of us," I reply. The ice cold pain still burning in my arm. The blade returns to the palm of my hand and her body falls lifelessly onto the floor.

I step past her body and approach the wall opposite the door I entered through. I throw a ball of light at the wall and an area big enough for me to step through crumbles to the floor.

Nial is the only thing remaining in my mind. *I want him dead.* My mind constantly reminds itself. Swiftly, I walk down the long white corridor and to another large room that seems to fill with Hunters and Huntresses from the games. My fellow candidates, the ones I grew up with.

Ivy steps forward, her emerald green eyes burning with sadness as she stares at me, her gaze never leaving my face, "We're sorry Devotion but you've brought this on yourself," she says, her voice quivering with sadness.

"Do you not understand?" I ask, my voice remaining strong, "They enslave elves and sicculets, there is no equality, they stole us from our parents at birth, experimented on us, killed half of the people we considered family and then forced us into an arena to kill other people, some of which could have been innocent"

"We truly are sorry," Ivy replies but something else rings in her voice. The sadness in her eyes, "I don't want to do this," she mouths, "they're forcing me to"

I nod to her, as a way for her to know that I understand what she is saying, "So be it then," I reply.

The first to attack is Bullet, he seems a little to eager to attack me to have been forced into this like Ivy has been. Swiftly I move and dodge his bullets as I approach him, the blades growing from the palms of my hand yet again. Sadness burns inside of me. I don't want to do this but I have to.

I have to get to Nial.

In a swift movement, I jump from the wall and slice one of the blades through his throat and his head falls to the floor. The next to attack is Moth, I remember talking to him in the library at the old training centre and I remember his favourite attack. He disappears into a cloud of smoke that he's created through magic.

I remain still, listening for his movements. A footstep appears behind me, I turn and with perfect precision, I stab him in his throat.

Dawn and Inferno are next, they move together as if they have suddenly become the perfect team. The first of Inferno's fire balls fly towards me and I dodge out of the way. The vines grow out of my tattoo and begin crawling along the floor as he throws the second ball of fire in my direction. I dodge again, hoping that the vines will move quick enough as the last of them falls to floor and it is no longer attached to me.

Dawn jumps in front of me, and begins to attack, throwing her fist at me. I dodge the blow. Silently, I know that Inferno will be moving behind me so that whilst Dawn is distracting me, he can kill me from behind. I hear his footsteps behind me as I dodge a second blow from Dawn. I jump above Dawn and fall behind her as Inferno throws another fire ball in our direction and without a second thought, I use Dawn as my shield.

I spin around on the balls of my feet to see her body engulfed in flames. She falls to her knees and then to the floor as the vines wrap around Inferno's neck and begin to choke him.

Before he can set the vines on fire, I charge towards him and stab him in his stomach with both blades causing them to slice through him so that his torso falls to the floor and the vines return to my skin.

Tears pour down my cheeks as I mourn their deaths. They were my family growing up and now I have had to kill them. I know I will never be able to forgive myself for killing them. Sadness fills my body but is soon replaced by hate.

This is Nial's fault!

I turn around to see Ivy crying, "He forced this," she cries. "He caused their deaths,"

"Then let me past," I say, my voice remaining strong as I approach her, "let me kill him,"

"He should be in the room through there," she replies as she stands and approaches the door. Gently she lays her hand on the screening pad and the wall opens as a door.

"Stay here," I command and she nods.

In a rough movement, I wipe away the tears and approach the white chair in front of me, looking out the window at the city that burns. The doors close behind me and I notice no guards. Clearly he believes I'd be dead now.

I turn the white chair and Nial looks up at me, his eyes filled with shock, "How?" He whispers.

I smile mischievously, "You forget I am the champion of this years games," I reply.

I can see the fear growing in his eyes before I perform the easy task of slicing through his throat, decapitating him with one of the blades. I approach a large device that I know is for announcements and I pick up the microphone and flick the switch, "It's over," I say, hearing it echo throughout the city. "Nial is dead,"

A elven male steps through a doorway and approaches me, "It's all over, you control every city," he says.

"How? We have one city left," I reply.

He shakes his head, "No, we just got word from Devote, they took hold of the Seneria this morning," he replies and a smile grows on my face. It truly is over.

EPILOGUE

I run through the trees, wild and free but its definitely not over, not like I thought it was. We will never truly be free not until the end of my days anyway. Maybe one day, my battle will finally be over and I'll be able to settle down, have children and be with Callum in a little cottage somewhere like Conquer and Innocence have, they're expecting their first child and don't have to worry about him or her being taken away and taken into the training centre.

But somehow I don't think that life is for me. Somehow I don't think that will ever be apart of my destiny, of my fate.

I jump from the trees and climb onto Mist's back. It seems she'll be the closet thing I'll be having to kids for a long time. She begins to run, her beautiful powerful body seems to hit speeds that are impossible for a horse.

There's somewhere I need to be and she knows exactly where I'm going and soon I'm there. Riding beside Callum as he runs in the form of a wolf. Sadly Savannah is gone, lost in the battle but Callum seems to be more at peace knowing that she is now in a happier place knowing her people are gaining more and more equal rights every day.

This is my fate, my destiny. To fight for the rights of my people, the elves and the sicculets and for lycans. I was born and trained for this and I realise that now. If I had the chance to change my fate, would I?

It's a very simple answer, no I wouldn't and I wouldn't change my past either but if I could change something I would have stopped all of this from ever happening. I would stop the slavery of my people. I would stop the games from ever happening. But would I change anything else? No for in the end, all of this has made me as strong as I am, its made me different, its made me who I am and who I will always be.

I'm not a killer, I'm not what the maker wanted.

I'm a saviour, my peoples saviour and I won't rest until I know that slavery has completely come to stop and my people have rights. But until that day, I must fight the slavers and those that believe my people don't deserve rights.

I am the perfect warrior. The perfect hunter.

For in the end I will always be the Huntress.